ALL HALLOWS' EVE
VOL VI
RETURN OF THE GARGOYLES

By

J.P. Carol

CONTENTS

Prologue

Chapter I	The Encounter	4
Chapter II	The Request	48
Chapter III	The Rumors of My Demise'	60
Chapter IV	Escape…Betrayal…Treachery	80
Chapter V	The Dark Castle and the Ides Of March	89
Chapter VI	Come One – Come all, Come Forth, Come Forward	126
Chapter VII	The Infamous Barnabas Bane	139
Chapter VIII	The Battle for Central Park	176
Chapter IX	Return to the Warriors' Dimension	255
Chapter X	Return to Hampton	284

Prologue

The Gargoyles and their Warriors have returned to their Sanctuary in New York City, after disappearing almost a century ago with no explanation.

And none too soon.

Along with the magical community and their Human counterparts, the Gargoyles prepare to confront the renegade Pre' and the Whre, keeping them from going through with their plan of taking over the Human world, one city at a time.

Starting with New York City.

The ancient Warriors, Witches and the Banshees have gathered together all of the magical creatures that still exist together at the Gargoyles' Sanctuary. The need to devise a plan before it's too late has intensified as reports of unexplained incidents throughout the city have increased, and Humans are slowly becoming aware that something….is not right in 'The City That Never Sleeps'.

Something very dark, menacing and deadly is unfolding. The Pre' and the Where were on the rampage and they had to be stopped.

Chapter I

The Encounter

As Jerome led Jesse and Thomas down the street, they dodged the multitude of pedestrians out on a Saturday morning in New York City and crossed the street to the park. Even though it was cold outside, the vendors were out in full force as they peddled their food and wares to Saturday morning visitors and residents alike. Thomas and Jesse were surprised at how many people were out on the streets before noon.

They skirted the edge of the park for about a block and a half while Jerome pointed out several things, he thought they would find of interest. Then they turned toward a stone bridge at one of the entrances that ran over a small stream, and then led right into the park. As they attempted to cross the bridge and enter the park, they were stopped by one of several Police Officers who were trying to redirect the stalled pedestrian traffic that had gathered around the bridge.

"What's going on?" asked Jerome as he tried to get a look at what was happening further into the park.

"Nothing to be concerned about, Sir," said one of the Police Officers as he continued to wave people away from the area. "Just a dead animal. We're moving it now. Please move along. The area is going to be off limits for about an hour or so until we can get the area cleaned up."

As Jerome, Thomas and Jesse stood at the foot of the stone bridge with the rest of the crowd that had gathered, they tried to see beyond the Police Officers stationed there, and the animal control truck that was parked on the other side of the bridge. They had even put up yellow crime scene tape around the area, while several investigators walked around what appeared to be the remains of the deceased animal. The animal remains had been covered by a large orange tarp, and appeared to be a bigger than the normal sized animal you would think would be found in Central Park.

"All of this for one dead animal?" said Jerome out loud to no one in particular. "Is it a horse?"

Then from over his left shoulder, another bystander who was also trying to get a look at what was going on responded.

"No, I don't think it was a horse," he said. "Although, it's big enough!"

Turning toward the disembodied voice, Jerome found that it belonged to one of New York's multitude of joggers who ran through the park on Saturday morning. He was dressed in long pants and a matching jogging jacket and wore a knit cap on his head to ward off the cold.

"Hey!" greeted Jerome as he silently admired the tenacity of joggers who were dedicated to running, no matter what the weather was like.

"Hey!" responded the jogger back.

Then both Gharvey and Catherine had noticed something going on over to the right of where they were standing.

"Master Jesse," asked Gharvey sensing that what had happened here was of importance. "Why do they have the area over there by those bushes blocked off?" she asked, as everyone's attention was drawn to an area just to the right side of the stone bridge, but further into the park.

"Dunno," answered the jogger as he too thought it was kind of strange. Several investigators were milling around a group of bushes that appeared as if they had been demolished. "Whatever is going on, it looks as if I'm going to have to run the perimeter of the park this morning…"

Then the jogger stopped midsentence. He quickly looked down, stunned at what he thought he had heard coming from the large, black Labrador standing next to Thomas.

"Did, did she…," stammered the jogger not sure what to think.

"Nah!" exclaimed Jerome, quick to dispel what the jogger was alluding to. "These two over here just like to mess with people, that's all," said Jerome quickly. "You have a good one, okay!" laughed Jerome nervously as he nudged Gharvey with his left knee.

"Yeah! Yeah, I will," said the jogger somewhat confused as he took off down the sidewalk, trying to avoid the crowd as it continued to grow.

Once the jogger had left, Jerome quickly turned to Gharvey and Catherine and made sure that they understood that talking in public around people who had no clue as to 'what' they were, was a 'no, no'!

"As in, 'Please don't do that again'!" exclaimed Jerome quietly.

For a minute there, he thought he was going to swallow his entire tongue when he heard Gharvey speak.

With that disaster averted, and realizing that entering into the park over the bridge was not going to happen any time soon, Jerome opted to enter the park at a another entrance little further down the street. They made their way through the crowd and walked another block or so down to the next entrance into Central Park.

As they approached the entrance, they heard a voice call out.

"Young man! Excuse me, young man!"

It was Jesse who finally realized that a carriage driver parked along the side of the street near the entrance, was trying to get their attention.

"Jerome!" exclaimed Jesse. "I think that man over there is trying to get your attention."

"What man?" asked Jerome as he turned around, searching the area for someone he might of known.

"Over here," called out the driver as he stood up inside of his open aired carriage and waved his arms. "Are you looking to give the boys a tour of the park?" he asked kindly.

"Thanks, but we were just going to walk through the park for a bit, then check out some other things," replied Jerome as he turned to go.

"Aw, but they can't come to New York City without taking a carriage ride, now can they?" said the persistent driver.

Jerome usually had no problem dissuading persistent vendors and peddlers. But there was something different about this one. He had the kind of face you trusted right off the bat. And his smile kind of drew you in whether you wanted to like him or not.

"Tell you what!" continued the driver. "I'll take you and the boys and your two pets around the park for a bit, then drop you off wherever you want after that," offered the driver. "I can even drive you down some of the streets of city that most people don't get to see!"

Not wanting to miss any opportunity while in New York, Thomas and Jesse tried to encourage Jerome to take the driver up on his offer.

"Com'on Jerome!" exclaimed Jesse. Let's do it!"

"What??" said Jerome, surprise that they might be interested in taking a carriage ride.

"Yeah!" agreed Thomas. "I've never had a carriage ride before. Besides, we can see more of New York by riding rather than walking."

"Yeah!" said Jesse, totally supporting Thomas. "And it is kinda cold out here!" noted Jesse as he wrapped his arms around himself and made a loud, shivering noise to make his point.

"Oh! So now you two are cold, are you?" questioned Jerome, realizing that not only was he was weakening, but that it did seem like a good idea. And he did include Gharvey and Catherine in the deal.

"Alright guys," relinquished Jerome as he walked over the edge of the street where the driver was parked. "We'll take a carriage ride!"

"Awesome!" "Whoohoo!!" yelled the two teens as they hopped into the back of the carriage without any encouragement, ready to see New York.

Thomas swung Catherine' carrying case off of his back and set it down on the floor of the carriage next to where Gharvey had settled herself.

"And there's a blanket to cover yourselves with if it gets a little chilly," said the driver, as he waited for the group to get settled in. Then he carefully pulled his horse and carriage away from the curb and into the flow of the traffic.

Jesse and Thomas settled back and listened to the 'clip clop' sound that the horses' hoofs made on the paved street as the carriage slowly made its way around the park. They pulled the thick blanket up over themselves, and settled in as the sights and sounds of New York City slowly meandered by.

"Thanks, Jerome!" exclaimed Jesse as he felt his excitement well up inside of him.

"Yeah, thanks a lot," chimed in Thomas, just glad that his parents let Jerome take them out to sightsee the city.

"You're welcomed, guys," acknowledged Jerome feeling kind of hyped himself.

It was kind of cool to see the two of them being so excited just to be out with him. It made him feel like a big brother. And being an only child, he didn't have many of those kinds of moments to relish. So, this was big for him, too.

Then Jerome realized that the driver hadn't quoted him a price on how much it was going to be to be to take them around the park. So he leaned forward and tapped the driver on the arm.

"Excuse me, how much for the tour for the three of us?" he asked, hoping it wasn't going to break the bank.

He wanted to make sure he had enough money to do some other things with Thomas and Jesse later on. And although it was already going on one o'clock, he felt that they could squeeze a few more things in before it got to be too late and they had to get back.

"Oh, don't worry about a thing, Son," answered the carriage driver as he glanced back over his shoulder and winked. "It's already been taken care of!"

"What?" exclaimed Jerome. "By who?" he asked.

No one knew they were going to take a carriage ride around the park.

"Heck! They didn't even know they were going to do this until just a few minutes ago," he thought to himself.

Then before Jerome could ponder the response of the driver any further, he continued.

"Son! You don't think that the Warriors or the Gargoyles would let you go about the city without someone to watch over you, now do you? I understand that you have your dog and cat to watch over you," said the driver. "But there's a lot going on right now. They felt it was better to be safe than sorry. I hope you're alright with that?" inquired the driver as he continued to steer his horse drawn carriage through the midday traffic.

Dumbfounded, Jerome could only nod his head in agreement. He had to admit, the magical community here in New York City was really on top of their game. He thanked the driver and sat back finding himself at a loss for words. But at the same time, he found it reassuring to know that they were constantly being looked out for. It felt good.

Seeing the look on Jerome's face, Thomas asked, "Is everything alright?"

"Yeah!" exclaimed Jerome with a slight laugh. "Everything is...great!"

"By the way," said the driver with a broad smile as he turned. "My name is Charlie. Sit back and relax and enjoy the ride. And I'll show you New York City like you've never seen it before."

And for the next five hours, that was exactly what Charlie did.

To Jerome's surprise, Charlie had even shown him some sights of the city that he hadn't seen before, even though he had been in New York for almost three years. He took them by several of the famous museums that New York was known for, and even showed them historical landmarks that Thomas and Jesse had only read about.

Halfway through the afternoon, Charlie pulled up to the curbside in one of the local neighborhoods and dropped them off. He directed them to one of the best known Italian restaurants in the city so they could grab a bite to eat, and told them he would be back for them in about an hour and a half.

"When you get inside," said the carriage driver. "Let them know that Charlie sent you. They'll take good care of you."

Glad to be able to get out and walk around for a while, the trio thanked Charlie and made their way down the street toward the restaurant. They were astounded by the sights and the sounds that they were experiencing. It was as if pieces of different cultures had all been gathered together and dropped right here in New York City.

And at every street corner and along the curbsides, there were vendors selling everything you thought you'd might want or need. For Thomas and Jesse, it was almost 'sensory overload' for them. But they didn't care. They were in New York City!

What could have been better?

After they found the restaurant, they were seated promptly after mentioning that Charlie had sent them. Even Gharvey and Catherine were taken in the back where they were fed and treated like royalty. The guys ordered and had their fill of pasta, meat sauce and the best garlic bread they had ever tasted. Then after lunch, they sampled a special Italian dessert called Tiramisu that Jerome and the boys literally inhaled.

When they had finished lunch, and Jerome went to pay, he was told the same thing that Charlie had said to him.

"Oh no! Don't worry about a thing," said the waitress with a wink. "It's already been taken care of. Have a good one, now!" she exclaimed as she turned and left with a smile.

"Wow!' exclaimed Jerome to himself. "He could get used to this, with no problem."

As they headed back to the drop off spot that Charlie said he would be waiting for them at, they stopped at a vendor where Jerome brought everyone a Gelato. This was the icing on the cake for Thomas and Jesse. A great tour of New York City by a horse drawn carriage, a fantastic lunch. And they were finishing it off with an Italian ice cream.

When they rounded the corner and looked down the block, sure enough. There was Charlie and his horse drawn carriage waiting for them, just like he said he would be.

As everyone loaded into the carriage, Charlie noticed that it was going on five-thirty. So, he decided to head back to the Lexington by passing through several areas of the city that bordered the far side of Central Park. This way they could see the city in all of it grandeur as it began to light up for the evening.

And light up it did.

The skyline of New York City was one of the most awesome sights at night that Thomas and Jesse had ever seen before.

And the moon!

Thomas and Jesse could see the brightness of the full moon as it began to rise and take its place in the night sky above.

"Would they have something to tell their friends when they got back to Hampton," thought Jesse to himself as he leaned forward and took it all in. "No wonder they called it the city that never sleeps".

There was always something going on, no matter what time of the day or the night that it was.

Around six thirty, as Charlie pulled his carriage up to the curb to the exact spot that he had picked them up at, he hopped out and tethered his horse.

"Well folks!" exclaimed Charlie as he put the steps down. "I got you back safe and sound. I hope that you all had a good time, and will come back to New York City again."

As everyone got out and thanked Charlie, they couldn't have been more satisfied with the tour of New York City that he had given them.

"It was great!" gushed the boys. "Yeah, awesome!"

Jerome reached out and shook the driver's hand and personally thanked him for the great afternoon.

"Thanks, Man!" said Jerome. "It was really appreciated. You showed us all a great time!"

"My pleasure, Sirs, and Ladies!" said the driver as he did a slight bow. "The Lexington is about two and a half blocks that way, back down the street," said Charlie as he pointed. "I'm sorry I couldn't drop you off right in front of the building. They only allow the carriages to stop at certain places on the street."

"Not a problem," said Jerome as he once again thanked the driver, and with Thomas and Jesse behind him, headed toward the corner so they could cross the street and head back toward the Lexington.

Even though it was only going on six thirty, and the sky above them had turned dark, there were still plenty of people out on the streets trying take in what they could of the city before it got too cold. And as the lights of the city lit up the skyline, Jerome, Thomas and Jesse made their way to the corner. With Gharvey beside them and Catherine nuzzled comfortably inside of the carrying case strapped on Thomas' back they sidestepped people as they made their way through the crowd.

Then in his attempt to keep up with Jerome and Thomas, Jesse accidently bumped into a young man standing near the corner.

"Sorry!" apologized Jesse, as he made his way around the young man, and caught up with Jerome and Thomas.

Then midstride, Jesse froze.

He wasn't sure what it was he had sensed when he touched the young man, but whatever it was, it caught him totally off guard. And then he heard Catherine hiss from inside of the carrying case on Thomas' back and start to thrash around.

At first, he wasn't sure he wanted to turn to confirm what he thought he had felt. But before he had clearly thought it through, he turned around.

There, standing like a statue amid the crowd as people moved about him, was a twenty-something young man with disheveled dark brown hair. He was dressed in worn blue jeans and sneakers and wore a navy blue jacket over a loosely hanging plaid shirt that hung out from underneath his jacket.

As Jesse stared at the young man, he felt there was something 'odd' about him. Something he couldn't quite place.

The young man continued to stand silently within the crowd as if he were frozen and couldn't move. His head was bent down, and the look on his face was the look someone would have if they were bewildered, or if they were confused and were trying to remember something they had forgotten.

The instant that Jesse had touched him, a connection had been made. In the flash of a few seconds, Jesse saw images of a wild pack of animals as they ran over the countryside, heading for a brightly lit city off in the distance. He could feel their intensity, their feral rage as they pushed their aching, tried muscles onward.

They had to get to the city!

They had to get to the Sanctuary!

And Jesse could feel the intensity of their elevated levels of pure animal adrenaline as it flowed through his body as well. They wanted one thing, and one thing only.

Revenge on the Gargoyles!

In that same instant, Jesse knew 'what' this young man was, and why he and the others who were with him, were in the city. Jesse broke the connection he had made with the young man just as quickly as he had made it, and caught up with Jerome and Thomas.

Jerome, realizing that Jesse wasn't right beside him, quickly turned just as Jesse ran up to him.

"Guys!" exclaimed Jesse as he pulled on Jerome's arm. "Run!! Now!! The Whre! They're in the city and they're heading for the Sanctuary!"

Without any questions, all three of them took off running across the street with Gharvey quickly keeping up beside them.

The young man, realizing that whatever had entered his mind was now gone, jerked his head upward, and quickly looked to his right. He eyes were about to betray him as they momentarily turned 'wolfen' and flashed yellow.

As people continued to move around the young man, trying to avoid bumping into him, he thought he heard someone call out to him from a distance.

"Colm! Colm!"

As a pair of hands shook the young man back to consciousness, a taller figure stood in front of him, calling out his name.

"Colm!! What's wrong with you?"

As the young man slowly came out of the fog he had been in, he looked wildly around himself.

"What!! What!!" he exclaimed loudly.

The tall figure that had been furiously shaking his shoulders, turned the young man toward him and spoke.

"What happened to you?" he asked quickly. "It looked like you went into some sort of trance or something. Colm, you almost turned!"

Still not sure what had actually happened to him, Colm, slowly shook his head trying to clear out the cobwebs.

"Someone, someone touched me," he said.

Then he quickly corrected himself.

"No! I mean, someone touched my mind!" he said, not believing his own words.

"What do you mean, 'someone touched your mind', Colm? That doesn't make any sense," said the older man, now wondering if it was a good idea to have brought some of the younger, more inexperienced of the Brood with them.

"Sense or not, someone got into my head!" exclaimed Colm, loudly. "I couldn't move unless he said I could! And he knows 'what' I am!" yelled Colm. "He knows who we are, and why we're here!" stated Colm nervously, fearing they had been discovered. "And there's something else," he said shakily.

"What?" questioned the older Sire.

"I smelled Gargoyle on him!"

Quickly, the two young men looked around them, trying to pinpoint just who it was that had somehow reached into Colm's mind and discovered their secret. They knew that whoever it was, if they indeed had been in close contact to the Gargoyles, they were probably on their way to warn them.

"We've got to find him, Colm!" said the older man as he continued to search the faces of the humans as they milled about them. "He cannot be allowed to get back to the Gargoyles and warn them! Do you understand?"

"But what about Delan's body?" asked Colm. "We can't just leave these Humans to dispose of him any way that they wish," he said. "He deserves a proper burial by his own kind."

"Don't worry. We will retrieve Delan's body in due time," said the older of the two men. "Right now we must find the one who knows why we are here! And we have to warn Faayn and the others!"

Then turning to the younger Sire, the older man asked, "Colm! Did he touch you anywhere?"

"Yes. On my right arm," answered Colm. "He bumped up against me as he passed."

With no regard to what the humans passing by may have thought, the older man grabbed Colm's right arm and breathed in a couple of times. Then turning his head upward, he began to inhale the air about them, trying to identify which direction the scent he was looking for, had gone.

As both men sniffed the air, Colm turned, and then stopped dead in his tracks. He was transfixed as he glared at three young men across the street from where they were, as they ran in the direction of the Lexington.

"There!" yelled Colm as he pointed at Jerome, Thomas and Jesse as they made their way through the crowd on the other side of the street. "He is there!"

"Quickly! Follow them!" shouted the older man.

As the two Whre made their way through the crowd, they rushed into the traffic on the street in an attempt to get to the other side.

Just as they attempted to cross the street, the sound of a horse whip snapping through the air caught their attention. They looked wildly around when they heard it again. This time the tip of the whip snapped and pulled back as it sliced a wicked line across Colm's face from his temple to the corner of his mouth, gushing blood.

Enraged, Colm covered the side of his face with his hand as he looked up and growled. In his anger, Colm almost found himself uncontrollably transforming into his true form when he spotted the carriage driver.

There, standing in his carriage on the side of the street, was Charlie as he readied his whip once again. As Colm crouched in the middle of the street holding the side of his face, cars and busses screeched to a halt. Pedestrians had started to gather wondering what was going on, and wondering why one of the carriage drivers had seen fit to take his whip and use it on someone.

The older Sire seeing that his younger counterpart was about to lose control, grabbed him. Dodging cars, and just barely avoiding getting hit, the two young men made it to the other side of the street and away from the carriage driver.

"We must stop them!" yelled the older Sire to Colm. "Are you in control?" he asked quickly.

Gaining control over himself, Colm nodded his head that he was fit. And despite the severity of the cut, the blood had stopped flowing, and the wound had already begun to heal itself.

Wasting no time, the two Whre took off running, trying to catch up with Jerome, Thomas and Jesse as they tried to make their way to the Lexington.

"Faster, guys!!" yelled Jesse as he let go of Gharvey's leash and let her run freely. "We got to go faster! Their gaining on us!"

As Jerome quickly looked back over his shoulder, he saw that Jesse was right. Even though he had been the star quarterback when he was in high school, the two young men were in fact not only gaining on them but had almost caught up with them. Jerome could have put out more speed, but then he would have left Jesse and Thomas behind, and that wasn't an option for him.

Then again, Jerome had already sized up the two young men that were chasing them and felt that he could take them if he had to. Not only did he have the height over them, but he also had the weight.

"All I had to do was to stop, turn around and deal with them."

Then Jerome thought about his idea.

"If Jesse was right and they were Whre, he wouldn't have a chance against them."

He thought twice as he took note that while in their human form as they currently were, they sure could run like the devil. And there was no reason not to think that they were probably still fairly strong without having to transform.

"Enough said!" screamed the voice in Jerome's head as he too continued to run.

They had ran at full speed for about two blocks, dodging people as they went. Finally, Jerome saw the Lexington rising in front of them, about a block away. As they sprinted down the last block, and crossed the street dodging traffic, neither Jerome, Jesse nor Thomas let up. Gharvey was already at least ten paces ahead of them.

"Don't stop, guys!" yelled Jerome as he saw the front entrance of the Lexington come into view. "Keep going, no matter what!"

As they continued to run full speed, Catherine tried to keep herself upright inside of carrying case on Thomas' back. As she was being bounced and bobbed around, she took a chance and unfurled her tail and aimed it at the younger of the two men chasing after them.

"Zappp!!!"

A staggered flash of yellow energy emitted from the tip of her tail and jolted the young man mid stride as he ran. For a split second he hung motionless unaware of what was happening to him. And then the next second, he dropped like a lead balloon onto the concrete sidewalk in a heap.

Glancing over his shoulder and seeing his younger counterpart fall, the older of the two Sires had moved himself forward, pushing himself harder. He possessed greater strength and speed than the younger one did and had come within five feet of one of the teens they were chasing. He had attempted to reach out and grab him just as the teen took an unexpected turn to the right.

Jesse quickly turned right following behind Jerome and Thomas, and had just barely slipped out of reach of the older Sire as he grabbed for him. The Sire, realizing that his prey had turned just in time to avoid being caught, came to an astonishingly abrupt stop in front of the Lexington. It was as if he had been going in fast motion one second, and then suddenly, all motion had stopped.

As he slid to an abrupt stop, the older Sire jerked his head to the right and drew back his lips as growled under his breath.

As Jerome, Jesse and Thomas made a sharp, right turn into the recessed entry of the Lexington, they quickly sidestepped the concrete planters that were set between the sidewalk and the front doors of the building.

And what they saw behind the concrete planters gave them relief.

There, standing shoulder to shoulder with the two Sentinels that had greeted them earlier, were three other Sentinels. They were all were standing in one line in front of the double doors that led into the Lexington. Two of the Sentinels quickly stepped aside allowing them and Gharvey pass.

Then they stepped back into formation, protecting the front of the building.

Neither Jerome, Thomas nor Jesse looked back to see if the two men chasing them had tried to follow them into the building. But of course, if they had tried to follow them, they would have to deal with the Sentinels first.

But of course, they didn't know that.

The older Sire strode into the recessed entry of the Lexington, his head was slightly hunched forward, as he was intent on continuing after the teen he sought.

It was then that he spied the Doormen standing between him and the entrance of the building.

All five of the Sentinels were standing in one line, with their legs slightly apart, and held their arms in front of them, slightly bent at the elbow. Their right hand was crossed in front of them as they grasped their left wrist.

At the time, it might not have seemed like anything one would take note of. That was until it appeared as if they were in some sort of formation.

And they were smiling at him. Not a broad, toothy type of smile. Just a gentle upturn of the mouth.

That was all!

"I will go through these 'Humans' if they try to interfere," thought the Sire as he approached the Doormen and stopped just short of where they stood.

"Let me pass!" yelled the Sire as he glared at the Sentinels, daring any of them to challenge him.

"After all, they were just 'Humans'," thought the Sire to himself. "Even without transforming into his 'wolfen' state, he still had superior strength and speed than they did.

The Sentinel standing in the middle of the group facing the older Sire, stepped forward toward the young man and stopped just out of arms' reach of him.

"There is nothing for you here, Son," stated the Sentinel as he stood his ground with the Sire, and kept eye contact with him. "Best be on your way. We don't want to have to put you down."

The Sire was caught off guard by the response of the Doorman. He had not expected such boldness from a 'Human'.

"Get out of my way!" yelled the Sire, now enraged as his face belied him and he began to transform.

As the Sire lunged, he could have sworn he saw the Doorman make an odd movement with his right hand.

And sure enough.

The Sentinel had dropped both of his hands, and locked his right arm out to the side. Instantly, something silver appeared in the palm of the Sentinel. A split second later, it extended itself out to become a long, gleaming, silver staff.

The Sentinel rotated the silver staff so all that was seen was a blur of silver twirling light. Before the Sire even knew what had happened, he was being struck square in the chest with the staff.

The Sire didn't have time to ponder what he thought he had seen. He was stopped dead in his tracks by a jolt of electrifying pain as it coursed throughout his body and literally lit him up like a Christmas tree. The energy that struck him was so intense, that had it lifted the Sire up off of the ground a few inches and held him suspended in midair for at least five seconds.

Colm had recovered from his brief encounter with Catherine's magic, and was watching from the other side of the concrete planters. He was awestruck as he saw the older Sire being struck and then fall into a limp heap onto the ground.

"Who were these 'Humans'," thought Colm to himself. "And how could they stop one of the Brood with a mere staff? This was truly unheard of."

Then, without warning, the Sentinel that brought the older Sire down, called out to Colm.

"Son!" he called out. "You there behind the planter! Come and get your friend and be on your way."

Not sure if he could trust the Sentinel not to do the same thing to him if he stepped forward, Colm slowly shook his head. He wanted to run to the others and report what he had witnessed, but he knew that he couldn't leave one of the Brood behind.

"Son!" said the Sentinel again. "It's alright! We're not going to do anything to you. Just come and get your friend, and be on your way."

Taking a chance, Colm slowly stood and stepped forward and approached the older Sire as he laid on the ground. Grabbing a hold of his pant leg, Colm dragged him out of reach of the Sentinels. And when he was a safe distance from where they still stood unmoving, he lifted his brethren up and helped him to limp away from the entrance of the Lexington.

~~~~~~~~~

Even thought they had made it to the safety of the Lexington, Jerome wasn't taking any chances. As he led the way, he flung open the tinted glass doors of the building and charged inside with Thomas, Jesse and Gharvey close behind him. He made a mad dash across the lobby, and headed for the corridor on the right side of the building. As he ran, he kept a close eye on both Thomas and Jesse, making sure that they were with him all the way.

As Jerome took the corner and turned toward the elevators, he stopped dead in his tracks.

The first thought that bombarded his mind was, "Which elevator do we take?? Which elevator do we take??"

Jerome thought that with everything that had just happened, now was not the time for his head to feel like it was going to explode with indecision.

Thomas and Jesse had turned the corner right behind Jerome and almost collided with him as he stood in the middle of the corridor.

Then Thomas yelled loudly as he quickly ran around Jerome, "The elevator on the left!" he called out as he ran. "It's the elevator on the left!"

As the three of them ran up to the elevator, Thomas and Jerome began pounding on the button panel trying to get the elevator to come.

"Com'on! Com'on!" yelled Jerome as he kept pushing buttons. "Where's the frickin' elevator when you need it?"

As Jesse stood behind Jerome and Thomas, all he wanted to do was to get back upstairs to the apartment and then to the Sanctuary. He wasn't sure for how long the Sentinels out in front were going to be able to fend off the two Whre that had been chasing them, but he felt they would to be able to handle them with no problem.

Then a terrifying thought hit Jesse.

"What if the other Whre he saw in his vision joined the first two, and the Sentinels weren't able to keep them from getting into the building? Aw Man!!" thought Jesse.

He knew they would be toast for sure if that happened.

Returning his attention back to Thomas and Jerome, Jesse couldn't help himself. He screamed out loud to no one in particular.

"Com'on guys!" he exclaimed. "Where's the elevator?"

He was hoping that the urgency in his voice would be heard and the elevator would just…come!

"I don't know!" said Thomas as he took in a deep breath and punched the button again.

As the seconds passed, it felt like minutes.

Still no elevator.

Then suddenly Gharvey started to bark wildly at the dark corridor that was to their left.

It was then that Jesse caught a slight movement from within the darkness of the corridor. As he held onto Gharvey's leash, he slowly turned his head and strained his eyes to see what it was that had caught Gharvey's attention. Then from out of nowhere, there were all of these voices in his head at the same time.

Angry voices calling for revenge!

Revenge for someone called, Delan!

And then he saw it!

There, hulking in the shadows of the corridor but just barely visible, was a dark figure. At first it looked as if it were crouching close to the floor. It was then that Jesse adjusted his eyes and realized that the figure wasn't crouching as much as it was slowly moving itself along the back wall of the corridor.

"And Oh my God!" screamed the voice in his head. "It was making its' way into the main corridor where they were standing!"

Thomas and Jerome were trying to block out Gharveys' barking as they focused on why the elevator wasn't responding.

But peering out from the carrier on Thomas' back, Catherine knew what was coming toward them, and she knew they were about to be in serious danger.

As Jesse gripped Gharvey's leash tighter to keep her from charging into the darkness, his horror flooded from his gut to his head as he got a clearer look at what it was that was slowly making its' way toward them.

"It couldn't be!!" screamed the voice in his head.

He couldn't believe his eyes! Coming toward them had to be one of the biggest wolves anyone had ever seen on all fours before!

And then Jesse's heart literally jumped out of his chest and exploded when he saw that it wasn't just one wolf that was making its' way down the corridor toward them. It was at least six or more of them! And their dull, yellow eyes were fixed solely on him and the others.

Jesse's voice stuck in his throat as he tried to mouth a warning to Thomas and Jerome.

But there was no need.

Both Jerome and Thomas had looked up at the same time when they heard the commotion going on behind them. And it was then that they saw what Jesse was seeing.

The Whre had somehow made it past the Sentinels!

And they had not only gotten into the building, but they now had their sights set on them!

Not only were they were heading straight for where Jesse and the others were standing in the hallway, but he could see that there was nothing but revenge in their eyes! And the sounds. They were making low gurgling, snarling sounds that would send chills down anyone's back.

When Jesse finally found his voice, all he could do was scream. His scream was so loud that it even startled him when he heard it.

"Ahhhhh!!!!"

"Quickly, Jesse," called out Catherine as she jumped out of Thomas' backpack and landed on all fours in the middle of the hallway. "Move to the side! Move to the side!!" she yelled, trying to get him and Gharvey to get out of the way so she could have a clear shot.

But Jesse found that he couldn't move! It was as if his feet were frozen to the spot where he was standing.

And then abruptly without warning, the Brood stopped their advancement toward Jerome and the others!

"Did I do that?" questioned Jesse quickly as he looked around.

As he slowly turned and looked in the same direction that the Brood was looking, it was then that he realized that it wasn't his scream that had caused them to stop.

The Brood had all but stopped and cast their stare beyond the elevator where Jerome, Thomas and Jesse were standing. It was as if something else further on down the hall had taken the attention of the Brood away from them.

Slowly turning at the same time, Jerome and Thomas joined Jesse as he looked to the right.

And there, coming from the other direction was Paytric, Remy, and Ziggy, along with Irina and at least five other Gargoyles. And there was another man keeping stride alongside Paytric that Jerome hadn't seen before. But from the other end of the hall, Faayn and the other Brood recognized the man with the Gargoyles and the Warriors.

It was Skalla, their leader!

And although Gharvey would have willing stayed in the hallway and fought until her last breath to protect Jesse and the others, she knew when the odds were against them., and this was one of those times. And she also knew that if there was another option available to them, to take it.

Catherine had given them another option.

Gharvey, realizing Catherine needed them to get out of the way, turned and leapt on top of Jesse, knocking him toward the elevator just as the doors finally opened. Jesse found himself stumbling past Thomas and Jerome and falling through the open doors of the elevator and onto the carpeted floor with Gharvey jumping in behind him.

Without hesitation, Catherine arched her thick tail and flipped off several bolts of magic at the oncoming Brood. Then she quickly turned and leapt into the elevator just behind Gharvey and Jesse. But she didn't have to stay and see if her magic had hit its' mark. As Catherine landed inside of the elevator, over her shoulder she heard the cries of several of the oncoming Brood as they yelped in pain.

They had not only been thrown up against the back wall of the hallway when they were hit by Catherine's blast, but magical flames were burning and shearing the fur right off of their backs and undersides. As they hit the back wall and slid to the floor, they twisted and contorted their bodies as they rolled on the carpet trying to put out the flames that were licking and eating at them.

Faayn paused.

He was shocked to see that the Gargoyles were not only using magical creatures against them, but that his father, Skalla, was also standing with them. He couldn't understand why his father would stand against his own kind with those who were not only their sworn enemy, but were responsible for his son, Delan's death.

Faayn snarled and bared his teeth as he reared back onto his hind legs and stood to his full height. And although he wasn't as tall as Delan or his father was, standing at all of eight feet, he still commanded respect.

"If it is a fight they want, then it will be a fight we will give them!" yelled Faayn to the Brood that followed him as he moved forward.

"But Faayn!" exclaimed one of the Brood standing to his side. "Skalla is with them! We must stand down! He is our leader!"

And most of the Brood that had followed Faayn agreed. With the exception of a few, most of the wolves behind Faayn began to withdraw.

Without warning, Faayn quickly turned. He snapped and growled as he spoke.

"For whatever reason, my Father has become soft and has chosen to stand with our sworn enemy. You chose to follow me to revenge Delan's death. You all will stand by your decision or die now by my hand! What will it be?"

As Faayn glared at the wolf that had spoken up, it cowered and backed away. It knew that Faayn would surely follow through with his threat without pause as did the others.

Faayn turned back to the Warriors and the Gargoyles that approached them. Spreading his elongated arms to either side, he stood with his legs apart as he growled and snapped. His fangs and claws were fully exposed as the hair along the back of his neck stood straight up.

Faayn was prepared to attack.

The remaining of the Brood reluctantly fell to either side of him and began to move forward. As their various shapes separated from the darkness of the corridor and became distinct, their dull yellow eyes glared.

Jerome, seeing that Gharvey had pushed Jesse into the elevator, reached over and grabbed Thomas and shoved him in behind the others.

"Not today!" shouted the voice in Jerome's head. If he could help it, nothing was going to happen to either Thomas or Jesse while they were with him!

Jerome literally threw Thomas into the waiting elevator. And before he could turn and move himself forward to step in behind him, he saw a quick movement on his left side.

And sure enough, when Jerome turned his head, he spied that several of Faayn's Brood had broken away from the pack and were heading straight for the open elevator door.

Several of Faayn's loyal followers saw that three of the Humans they had cornered in the hallway of the Lexington were trying to escape into one of the elevators. Not wanting any of those that were possibly responsible for the death of Delan to get away, the two wolfs quickly bound forward.

And they were moving fast!

As the Warriors drew their short swords and quickly moved forward toward the Brood, Paytric saw that Jerome was the only one left standing in the corridor between them and the attacking wolves. Both Thomas and Jesse along with Gharvey and Catherine were already safe inside of the elevator.

"Move aside Jerome!" cried out Remy as he moved forward with the group, his short sword ready.

But Ziggy saw that two of the wolves were making a move to stop Jerome from getting to safety. Moving quickly, Ziggy drew his short sword and charged at the first wolf as he ran along the side of the hallway toward Jerome. His only hope was that he got to Jerome first before the wolf did. Jerome went to dive into the elevator, but the wolf was moving too fast.

From inside of the elevator, all Thomas and Jesse could do was to stare wide eyed as their hearts fell.

As the elevator doors quietly began to shut with a soft 'hissing' sound, they saw Jerome turn toward the lunging wolf as it went for his throat. All Jerome could do was to open his mouth to scream, but there wasn't time for any sound to escape.

The wolf was on him before he knew it!

"Jerome, look out!!" "Nooo!!"

Thomas and Jesse both screamed as they tried to move forward to try and help Jerome.

At that same time, Thomas and Jesse thought they saw something white and hazy began to swirl around Jerome just as the wolf went to snap at his neck.

It was then that they saw Ziggy as he seemed to literally leap through the air sideways from behind Jerome and the attacking wolf as his short sword sought its' mark. While the wolf was moving at an incredible speed, Ziggy was faster.

But before they could tell if Ziggy had gotten to the wolf before it was able to harm Jerome, the doors of the elevator tried to shut.

Everything was happening so fast, Thomas and Jesse weren't exactly sure what they actually saw. But just before the elevator doors could close completely, a set of oversized, curved claws from the second wolf had caught the doors and were trying to pry them back open!

Thomas and Jesse found themselves jumping back in shock! Gharvey began to bark wildly as Catherine arched her back and hissed.

They had just witnessed one of the wolves as it attacked Jerome and was hopefully brought down by Ziggy. And they weren't quite sure what it was they had seen engulf Jerome at the same time. But now with the possibility of a full-blown war going on in the corridor outside of the elevator they were in, another wolf was trying to pry the elevator doors back open to get at them!

"Auntie!" screamed Thomas as he and Jesse backed themselves up against the back wall of the elevator.

With the elevator doors only opened an inch or two, Catherine aimed her tail at her intended target. As she shot off a blast of magical energy, it partially hit the wolf trying to get into the elevator as it yelped and lessened its' hold on the door, but not entirely. The magic infusing the elevator and the doors was holding.

And then without warning, Catherine's magic began to ricochet off of the walls of the elevator as it bounced from one wall to the other just barely missing its' occupants.

"What happened?" screamed Jesse as he and Thomas tried to lay as low on the floor as they could trying to avoid being hit by the errant magic blast as it zigzagged back and forth.

"I should have guessed!" exclaimed Catherine as she too tried to elude her own magical blast. "They must have put protection spells on all of the entrances into the Sanctuary," yelled Catherine as she ducked quickly. "The walls of the elevator must be infused with magic to repel any spells. Do not worry, though!" exclaimed Catherine as she huddled in the corner with Gharvey. "I am sure that it will dissipate soon!"

"Not soon enough!" screamed Jesse as he ducked to the right just in time to miss the staggered bolt of magic as it whizzed by his head.

Then Gharvey yelped as the blast of magical energy zipped past her just missing her left ear.

As Catherine tried to reassure the boys that the magical blast would fizzle out soon, they heard a loud growl. Looking up, they saw that Catherine's magical blast had all but missed its' target. The attacking wolf had recovered and was still trying to pry the doors of the elevator open.

It was intent on getting to them by whatever means necessary!

"Let me try, Auntie!" shouted Thomas.

Even though he had a long way to go in learning how to wield his magic, he had learned a few tricks in the process.

"No, Thomas!" exclaimed Catherine quickly. "Any kind of magic spell you try to cast will be repelled."

"But we can't just sit here and wait for it to break through!" cried out Thomas as he tried to push himself further back against the wall as the magical blast whizzed by his face.

As far as they all were concerned, waiting for the wolf to break in was not something any of them was looking forward to!

"Maybe I can stop it!" exclaimed Jesse as he leaned forward and tried to focus on the wolf.

He wasn't sure that what he was going to try would work, but right now, they were out of options.

As the wayward bolt of magic began to fizzle and fade the more it bounced off of the walls of the elevator, Jesse made his move. He tried to block out the growls of the wolf as it continued to try and pry the doors of the elevator open with its' claws. He got as close as he dared and looked into its' eyes through the small opening.

He tried to concentrate as he entered the wolf's mind.

At first, Jesse was bombarded with hundreds of images he couldn't make out. They were all overlapping onto each other and blurred to where he couldn't tell one from the other. And anger. Jesse felt the anger and the rage of the wolf as he pried further into its' mind.

Then Jesse felt something.

But it wasn't coming from the wolf.! It was something in the back of his own mind!

Jesse tensed up as he realized that while he was trying to get into the wolf's mind, someone had entered his! But it didn't feel threatening to him. Jesse realized that it felt soft and warm. Almost soothing.

"Jesse! Jesse! You can do this!" the female voice said. "Sweep away everything that you see before you and concentrate on controlling his actions."

It was then that Jesse recognized the female voice he was hearing inside of his head. It was the same voice he had heard three years ago when he had the vision of Thomas in the Warrior's dimension when he and Pauly were flying above the fog bank.

It was Samantha, Thomas' birth mother.

She and Thomas' birth father, Mal-lor had been working with the two of them on learning how to handle their abilities. And although for Jesse it was a slow process, Thomas' birth mother had helped him learn how to focus on whatever it was he was trying do. And right now, it was something that he needed to put to the test.

And it felt good to realize that she was still there with them in spirit when they needed her. And that was speaking literally since both she and Mal-lor had remained earthbound as spirits to watch over Thomas.

So, Jesse concentrated harder with encouragement from Thomas' birth mother, and found that he could easily move the images he was seeing aside. He then placed a thought into the wolf's mind.

"You don't want to hurt us!" he said. "As a matter of fact, you will protect us from harm. That is what you want to do! Protect us! You will protect all of us!"

As soon as Jesse had finished placing the thought into the wolf's mind, the wolf stopped snarling and snapping through the small opening between the doors of the elevator. It whimpered a few times as it eyed Jesse through the crack, and the look in its' eyes had gone from angry and vicious, to gentle and calm.

And then they heard scraping sounds as it withdrew its' claws from between the elevator doors and let them close completely.

All of the time that Jesse was staring down the wolf, Thomas was holding his breath. He was just praying that the wolf didn't get through the doors before Jesse had a chance to plant his suggestion in its' mind.

Seeing that Jesse was able to deter the wolf and make it back off, Thomas breathed a sigh of relief. For a minute there, he thought he was going to burst if he had to hold his breath another minute.

"You did it, Jesse!" exclaimed Thomas out loud as he slapped Jesse on the back. "You did it buddy!"

Yes, he had done it. But he still felt as if he had failed.

Jesse slumped down onto his knees as he knelt in front of the elevator doors and just nodded his head. And then he leaned forward and broke down as he started to cry.

"Yeah, I did it!" he said in between his sobs. "But not in time to save Jerome! Not in time to save Jerome!"

He couldn't shake the last image he had of Jerome as he stood on the other side of the elevator doors as they were closing. All he could see was the first wolf as it lunged at him, going in for the kill. And even though they saw Ziggy go after the wolf, for some reason to Jesse, it didn't seem as if he had made it in time to save Jerome.

Thomas fell back onto his heels as the reality of what Jesse was saying sunk in. He had been so relieved to see that Jesse had saved them from the attacking wolf, he had all but forgotten what they had just witness happen to Jerome.

"Oh My God!" exclaimed Thomas. "Jerome! Maybe…maybe Ziggy got to him in time…?" mumbled Thomas as emotion began to flood his body.

But then he realized the same thing that Jesse had. The wolf was on top of Jerome a split second before Ziggy had gotten there to bring it down.

Catherine, also distressed that she couldn't do anything more to help Jerome, quietly approached the two emotional teens.

"Jesse! Thomas!" she said softly. "There was nothing that either of you could have done differently."

And then to Jesse she said, "And even if you could have done something more, Jesse, there is no guarantee that it would have saved Jerome. With all that was going on, you cannot put the fate of the whole world onto your shoulders alone. Sometimes…things happen."

Thomas slowly moved himself next to Jesse and put his arm around his shoulders. He couldn't help himself as he too felt the tears began to fall from his eyes. After everything they had been through together, this was the first time that one of their group had fallen. They all knew that it was a possibility, but there was nothing to prepare them for the flood of emotions that would bombard them when it finally did happen.

Catherine watched the two teens as they consoled each other. She knew that at that moment, there were no words that could be said that would make any difference in how they felt. She knew that they needed to grieve in their own way.

She hopped as lightly as she could into Jesse's lap, as Gharvey slowly rose up on all fours and made her way over to the two teens. As she sat down next to Thomas and leaned herself up against him, she put her head in his lap. She whimpered softly to let them know that she too was grieving.

As the four of them sat in a group huddle in the middle of the elevator consoling each other, they could feel the elevator move as it quietly made its' way to the thirtieth floor. Everyone was so overcome with grief that no one had noticed that none of them had pushed the buttons that would take the elevator up.

Yet it was moving.

It was Thomas who realized it just as the elevator stopped and the doors opened. In his heart and mind, it almost didn't matter anymore.

They had lost Jerome! They had lost their friend!

As the doors of the elevator silently slid open, they revealed Thomas and Jesse huddled together in the middle of the floor sobbing, with Gharvey and Catherine by their side.

Lillian and Jonathan Gates quickly rushed into the elevator as Amanda and Angi followed behind them. They gathered up the two distraught teens and helped them out of the elevator and into the hallway. Vi quickly scooped Catherine up into her arms, and took a hold of Gharvey's leash and followed the group as they made their way to the door of the apartment.

Lillian Gates and Amanda were both trying to calm Jesse down while Jonathan Gates drew his son close. As Thomas' mother turned to her husband, he gave her a nod that he had Thomas and they were okay, and that she should try and look after Jesse.

"Jerome!" cried Thomas as he let his father hold him. "Dad, we…we lost Jerome!"

"We know, Son! We know!" he said. "It's okay! Do you hear me?" he said quietly as he whispered into Thomas' ear. "It's okay. Everything's gonna to be alright! It's gonna be alright!"

Jonathan Gates wanted to break down and weep himself.

It was hard enough to lose someone as close as Jerome and the boys had become. But to see his son and his friends experience these types of things at such a young age. It just didn't seem right. But Jonathan Gates also knew that there were things happening in the world today that they didn't have any control over. And all they could hope for was to do their best. And at certain times, even their best wasn't going to be good enough. Bad things were still going to happen. And when they did, they just had to be there to give the love and support to those that needed it.

Like now.

Jonathan Gates just hoped that it would be enough.

As Amanda and Lillian Gates walked beside Jesse, he found that his feet felt as if they weighed a hundred pounds each. He just couldn't lift them to move himself forward. At that moment, he just didn't care anymore. Especially if it meant that more of his friends might get hurt or worse.

He didn't understand 'why' any of this had to happen. It didn't make any sense to him.

Once inside of the apartment, the group made their way to the side hallway where the waterfall was, and entered into the 'Gateway' that led to the Sanctuary.

Jesse just wanted to go somewhere and lay down so he could curl up into a tight ball and sleep. That was all he wanted to do.

Thomas held onto his father hoping that he wouldn't have to let go anytime soon. It felt safe in his father's arms, and he just wanted to stay there for as long as he could.

~~~~~~~~~~

As Ziggy ran alongside the right side of the hallway toward the wolf he had spied, he felt his 'Witches' Ride' surge upward and embrace his whole body. It was what happened to Warriors when they were in the mists of battle. That swelling of pure adrenaline times a hundred, that would flow throughout a Warriors' body and empower them with superhuman strength, aggression…purpose.

He had also learned to focus and control the energy of a 'Witches' Ride' while training with the Warriors. It was all important not to lose control of that surge of pure adrenaline once it began to course throughout your body. Controlled, it made you fight harder, fiercer. Uncontrolled, it could spell your own downfall.

A lesson that every Warrior learned, as he had.

As Ziggy leaped through the air toward the charging wolf, he saw it go for Jerome's throat as it drew back its' lips and bared its' fangs. Since Ziggy was behind Jerome and the wolf, he raised his short sword upward and brought it down at a forty-five-degree angle, over and in front of Jerome's right shoulder. He aimed for the chest of the attacking wolf that was open for his short sword to find its' mark.

But just as he went to strike, Ziggy saw the jaws of the wolf as they went to clamp down around Jerome's neck. As Ziggy heard the force of the jaws of the wolf snapped shut and close, he yelled out.

"Noooo!!!"

He hadn't made it in time!

Losing control of his emotions, Ziggy thrust the silver short sword deep into the chest of the wolf with such force that it came out through its' back. Falling to the floor, the wolf in its' final seconds realized that his jaw had clamped down not onto Jerome's throat, but onto nothing but thin air.

Ziggy was just as surprised as the wolf had been when he hit the floor. With a heavy heart, he quickly rolled over expecting to see the torn and brutalized body of his friend lying beside him and the wolf.

But Jerome's body wasn't there!

Only the impaled wolf was laying on the floor on its' side. And swirling around it and Ziggy was a somewhat opaque, yet slightly translucent, smokey haze. As Ziggy stared in disbelief, within seconds the haze slowly twisted and curled itself through the air and then rose toward the decorated ceiling of the corridor and then dissipated.

"Was that…was that Jerome's lifeforce that he was seeing?" thought Ziggy to himself.

Then he heard the Warrior yells as Paytric, Remy and Skalla, and the Gargoyles rushed by him to encounter Faayn and the rest of the Brood. And like a true Warrior in the mists of battle, Ziggy quickly regrouped himself, retrieved his short sword and bound to his feet. As Ziggy rushed forward with the rest of the group, he knew would have to mourn his friend, and ponder what he had witnessed, later.

For now, there was a battle to be fought, and a friends' life to be avenged!

Chapter II

The Request

As Paytric and Remy watched, they saw Ziggy leap to the defense of a friend like a true Warrior would. But even they could see that there was too much distance between Ziggy and Jerome for him to have made it in time.

The wolf was closer to Jerome than Ziggy was.

They watched in horror as the wolf went for Jerome's throat just seconds before Ziggy was able to thrust his short sword deep into its' chest. They themselves were too far to the left of the hallway to have been able to help. As they watched Ziggy and the dying wolf fall to the floor, Paytric and Remy stared down the approaching Brood.

"They will pay!" shouted Paytric under his breath as he and Remy also drew their short swords.

With heavy hearts, Paytric and Remy gave a battle cry and moved forward to meet Skalla's youngest son and the Brood that followed him.

Skalla seeing that a battle was inevitable, swiftly moved ahead of the Warriors and the Gargoyles and quickly transformed himself into his true form. Startled, the Warriors and the Gargoyles halted their charge as did Faayn and the rest of the Brood.

Skalla stopped just in front of the Warriors and the Gargoyles and the oncoming Brood. In his true form, he was crouched in the middle of the corridor with his head down as his body heaved up and down, pumped with emotional adrenaline.

The gray and black fur along the back of Skalla's neck stood straight up as the largest wolf Paytric, Remy or even Irina and her kind had ever seen, crouched in front of them…waiting.

Skalla was truly a rarity, even for his kind.

His father when he was alive, was well known among all of the other Brood clans. And up until his passing, he was larger in stature and girth than any of the Brood clans had ever seen before.

But then there was Skalla. When he was younger, he was always larger than the other Sires. Then he grew swift and in no time even surpassed his own father's height.

And now here he was, the only thing between two factions bent on attacking each other. One, his sworn enemy. The other his renegade son, Faayn, and the misguided Sires he had persuaded to follow him.

"And follow him they did," thought Skalla to himself. "They had followed him under false and misleading information. It was time that it end here and now!"

Raising his head, he drew back his lips and roared a warning to his youngest son and those that followed him. Then he slowly stood to his full height, all of ten plus feet as he literally dwarfed those standing around him. His arms were thick and muscular and had elongated to where they almost reached the floor. As he stood with his legs apart, his thick haunches were enormous and stout as they supported his massive frame. He just missed hitting the twelve foot ceilings above him by barely a foot or so.

Turning to his son, Skalla spoke.

"Son, you have offended me and all Whre by your actions," he said solemnly.

Faayn, heaved his chest forward as a challenge, would not back down.

"It is you, Father, who has offended us, your own kind!" he yelled. "You stand with our sworn enemy against your own! You stand with those that I saw with my own eyes, bring down and feed upon your own Son, Father! They fed upon Delan! The Gargoyles fed on Delan while I watched! And you stand here defending them!"

Faayn's voice bellowed throughout the corridor as his emotion and agitation began to rise. The rest of the Brood joined in as they howled their anguish.

"Tell me, Faayn," said Skalla. "Did you tell the Sires that follow you, why you and your Brother were in the City? Did you tell them that you and Delan had been hunting within the city for some time now, breaking my law. And that the only reason Delan is dead, is because of his own arrogance and defiance of my rule!"

As the other Sires standing with Faayn listened, they all looked to Faayn for a rebuttal. When there was none, they began to instinctively retreat away from his side.

He had lied to them!

He had roused them into a fighting fury to follow him into the city to avenge the death of Delan. But in truth, Delan and Faayn were caught in the wrong. They had gone against their father's decree, their own father's word not to hunt within the city. And now with a lie, he had involved them in his wrongdoing.

"Why Faayn?" asked Skalla. "It is one thing to break my law and a pact that had been in place for centuries. But to rouse the Sires to fight with a lie that would further damage that which may now not be repairable. Why?"

"You have become weak, Father!" answered Faayn, arrogantly. "Your own Sons could see it! And yes, you are right! We have been hunting the humans in the city for quite some time now. We have only taken the weak and the forgotten. But even though they are weak and forgotten, their blood be Human! I bet you have forgotten what human blood tastes like, haven't you, Father?" taunted Faayn. "I bet you have forgotten how sweet the nectar of humans is. The thrill of the chase, and how thirst quenching it feels as their blood flows through your body as you take it in. The sweet taste of their flesh."

"Stop!!!" yelled Skalla, unable to listen to anymore. "You no longer have the right to be called my Son!"

"I am Whre, Father!" Yelled Faayn as he now stood alone facing his father. "We are all Whre! And as Whre, we are meant to hunt Humans!"

As the Warriors and the Gargoyles stood their ground behind Skalla, they listened. They could appreciate Skalla's dilemma and now understood why he requested what he did of Irina. It was the only thing he could do to possibly save the rest of the Brood from his sons' treachery. And even though he stood tall, Paytric could see that the shoulders of leader of the Whre were slightly slumped forward as he spoke to his son for the last time as a father.

"It is by my decree that you, Faayn, are no longer my Son."

The gasps from the Sires that had backed off could be heard throughout the corridor as Skalla continued.

"And you are no long of the Whre. No Brood of the Whre will ever acknowledge you. By disowning you, you have no clan, no rights. And because you have broken the most sacred of our laws, my law!" shouted Skalla. "You shall be punished. And by Whre law, your own Brood will exact the true death upon you."

"You will have me put down, Father?" exclaimed Faayn, not believing what he was hearing. "I was doing that which I knew you would not! Avenge Delan! And now you have led me and the others into a trap!" he yelled. "I wondered how we made it past the Sentinels so easily."

Ignoring Faayn's words, Skalla turned to Paytric and the Gargoyles.

"Is my request still granted?" he asked.

Irina stepped forward and slowly nodded her head.

"It is!" she said.

'Then so be it!" exclaimed Skalla as he felt the sadness sweep through his body.

Stepping from behind the Gargoyles were the Whre that Skalla had brought with him to the city. One of the men had a metal band in his hands with short sliver spikes running along the inside.

Turning back to Faayn as he stood in front of him, Skalla spoke to him once more.

"Faayn. Unless you are going to challenge me here and now, transform and allow yourself to be 'banded'."

"But, Father…I, I" Faayn stumbled over his words.

He now understood what was happening. Skalla, his father, had condemned him to death. And not just any death. He was going to be 'banded' so he could not transform and then subjected to a punishment that had not been initiated for as long as he or any other Whre could remember.

"I no longer have any Sons," stated Skalla simply. "Transform! Or as your leader, I will bring you down myself!"

As the other Whre moved toward him, Faayn's mind was quickly weighing his options.

"He would not be put down without a fight!" yelled the voice in his head. "He would not!!"

But he saw that at that moment there was no other choice for him but to transform and suffer the humiliation of being disowned and 'banded' in front of the other members of the Brood that had followed and looked up to him.

But he had a plan.

As he transformed and stood naked in front of the onlookers, he glared at his father. He allowed himself to be 'banded' and his wrists shackled and attached to the front of the metal form around his waist.

"How could his own Father allow this? How??" yelled the voice in his head.

And then as he stared down his father, he smiled.

His eyes had the look of a man who at that moment, had nothing to lose. While he was figuring a way out of his current situation, in the end he swore to himself he would make his father pay!

As the other Whre secured the metal band around Faayn's waist, the short sliver spikes were driven into his flesh. As he screamed, the short silver spikes delivered a searing pain that was almost unbearable as it brought him to his knees. His eyes began to water as the pain found its' way to his head and made him feel as if it were going to explode.

He began to foam at the mouth and his vision blurred as the pain only intensified as he knelt in front of his father. His eyes flashed as they turned a deep, dark, yellow color.

"Father!!" yelled Faayn. "Please!!"

As Skalla transformed and stood in front of Faayn, all he could do was to look away. He felt his heart break as his own son, his last son, was being led away. 'Banded' as the decree of the true death for a Whre was to be initiated by his own kind.

Irina had granted a distraught and betrayed father his request.

She would allow the Whre to deliver punishment to Faayn by their own law and by their own hand, in order to save the rest of the Brood from being wiped out for breaking the pact.

Faayn felt himself being lifted by his shackled arms as they led him back down the corridor away from the Warriors and the Gargoyles. The Whre would transport him back to the Den of his Brood, and by the light of the full moon that night, they would deliver onto him the true death for a Whre.

His father had made a promise to the Gargoyles. And by his word, it would be carried out.

As the other Sires that had followed Faayn transformed, they too were escorted out of the corridor. Although they would not suffer the same punishment as Faayn, they knew that they were surely going to be dealt with harshly for their betrayal.

As one of Skalla's followers handed him something to cover himself with, he turned to the group of Warriors and Gargoyles and spoke.

While his voice was filled with emotion and remorse, he tried to steady himself.

"Thank you, Irina. I will forever be indebted to you for granting my request," stated Skalla humbly. "Perhaps I have not been the leader that my Sons felt I should have been. But I 'am' still the leader of the Whre. And the rest of the Brood will come to understand that no further disloyalty will be tolerated.

The pact that you and my Father had come to an agreement on still stands. And with my last dying breath, it will be upheld by the members of my Brood."

Acknowledging Skalla, Irina bowed slightly and said, "So it will be."

Turning to Paytric, Skalla gave the Warrior a slight smile and bowed.

Perhaps in another time, another place, he felt that he and Paytric would have been good friends and confidants. But he knew that was something that he would never come to know.

As the remaining Whre made their way down the corridor, they stopped to retrieve the one fallen Sire that Ziggy had brought down. Skalla followed behind them, truly dreading what task he had agreed to put upon his Brood that night. It was something he was not looking forward to.

Paytric and Remy watched the leader of the Brood as he exited the corridor, then turned their attention to a situation they themselves were not looking forward to.

Irina was the first to speak.

"We grieve for your loss Paytric," she said.

Even JoSen, one of her fellow Gargoyles, who had leaped across the hallway and had also tried to make it to Jerome before the wolf did, knew that the wolf was in too close proximity of Jerome for either him or Ziggy to have made it in time. But still he tried.

At least his presence in front of the elevator door with Ziggy help to block the other wolves.

"Thank you, Irina, JoSen," said Paytric.

Then he asked, "Do you know what that was that we saw Jerome dissipate into?"

"I do not," answered Irina solemnly. "I have never seen such an apparition such as that before."

The fallen Sire that had attacked Jerome just seconds before Ziggy was able to bring it down had been removed. But the question was, 'where was Jerome?'

"Paytric! I don't understand!" exclaimed Ziggy angrily as he walked back to the spot in front of the elevator where he, Jerome and the fallen wolf had landed. "He was here! Jerome was here and then…he wasn't!"

Ziggy paced back and forth not understanding what had happened. He was hoping in his heart that through a magic spell, someone had transported Jerome from the lobby and away from the attacking wolf. But as he looked around, Ziggy could see that there was no one in the lobby that could have cast such a spell.

Catherine was with Thomas, Jesse and Gharvey inside of the elevator as it made its' way to the thirtieth floor. Granna was in the Sanctuary with her sisters, and as far as he knew, Cherese was still out with the girls shopping.

"Was what he saw the essence of Jerome's life as it slipped away?" questioned Ziggy as he continued to pace. "If that were true, then the question was, 'Where was Jerome's body?' And with all the magic that surrounded them, could none have been spared to save Jerome?"

The feeling of loss was overwhelming for Ziggy as he knelt down and dropped his head onto his chest. He felt his breathing become shallow and quick as he tried to gasp for air. He felt as if he was suffocating.

"This can't be happening!!" shouted the voice in his head. "It can't be!!"

As Paytric and Remy stood beside Ziggy, they placed their hands on his shoulders allowing the young Warrior time to gather himself. They knew all too well that at one time or another, they as Warriors all had to face the loss of someone. It wasn't something that they would wish upon anyone, but it was what it was.

After a few moments had passed, Ziggy lifted his head and wiped away the tears he had shed for a good friend.

"How was he going to tell Cherese? And his parents! What about them?"

As the realization of what he had to face raged through his mind, he slowly shook his head from side to side in disbelief.

"He could battle the entire Whre until he fell if he had to," he thought to himself. "That's what a Warrior does! That I can do! But this!" he lamented. "This was going to be the most difficult thing he was ever going to have to do."

And in truth, Ziggy wasn't sure he was up to it.

Irina and the rest of the Gargoyles bowed solemnly and began to make their own retreat out of the hallway. She knew that the Warriors would need time to grieve the loss of one of their own. And however long they needed, they would have.

"We will leave you so that you may return to the Sanctuary and your friends," said Irina. "We are sorry!"

As Paytric and Remy helped Ziggy to his feet, they led him to the same elevator that Jerome had been standing in front of only moments before.

Even Paytric as baffled as to what he and the others had witnessed.

"Surely it had to be some form of magic that had occurred," thought Paytric to himself.

But like Ziggy, Paytric knew there was a slight chance of that being the case. And although it pained him greatly, he knew that Jerome was in fact gone.

Chapter III

'The Rumors of My Demise…..'

As Cherese stepped into the bedroom that she and Jerome shared, she tossed the two bags of 'great buys' she and the girls had found onto the bed. She and the other girls had spent the whole afternoon just going from one fabulous store to the next, looking, trying on and of course, buying! She couldn't remember when she had had so much fun with friends.

As she turned and headed for the door to go back out into the great room and join the others, she was stopped dead in her tracks. It was as if she had turned and slammed into an invisible wall.

The impact caused her to stumble backwards and double over in pain as her gut told her…something had happened.

Something bad!

And then in an instant she knew that it involved Jerome. She couldn't quite put her finger on it, but it felt as if Jerome was…gone! But something was off. Something wasn't…quite right about it.

~~~~~~~~

As Lillian Gates entered the Sanctuary's great room, she saw that the other Watchers and Wau-douns along with Jerome's parents had just arrived. Even Mr. Chisum, the school bus driver from Hampton was there with his daughter Stephanie. Although Thomas and Jesse had seen Mr. Chisum at school over the last couple of years because he had continued to drive the school bus, it had been a while since they had seen his daughter. She was one of the first Watchers they had met during the battle in Hampton, other than Thomas' parents. They remembered her well.

Lillian Gates and Amanda walked a distraught Jesse to the nearest couch and sat him down while her husband sat Thomas down on the other couch.

Amanda sat next to Jesse and pulled him close. She tried her best to hug his pain away. If she could, she would have taken it all away. But she knew there was nothing she could do for Jesse but to let him cry and get it all out.

Seeing that Jesse was in good hands, Lillian Gates slowly made her way over to her husband and her son. Mr. Gates continued to talk softly to his son as he rocked him back and forth like a baby.

"At this moment, he is my baby boy," thought Jonathan Gates to himself. "And he needed nurturing."

Angi quickly moved over to the couch and wrapped her arms around a trembling Jesse as Amanda tried to comfort him.

They had all lost someone very dear to them that day. The question was, how were they to go on?

"What's happening?" "What's going on?"

The new arrivals were stymied by the emotional scene they saw before them as they threw questions out looking for an answer.

As Vi stood on the steps leading down into the great room still holding onto Gharvey and Catherine. She couldn't stop the tears from falling as Kenadi approached her and gathered her in a hug, They couldn't believe what they had seen through a magical portal the Wielders of Magic had opened up just as the confrontation that was going on in the lobby got started.

Just as Jerome made his move to enter the elevator behind Thomas, they saw the two wolves make their move just as Ziggy and one of Irina's Gargoyles matched them. Everything happened within a matter of seconds, that even Granna's two Wielder of Magic sisters didn't have time to cast a spell to help Jerome.

Then Vi thought about Cherese!

"Oh My God!!" screamed the voice in her head. "What about Cherese?"

Cherese had just left the great room of the Sanctuary to go into her and Jerome's bedroom before Helen and Mrs. Whitehall had opened the magical portal. They wanted to observe what was going on downstairs even though the sisters had been directed to stay in the Sanctuary and protect everyone there, until the situation with the Sires of the Whre could be contained. But they felt that if things didn't go as planned, they wanted to be ready to intervene if they had to. So, Cherese hadn't seen what the others had witnessed.

Lillian Gates looked up into the faces of Reginald and Carolyn, Jerome's parents as they approached her. She felt her heart break as she just shook her head slowly. It wasn't her child that was lost that day, but it felt like it. And she knew her friends were going to be devastated by the news.

"Lillian, what…what's going on?" asked Jerome's mother as she stepped closer. "What's happening?"

Then as she looked into the faces of those around her as an overwhelming fear swept over her.

"Why isn't someone saying something?" said Jerome's mother in a strained voice as she quickly stumbled back with a frantic look on her face. She felt a sharp, stabbing pain in her stomach as her husband, Reginald reached for her.

"Carolyn, what's wrong, baby? Are you okay?" he asked as he too started to feel as if something bad had just happened. Something very bad.

All Carolyn could do was to shake her head from side to side slowly as she immediately looked around the room and into the faces of those she had come to know as friends.

"Where's Jerome?" she asked in a shallow voice. "Where…is…Jerome?"

Jonathan Gates slowly rose from the couch where he had been sitting with his son, and reached out to the two as he approached them. He knew what they were going to go through since he and his wife gone through almost the same thing with Thomas.

"Carolyn. Reginald."

They thought they had lost Thomas to the Dark Dimension three years ago, but this was different. They were able to rescue their son before anything bad had happened to him. The same was not to be said for Jerome.

"Something has happened," he said as emotion filled his voice. "And I am…so sorry!" he lamented.

"What are you talking about, Jonathan?" said Reginald as he too began to feel that something was not right. "Where's Jerome, man? Where's my Son?"

"He…he didn't make it, Reginald," answered Jonathan Gates slowly as he tried to forget the image of Jerome's face, and the look in his eyes as the jaws of the first wolf went to clamp down onto his throat.

All Jonathan Gates could see was the shock and scared look in Jerome's eyes as he seemed to be thinking, 'This can't be happening! This…cannot be happening!"

And now he had to endure the look in Jerome's parents' eyes as the realization of what he was saying dawned on them.

"He was protecting Thomas and Jesse," continued Jonathan Gates in a strained voice.

"Are you telling us that our Son is…is dead?" asked Reginald as he felt his knees begin to give way.

Carolyn turned her head into her husbands' shoulder as she fell into him. She didn't want to hear the answer that she knew was coming. It was something that no parent wanted to hear.

All Jonathan Gates could do was to slowly nod his head.

As everyone's heart went out to Jerome's parents, several of Reginald's retired buddies from his old military squadron, made a move toward him. They knew that the man they affectionately called 'Reggie', was hurting. They knew that it was 'God', country, and family that was important to him, and he would die to defend them.

And now they had to look on while he was emotionally brought down after hearing that his son was gone.

As Kenadi stood on the steps leading into the great room, she reached out to hug a crying Vi as she too broke down.

No one could believe what had happened.

Just then, Paytric, Remy and Ziggy came through the 'Gateway', and stood next to Kenadi and Vi. Kenadi turned to her brother and let herself and Vi be drawn to him as he tried to comfort them the best that he could. As they took in the emotional scene before them, everyone could see from the look on the Warriors' faces, that they too were distraught by what had just happened.

And Ziggy!

He looked as if he had been drawn and quartered several times over.

One of their own had fallen defending those he had sworn to protect…like a true Warrior would have.

Suddenly, from just beyond where Vi and Kenadi were standing with Paytric and the others, a voice spoke.

"What's going on?"

Everyone in the room turned toward the voice, fully expecting to see Cherese.

In an instant, the whole room erupted.

"Jerome??" "Jerome!" "Oh My God, it's Jerome!"

As everyone made a move toward Jerome as he entered the great room with Cherese by his side, the feelings of elation were overwhelming.

Carolyn and Reginald made their way to their son's side first as the rest of the group followed suit.

As they hugged and kissed him, they didn't know, nor did they care what had transpired earlier. All they knew and cared about was that their son was alright. He was alive!

"What happened?" "How did you get away?"

The questions poured out as did the feelings of relief that Jerome was in fact alright.

"Son! Son, you sure you're alright?" asked Reginald. "Are you sure?"

"I'm okay, Pops!" exclaimed Jerome just glad to be there. "I'm okay!"

"Baby, I thought we had lost you!" cried Jerome's mother as she held onto him, not willing to let go. "I thought...!"

"No, Mom. I'm, I'm okay!" said Jerome as he hugged her back.

As everyone rallied around him, it was beginning to feel like a joyous reunion.

The stunned look on Paytric's face was only matched by the look on Remy's face. They couldn't believe their eyes as they stood staring at a healthy Jerome who was very much alive!

And then in the fashion true to Jerome, he announced with a broad smile, "The rumors of my demise…have been greatly exaggerated! At least this time!"

Ziggy wasted no time as he made his way to stand in front of his best friend, and what he had hoped wasn't an apparition. As he gathered him in a bear hug and held on, he did his best not to break down and cry in front of the Warriors and everyone else who was gathered around Jerome. But he was beyond overjoyed to see him alive.

"Dude!" exclaimed Ziggy as he whispered into Jerome' ear. "I tried to get to you in time!" he said. "I did! I'm so sorry!"

"I saw you, Man!" said Jerome to his friend as he hugged him back. "I saw you. You looked cool too, flying through the air like that. Where'd you learn that from?"

As the two friends stepped back from each other, they couldn't help to laugh at the humor that Jerome had injected into a otherwise awkward situation.

"Thank you, Man, for coming to help me!"

"Next time, I'll be quicker!" said Ziggy as he slapped his friend on the shoulder. "I promise!"

"Let's hope there won't be a next time, okay!"

"Here's hoping!" exclaimed Ziggy, as he reached over and hugged Jerome once again.

Lillian and Jonathan Gates rushed forward but were almost knocked over by Thomas as he made his way to Jerome. And Jesse had moved ahead of them all by leaping over the back of the couch he had been sitting on just moments before.

They couldn't believe it! How was this even possible?

They had witnessed the horrible scene outside of the elevator when the wolf went for Jerome's throat. It was then that they realized the only reason that Jerome could possibly be standing before them, had to be because Ziggy had somehow felled the wolf before it could rip out his throat.

As the questions swirled around in their heads with no apparent answers, they dismissed them all and decided to dwell in the moment.

Jerome was alive! And that was all that mattered.

J.D. and her sister Laura, along with Helen and Mrs. Whitehall, all stood with the other Watchers and the Wau-douns as Jerome's miraculous return was celebrated.

Angi and Amanda were so dumbfounded that they just stood staring at each other with their eyes as wide as saucers, unable to comprehend was happening. They too had witnessed what had transpired downstairs in the corridor. For all intents and purposes, Jerome should have been dead.

"But he was alive!" they thought to themselves. "Jerome was alive!"

Then, when they realized that they weren't going to have to relay to Cherese what they had witnessed, the feeling of relief that lifted off of their shoulders was beyond description.

After they both had recovered as best as they could, they made their was over to where Jerome was standing with Cherese by his side.

As Amanda reached out for Cherese, she whispered in her ear, "You okay?"

Nodding her head that she was, Amanda stepped back and eyed her friend carefully.

She had come to know Cherese fairly well during the last three years. And just looking at the strained look on her face, Amanda could tell that Jerome's appearance had thrown Cherese for a loop too.

"Jerome."

It was Paytric who had moved himself forward and placed his hand onto Jerome's shoulder.

"By our Creator! Is it really you?" he asked as he gave Jerome an intense look, just as stymied by his appearance as the others were.

Jerome nodded his head confirming that it was in fact him. Actually, he was glad that he still had a head to nod after he almost lost it.

"Jerome! I am so glad to see you!" said Jonathan Gates shakily as he stood next to Paytric and Remy. "But I have to ask. I mean, we all need to know.

What happened? We were watching from up here, and from what we saw…I don't understand how you can be here! Son, you have to explain this to us!"

As everyone quieted down so they could give Jerome their undivided attention, he coyly looked over to his left at Cherese.

He squeezed her hand lightly, letting her know that he might need help in explaining to his friends something that he didn't quite fully understand himself. But he would try.

"Well, I didn't mention this to anyone because…I wasn't really sure what was happening."

"What are you talking about, Son," asked Reginald as he and Jerome's mother looked on with a confused look on their faces.

It was Amanda who put her finger on what Jerome was eluding to immediately.

"You started to develop an ability didn't you?" she stated with a questioning tone.

Jerome just nodded his head as he smiled slightly.

"Yeah! So it would seem."

"That's why when I brought down the wolf in the corridor, and I landed on the floor next to it, you weren't there." said Ziggy as the type of ability that Jerome seemed to have developed began to come to light.

"Yep!" exclaimed Jerome. "It seems that I have begun to develop the ability to…" Jerome paused for a second, and then he continued. "How do I say this?" he said hesitantly. "I've developed the ability to disperse myself at will. Go figure!"

"You mean, disappear!" exclaimed Jerome's mother as she stood by his side.

"Well," stammered Jerome as he fumbled with the words that would explain what he meant. "Not exactly disappear, disappear like the 'Invisible Man' does. I kinda...disperse! Like into a cloud of mist!"

"That's what we saw just as the elevator doors shut!" exclaimed Jesse as he looked over at Thomas for confirmation. "Just as the wolf leaped on you and went for your throat, we saw this sort of haze wrapped itself around you."

"Actually, the haze you saw 'was' me!" said Jerome as he looked around at the group as they stood before him.

He knew that what he was saying sounded weird if not crazy, but it was what it was.

"Wow!" exclaimed Thomas and Jesse in unison.

As far as they were concerned, that was a really 'cool' thing to be able to do!

"Heck!" they thought to themselves. "You could come and go anywhere you wanted, whenever you wanted. And if no one was the wiser, that particular ability could prove to very useful."

"Especially with a certain girl named Shelby," thought Jesse as she thought about her for the first time since he had arrived at the Lexington.

He could kind of check in on her and some of her girlfriends and see how she really felt about him.

"Now that would be really interesting!" Jesse mused to himself.

Lillian Gates turned to Jerome and asked, "When did you first realize that you could do this, Jerome?".

Thomas' parents were trying to keep a running timetable on how long it actually took for abilities to present themselves in those that had stayed in the Warriors dimension over a certain amount of time, and what abilities actually presented themselves. In Jerome's case, it was just over three years, much later than the others. And as far as they knew, Ziggy still hadn't shown any signs that he had developed any abilities like the others.

"Actually, it was about two months ago," explained Jerome.

"What was the situation that first brought it forth?" asked Jonathan Gates, trying to get as much information as he could.

Jerome paused at Jonathan Gates' question. He didn't want to go into a full explanation of exactly how it had happened because, well…it was kind of personal, and between him and Cherese. How could he explain to his friends, some of their parents, and his own parents, that the first time he had transformed was when he was in an 'aroused' situation with Cherese".

"Well…you see," started Cherese not really sure how to explain it herself. "He was…we were fighting.

And, after a while we realized how, silly it was, and ah…we made up…!"

"Yeah! We kinda found out that when I'm in a highly…emotional state, my body does this weird thing!"

Jerome tried to laugh it off as Cherese laughed with him hoping to sidestep the awkwardness of the situation.

J.D., standing next to her sister, Laura put into words what Cherese and Jerome couldn't.

"You were making love when it happened!"

She had said it in such an innocent, yet 'to the point' way, that for a few seconds the silence in the room was deafening.

As a matter of fact, it was so quiet, you could hear the crickets chirping.

Laura, realized that her sister, even though she was speaking the truth, had made an awkward situation even more so.

"J.D.!" she exclaimed as she turned to her younger sister. "There are children present! Humans don't discuss such things openly in mixed company like that! Sorry!" apologized Laura to the group.

Everyone looked from Cherese to Jerome and then tried to act as if they hadn't hear what J.D. had said. Some even cleared their throats and laughed nervously, wondering what they were supposed to do next.

Then it was Thomas who chimed in.

"Oh don't worry, Laura! Jesse and I are sixteen now!" he exclaimed proudly. "We know all about that kind of stuff. Especially Jesse! Right!" said Thomas as he nudged his best friend as he stood next to him.

"Say what!!??" exclaimed Amanda as she eyed her younger brother. "How, how do you know about, you know…this kind of stuff?" she asked.

She knew that she and Jesse hadn't been as close as they had been after the incident in Hampton a few years back.

"But how could she have missed this?" she asked herself. "My little Brother…!"

She couldn't believe it!

"Thanks Thomas!" lamented Jesse as he gave his best friend that, 'I'm gonna get you for that!' look.

"Well, it's official!" exclaimed Angi as she leaned over to Amanda. "He's not your 'little' Brother anymore, that's for sure!"

"Angi!" exclaimed Amanda to her best friend. "I really don't need to hear that right now!"

"Yeah…but I'm just sayin'!"

"Well, don't say it! He's my little Brother!" bemoaned Amanda hoping if it wasn't said out loud, then maybe it wouldn't be true.

Then, turning to her brother she asked quietly, "Jesse…does Mom and Dad know?"

"Know What!!" exclaimed Jesse. "There's nothing to know."

Then turning to Thomas, Jesse cried, "See what you've started!"

Thomas just shrugged his shoulders not understanding what the problem was.

Then Jonathan Gates turned to his wife and asked, "I thought that when Jerome and Cherese were fighting, that was when he changed?" he asked. "Did I miss something?"

"Yes, Jonathan, you missed it!" exclaimed Lillian Gates as she turned her husband around and led him back into the great room. "And we may need to have another talk with our Son, too"

"Well Son!" exclaimed Jerome's father as he looked intently at him. "Whatever it is you've developed from being in the Warrior's dimension, I thank God that it presented itself at a time when it was truly needed."

"I know that's right, Pops!" said Jerome as he smiled broadly at his parents.

As he and Cherese followed everyone into the great room, he thought back a couple of months earlier, to when he first discovered that his body would transform itself into wisps of mist whenever he was in a highly…emotional state.

The first time it happened was when he and Cherese were having 'make up sex' after an argument. He really didn't feel that he had to explain to his friends exactly how it had happened the first time, but just to suffice that it happened.

One day when they were alone in the apartment, they just blew up at each other over something that was so silly he couldn't even remember what it was about. But by that evening, he was missing her, and it was that feeling he didn't like. By the time he had made his way to the bedroom to talk to her, she was on her way to talk to him.

Apparently, she was having the same feelings as he was.

All he knew was that one thing led to another, and before long, they were deeply and passionately making love like they had never done before. They didn't even realize that Amanda and Angi had returned to the apartment. And after hearing noises coming from the bedroom, they quickly made their departure to give the two their privacy.

Jerome had had 'make up sex' before with a couple of his former girlfriends. And as other guys would attest to, there's almost nothing like it. But none of that could compare to what he and Cherese experienced that night. As an afterthought, he figured that it could have had something to do with the fact that Cherese was a Witch, and that just may have intensified the situation.

"But no matter!" thought Jerome to himself.

To him it felt like everything sensual between them, had been all rolled up together and magnified a thousand times over! There were so many sparks flying in the bedroom that night with him and

Cherese, he was surprised that no one had called the police on them.

It was during that time that Jerome had his first experience with his new ability.

All he remembered was looking down at Cherese with the greatest feeling of love and desire he had ever known. And in an instant, all of those emotions and feelings just seemed to explode inside of him. It was like nothing he had ever experienced before.

Then, as the feeling swept over him, he saw the shocked look on Cherese's face as he seemed to just dissipate into a soft, swirling mist. He felt himself float upward for a minute, and then come back down as he returned to his human form. And although it was for only a moment or two, that was enough.

After he was fully back into his Human form, he rolled over next to Cherese, stunned! All he remembered was Cherese's wide-eyed look as she looked over at him for a second, and then returned her gaze to the ceiling above them.

"What was that!!??" she exclaimed shakily, afraid to look over at him for fear that he would disappear again.

"I dunno!!!" said Jerome quickly, not sure what to make of what had just happened.

"Uh! Okay!!!" said Cherese, content to leave it at that for the time being.

She wasn't even sure if she could handle an explanation from him at that moment.

All Jerome knew was what he had felt. It was as if every cell in his body had just separated from each other and changed into something light, airy and see through. That was when he seemed to float upward toward the ceiling although he was still very much aware of everything that was going on around him.

When they had both recovered, they were able to discuss what they had experienced with each other. It was quickly determined that Jerome was in fact developing an ability as an aftermath of being in the Warriors' dimension. And although it was three years later, it was emerging just the same. To what degree he could transform and control it, was something that was yet to be determined.

"Was it only when he was in a highly aroused state, or were there going to be other times when his body would change? And if so, what were they?" thought Cherese to herself.

Whatever the answer was, Cherese was willing to put Jerome to the task whenever necessary, to find out.

As Lillian and Jonathan Gates made their way back into the great room, everyone followed suit. along with Jerome's parents. They were all relieved that the conflict between the Whre and the Pre' had turned out the way it had before it had spilled out into the Human world.

The situation with Skalla's son, Faayn, and the young Sires of the Whre had been resolved. The Gargoyles had granted clemency for Skalla and the rest of his Brood. But only if those responsible for breaking the pact that had been agreed upon hundreds of years ago between the Gargoyles, the Whre and the Pre', were punished.

Delan and Faayn.

And since Delan had already been felled by one of the Gargoyles in Central Park, that left only Faayn to be dealt with. It had been agreed that Faayn would suffer the true death for a Whre, by the hands of his own kind. It was the only thing that would stop the Gargoyles from wiping the Whre out, entirely.

"And what better sacrifice for the Son of the Whre leader to make, other than giving his own life to preserve the continuance of his fellow Whre," thought Skalla to himself, as he delivered the sentence to Faayn, his last remaining son. "And what better way for his Son to pay penance for his betrayal to his kind."

Granna and the others had dealt with the Pre' in the caverns below New York City, after they had mounted the rescue of Cherese and Sean, and captured two of their leaders and one follower. The others in the cavern had been wiped out, with the exception of the girl named Givant, who had escaped. But the magical community was on the lookout for her and any others that may have been missed.

And most importantly, Jerome was alright.

Due to the emergence of a new ability, he was able to escape being mauled to death by one of the young Sires of the Whre when they had attacked him in the lobby of the Lexington. Not only was he alright, but he had protected Thomas and Jesse.

All was as it should be. Or so it seemed at first.

Chapter IV

Escape…Betrayal…Treachery

8pm

As everyone regrouped in the great room, there was a feeling of relief and joy as they celebrated the return of Jerome from what everyone had thought was a sure death sentence.

Mrs. Whitehall announced that she and her Wielder of Magic sister, Helen, along with Laura, were going to check the perimeter of the Sanctuary to assure everything was as it should be. Paytric and Remy along with Jerome's father and his 'Special Forces' buddies who were now part of the Wau-douns, gathered around the large Mahogany dining table.

It was a relief to them to hear that because of the course of events that had happened just before they arrived, they had sidestepped a potential fight. Being former members of the Special Forces, Jerome's father and his retired buddies were always ready for whatever it took to defend their homeland. But if a confrontation could be avoided, that was something to be thankful for.

Lillian and Jonathan Gates found several comfortable chairs along the side of the great room where they sat along with Jerome's mother, Carolyn.

As Lillian Gates sat down, she saw Jerome's mother grasp her hands in front of her and bow her head. She was silently saying a prayer thanking God for delivering not only her son from harm, but for all those that were present. Lillian Gates leaned forward and put her hand on top of Jerome's mothers' hand and bowed her head too.

"Too many times we forget to give thanks for that which has been received," said Thomas' mother quietly as she joined Jerome's mother in prayer.

"Amen to that!" exclaimed Carolyn as she looked up and smiled at Thomas' mother, then bowed her head and continued to pray.

Jonathan Gates just looked over at the kids as they gathered in front of the large fireplace in the great room rejoicing at Jerome's return, and quietly said his own prayer.

"For Thomas and Jesse's safety, for Jerome being there to watch over them when they needed him to be, I thank you, my Lord," he said quietly under his breath. "And for whatever this new ability Jerome has developed, and it's timely emergence that saved him. For all of that, and so much more, I am so grateful that you are indeed looking out for us, and what we are trying to do. Thank you!"

As everyone settled in around the fireplace, they were anxious to hear exactly 'how' Jerome got away from the wolf in the corridor and made it up into the Sanctuary. Especially since entry into the Sanctuary was through the one elevator that Thomas and Jesse had taken to the thirtieth floor and the apartment. And as far as they could determine, Jerome wasn't in the elevator with them.

"So, how did you get here…in the Sanctuary, I mean?" asked Ziggy as he sat down next to Jerome. "Cause' Dude, the last time I saw you was downstairs in the hallway just as the wolf was going for your jugular. And then…pouf! You were gone!"

"Yeah!" exclaimed Angi as she chimed in with Ziggy. "With all of the magical protection around the Sanctuary, much less throughout the Lexington itself, how did you get pass them?"

"I don't know, guys!" answered Jerome as he relaxed a bit, just happy to be with his friends after his ordeal. "All I know is that I had the most intense feeling that I had to get back here to the Sanctuary, no matter what," explained Jerome. "It was as if that desire drew me here. I didn't feel any barriers or anything trying to stop me from entering. If there were any, I didn't feel it. All I know is that I found myself materializing in the bedroom where Cherese was."

"All right, girlfriend!" exclaimed Amanda as she directed her gaze to Cherese. "What did you do?"

"What?? Wait a minute!" exclaimed Jerome. "You think Cherese had something to do with me getting past the magical protection around the Sanctuary?"

"Well let's see!" said Amanda in a matter of fact kind of way. "The only way to get past the kind of magical barrier or protection spell that's around the Sanctuary, is if you counter it with something pretty strong. And I don't know if you've noticed, but my girl here is on the way to becoming a pretty strong Wielder of Magic, in her own right."

"Whoa!!" "Is that true?"

As everyone's attention turned to Cherese, she relented.

"Okay, fine! I may have done a little 'somethin' somethin' when I realized what was happening to him," she admitted.

"How did you know something had happened to him?" asked Amanda.

"Well, at first I had this sense that he was...'gone'! I mean, it hit me like a 'ton of bricks' and I didn't know what to think! Then inside of the confusing feelings I was having, I started to sense something else. Something, familiar that felt as if it was reaching out to me. Then I could sense that it was Jerome. So, I reached back and pulled him to me. I mean, what would you have done?"

"The exact same thing, Cherese," said Angi in support of her friend. "I would have done the exact same thing, without a doubt!"

"Well, Baby Girl!" gushed Jerome as he looked over to Cherese. "I guess I owe you my life."

"And that cute, tight butt of yours, too!" responded Cherese as she nudged Jerome and smiled at him in a playful way.

As the two gave each other a look that the others knew all too well, everyone surrounding them immediately chimed in.

"Oh, God! Here they go again!" "Yeah!!" "Ah, com'on, guys! Not here!"

"What!!" exclaimed Jerome and Cherese together.

The only two that beat out Jerome and Cherese in the 'lovey-dovey' department were J.D. and Sean. And that was saying something. Everyone broke out into laughter, relieved that the stress of the crazy day they all had experienced while in New York City had lifted.

Laura had returned from securing the perimeter of the Sanctuary with Mrs. Whitehall and Helen. Then the Wielders of Magic provided everyone with light refreshments, and for the next two hours they continued to converse and enjoy the company of each other, glad to put the day behind them.

At around ten o'clock, Irina and several of the Gargoyles abruptly appeared inside of the Sanctuary. Paytric was the first to disengage himself from the conversation he was in and rose to approach them. As he stopped in front of Irina, she leaned down and spoke to him in a hushed voice.

Immediately, all conversation in the great room ceased.

As everyone looked on, Paytric's body language suddenly changed as he quickly looked back over his shoulder with a concerned look on his face. Then turning back to Irina, Paytric simply nodded his head slowly as the Gargoyles took their leave as abruptly as they had appeared.

At that moment, it seemed as if the air inside of the Sanctuary had become profoundly heavy and intense. The Gargoyles had appeared for a reason. They had a message to give to Paytric . A message of great importance that would change the elated feeling of all those within the Sanctuary.

"Paytric. What is it?" asked Jonathan Gates as he rose from the chair he had been sitting in. "Is something wrong?"

"Brother!" exclaimed Remy as he too approached Paytric as he stood with his back to the others. "Has something happened?"

Turning to face everyone, Paytric took in a deep breath, and then spoke.

"It would seem that Faayn has escaped his Father's men, and is now loose within the city."

"Then we are on the hunt?" asked Remy as he, Ziggy and Kenadi all stepped forward.

Even Jerome's fathers' retired buddies from his old Special Forces group stood up, ready to be dispatched. They may have been retired from the military, but they were now part of the Wau-douns, and that meant standing to protect humans whenever they were needed.

"Yes, we are on the hunt!" said Paytric. "But it is no longer a hunt for just one Whre."

"What do you mean?" asked Ziggy as he stood next to Remy. "Did some of the other Sires follow him?"

"Yes. But it seems that when Skalla's men were escorting Faayn through the underground tunnels that lead to the outskirts of the city, the Pre' were waiting for them. They helped Faayn and the Sires escape from his Father's men."

"The Pre'??" "How??" "You've got to be kidding!" "I thought that we got them all when Cherese and Jerome were rescued?"

The responses from everyone in the room were all voiced at one time to Paytric's announcement.

"Obviously, there seems to be some questions we need to have answers to," said Paytric with a concerned tone to his voice. "One of them being, why would the Pre' help a Whre, one of their oldest enemies, escape his own kind. The other is, just how many of the Pre' are there left? I too thought that their numbers were few, and they had been basically eliminated in the rescue."

"Granna and her sisters have two of the Pre' leaders confined along with one of their followers," said Lillian Gates. "I believe we may need to have a talk with them, find out what's going on."

"You may be right, Lillian," said Paytric as he cautiously looked around the room. "It appears that we may have celebrated our victory too soon!"

"I'll go and get Mrs. Whitehall and Helen," said Lillian Gates. "Before we leave to talk to the Pre' leader, I want to make sure that the Sanctuary is secure. At least we'll know that the children will be safe here."

"Good idea, Lillian," said Jonathan Gates.

"If you don't mind, I'll go with you, Lillian." It was Carolyn, Jerome' mother. "I guess if I'm going to be a part of the Watchers, it's time that I start participating. What do you need me to do?"

"Thank you, Carolyn. It's always good to have your help," said Lillian Gates.

As the two women left the great room in search of the Wielders of Magic, Carolyn reached out to her husband, Reginald, and gave him a light hug. It was just her way to let him know that she was with him and her son in what they were trying to do.

Jonathan Gates turned to those gathered by the fireplace and spoke.

"Okay guys, listen up!" he said. "Paytric has something he needs to talk to you about, and we're going to need your undivided attention."

As Jonathan Gates stepped aside, he relinquished the floor to the Warrior.

Stepping forward, Paytric knew there was a lot to be thankful for this day. But he was also aware that the day was yet to be over. They had to track down Faayn and the small group of Sires that decided to escape with him. In addition, they needed to know why the Pre' would openly attack the Whre to free Faayn.

"Something wasn't quite right with this," thought Paytric to himself.

And deep in his gut, he had the feeling that they were about to uncover something that no one would have thought possible. He just didn't know what it was. But he knew that when it all came to be revealed, they had to be ready for anything that might come their way.

He quickly explained to everyone that the Gargoyles and Skalla's men were already on the hunt for Faayn and the Sires that had escaped, but they also needed to discover why the Pre' had freed him. From what the Gargoyles were told by Skalla's men, it appeared that the two enemies now appeared to be working together.

How this came about, Paytric had no clue. But it was something that they needed to understand quickly, before all hell broke loose in New York City.

Chapter V

The Dark Castle and The Ides of March

10:30pm

Paytric couldn't shake the feeling that something big was about to explode in their faces, and without accurate information, they couldn't prepare for it. After Lillian Gates and Carolyn had returned with the Wielders of Magic, they set about to find the answers that they needed. Paytric and Ziggy prepared to leave the Sanctuary with Mr. and Mrs. Gates, Mrs. Whitehall and Jerome's mother to talk to the three Pre' that had been captured.

The others were going to be transported out into the city in teams by Laura and Helen. They were to search the city and the underground tunnels along with the Gargoyles and Skalla's men. They had to track down Faayn and his Sires along with the Pre' that had helped them. And they had to find them at all costs. Paytric knew that if the Gargoyles found them first, they would be given no quarter, and they would possibly lose the opportunity to know what was really going on.

Remy would lead Jerome's father and part of his 'Special Forces' group, while Laura went along as their magical contingent. Kenadi went with the remainder of the 'Special Forces' group along with Helen. One thing they did not want, was to attract any undue attention not only to their presence, but to what they were doing. Although they looked somewhat out of place even for New York City, it would be an even harder thing to explain to the police that they were hunting a group of werewolves, who were possibly in the company of Vampires.

And then of course, it would be a whole different thing to try and explain who 'they' were.

A group of men who were retired 'Special Forces' hunting the streets with Ancient Warriors and a Witch and a Banshee. If it were Halloween in New York City, that explanation would've had a better chance of flying than it did today!

But with Laura and Helen along with each group, they could magically sidestep any of those unforeseen situations.

"What about us?" "Yeah! What do you want us to do?"

Amanda, Angi quickly spoke up, not wanting to be left out.

"We can help!" exclaimed Vi as she too stood, still cradling Catherine in one arm, and with Gharvey standing beside her.

Standing next to Vi, Thomas and Jesse both jumped up to voice their request to join in.

"We want to go too, guys…!!" chimed the two teens in unison.

Before they could even finish their sentence, everyone in the room quickly cast a look in their direction that said, "You've got to be kidding!!'

Thomas and Jesse instinctively stepped back.

It was undeniable that the feeling of everyone in the room was that the two of them had already been in the mix of far too many things already. And maybe this was the time that they weren't.

"Wow, that was an emphatic, 'No', without any words being spoken!" whispered Jesse as he leaned over toward Thomas.

"You got that right!" said Thomas as he agreed with his best friend.

And then to the rest of the group he said, "I guess we'll just have a seat and...wait for you to...come back!" said Thomas.

"Yeah!" agreed Jesse, as both he and Thomas quickly backed away and found a seat on one of the couches. "We'll be waiting right here for you!"

As everyone returned their attention to Paytric, he continued.

"Right now, we need you to stay here and regroup," said Paytric. "With Cherese and J.D. here along with Catherine, you will have magical protection if you need it. Besides, I think that Jerome may need the time to rest considering what he has been through."

"I'm, I'm fine," recanted Jerome, not wanting to be the reason that kept him or the others from going on the hunt with the Warriors.

He was a little shaky after what had happened, but he was still good to go!

"It is more than that," stated Paytric simply.
"Reginald and his men, along with the others have all experience in hunting that which does not wish to be

found. Even the Watchers do! As of yet, none of you have developed such skills. Besides, I hope that I am wrong, but if we do not track down Faayn and his Sires quickly, I feel that we may have need of all of your skills before too long. I fear something else is going on, and we need to get to the bottom of it as quickly as possible."

"And the Pre'?" asked Angi. "What about them?"

"That is the wild card Angi, that we have yet to figure out!" answered Paytric as he turned to leave. "We will be in touch with you through Cherese or J.D. Until then, we are counting on all of you to hold down the Sanctuary! If things go wrong out there, it may come down to us needing someplace to fall back to that is secure."

With that ominous assessment, Paytric left the great room saying, "May the Creator be with us all tonight!"

Within seconds, amid the appearance of 'portals', and the swirling of magical thresholds, the great hall emptied.

Amanda, Angi and Vi, along with Jerome, Cherese and J.D., all looked at each other as they stood alone in the great room of the Sanctuary. Thomas and Jesse were still sitting on the couch as they quietly observed from the sidelines.

After a few moments of silence, Cherese was the first to speak.

"Well, I think Paytric is right! The Whre and the Pre' have been enemies for as long as anyone can remember. Why would they all of a sudden start working together now?"

"You're right!" agreed Jerome. "It doesn't make any sense. Why now?"

Then from out of nowhere, a voice simply said, "I think I know why."

As everyone turned in direction of where the voice had come from, they realized it was Jesse who was speaking. And as he sat next to Thomas, he had the oddest look on his face.

Even Thomas did a double take as he stared at Jesse.

"You do!!" he exclaimed in shocked voice as he turned toward his best friend.

"Yeah! At least, I think so."

Amanda moved over to her brother and sat down on the other side of him.

"How is it that you think you know this, Jesse?" asked Amanda intently. "How could you know this?"

It was then that Jerome realized what Jesse was alluding to.

"Oh, my God!" exclaimed Jerome as it finally dawned on him. "Earlier today when the two Sires were chasing us. Just before they spotted us, Jesse said that he had bumped into one of them. That's how you knew the Whre were in the park?"

Jesse just nodded his head.

"You got a hit off of him, didn't you?" exclaimed Jerome.

Again, Jesse nodded his head in acknowledgement.

"A hit!" exclaimed Vi, not understanding what Jerome was talking about. "What do you mean a hit?"

"A vision…an image of the people and the things that the Sire knows about, experienced," explained Jerome. "When Jesse touched him, he must've tapped 'into' him! Connected to him."

"What did you see, Jesse?" asked Amanda as she carefully pressed her brother for more information. "Can you tell us what you saw?"

"I, I think so!" answered Jesse as he tried to concentrate on the images, he remembered flashing through his mind when he bumped into the young Sire in the park.

He remembered feeling the rush of pure adrenaline from the Sire when he was running with the other wolves as they made their way across the open field toward the light of the city. He could feel the anger that the Sire felt at the loss of one of their own. He could feel it well up from the Sire's gut and exploded into his legs and his chest as that rage pushed him onward, despite his exhaustion.

The more Jesse concentrated on what he had 'channeled' from touching the Sire earlier, the more he was beginning to experience and feel what the Sire had felt, what the Sire had wanted. Before Jesse knew it, he felt himself wanting the same thing.

"They had to get to the city! They had to make the Gargoyles pay!"

And now Jesse wanted that too!

As he sat on the couch staring straight ahead, Jesse's breathing began to come faster and faster. His chest began to heave, and his head dropped forward onto his chest, as his eyes rolled upward into his eye sockets. Jesse could feel the rage that the young Sire had felt, rise up inside of him! And from deep within his throat, he felt a growl angrily roll forward and emit from his mouth as he drew back his lips, bared his teeth and snarled.

"Grrrrrrh!!!"

Instantly, everyone surrounding Jesse screamed and jumped back in surprise at the change in Jesse's demeanor. Even Gharvey had instinctively leaped over the table in front of the couch where Jesse was sitting, when he abruptly growled at everyone. Catherine hissed and followed suit as she leaped out of Vi's arms and landed onto the back of one of the side chairs.

Thomas wasn't exactly sure how he had made it so far from Jesse and the others as quickly as he had. But when he looked up, he was standing behind the group on the other side of the room in the hallway, a good distance from where he had been sitting with Jesse on the couch.

"At least I won't be the last one to leave a burning room!" thought Thomas to himself as he maintained his distance.

Jesse was like a brother to him. But what had just happened was a little weird, even for him.

And for a second, just a second, J.D.'s Grimshaw momentarily phased in, ready to protect her.

"Whoa!!" screamed Jerome as he and the others backed further away. "Girl, keep that thing under control!" he yelled quickly.

"It's alright, Jerome," said J.D. calmly. "My Grimshaw will only attack if I am in danger. And even then, I still control it. I would never allow it to hurt Jesse, or any of you."

"Yeah, okay, if you say so!" said Jerome shakily. "But make it go away, okay! We're alright! We're fine here," said Jerome as he eyed J.D.'s Grimshaw with an uneasy look.

As the Grimshaw became translucent, and its shape and substance faded, Jerome returned his attention back to Jesse.

"And what was that Man!!??" exclaimed Jerome to no one in particular, as he leaned forward to check Jesse out from in front of the fireplace where he had ended up. "You 'growlin' at us now?"

Amanda, Angi and Cherese had made their way to the other side of the coffee table to where Vi and J.D. were standing. Everyone kind of held their ground where they were, as they all stared at Jesse who was still sitting on the couch, growling under his breath.

"Jesse?" called out Amanda, softly to her little brother as she leaned forward onto one foot.

No response.

Then she yelled, "Jesse!! Are you still with us, Squirt?"

Amanda wasn't sure what had happened, but she knew that she couldn't just leave her brother like he was. If she didn't know any better, it seemed as if Jesse's ability had allowed him to connect with the Sire that he had touch, on a level to where he was inadvertently channeling the Sire and his behavior. And what was weird, was that it had been hours after he had made contact with the Sire.

It was almost as if the connection Jesse had with the Sire, had begun to take him over. Change him.

Catherine arched herself as the hair along her back stood straight up. This was something she had never seen before. But as she positioned herself on the back of the chair she had landed on, she was ready to 'zap' Jesse with a magical spell, if she had to. She knew that he wasn't himself, so she was prepared to cast a spell that would knock him out to keep him from doing harm to himself, or to anyone else.

But to everyone's relief, a few seconds later, Jesse had stopped growling as abruptly as he had started. He slowly lifted his head and looked around with a dazed look on his face.

"Why is everyone looking at me like that?"

At the moment, Jesse felt it was a valid question.

Especially, since they were all staring at him with the oddest look on their faces. And when he saw that Catherine was poised and ready to 'zap' him, well then he really got scared!

"And Thomas!" he thought. "Why was he standing way over in the hallway looking all nervous as if he was ready to 'cut bait' and run at the drop of a hat?"

"Jesse? Are you alright, squirt?" asked Amanda asked again as she slowly approached her brother.

"Yeah!" exclaimed Jesse. "Why? What happened?" asked Jesse nervously, as he realized he must've missed something. Something big!

"Well, for one thing, after we asked you what you picked up from the Sire, you got real quiet, and then you started to 'growl' at us," stated Jerome. "And I have to say, you got kinda scary there for a minute, Jess!"

"I'll say!" "Yeah!" agreed Angi and Vi as they continued to keep their distance, not sure if Jesse was in fact back to normal.

"And you even made our girl here, and her…Grimshaw go on the defensive, man!" exclaimed Jerome a little on edge. "Not cool!"

"Com'on, guys!" exclaimed Jesse with a slight laugh as he looked back and forth at the group as they continued to maintain their distance. "I, I don't…growl!"

Then from the hallway, Thomas called out, "Yo, Jess! Trust me, you growled, buddy!"

"And, and you did this thing with your eyes where they kinda rolled up into your head. And then you bared your teeth at us, like a wolf would do," said Vi nervously.

"Really??" said Jesse quietly, praying that he wasn't beginning to turn into a Whre.

"Heck! I only touched him for a second!" his mind screamed. "It wasn't like the Sire had bitten him or anything like that. Why would I be acting like a wolf?" Jesse asked himself.

"Okay, Jesse," said Amanda soothingly as she cautiously made her way back to her brother's side and sat down next to him. "It's going to be alright, squirt. You don't have to think about the Sires, what they were up to, nothing! Just forget that we asked, okay!"

"Yeah, Dude!" exclaimed Jerome. "Just don't growl anymore, okay! I got some serious chills from that!"

"Then you don't want to know what I found out?" asked Jesse as a spark of mischief flared in his eyes.

"What??" exclaimed everyone at the same time as they moved in closer. Even Thomas came into the great room from where he had been standing.

"Wait a minute! You mean you know what's going on?" asked Amanda quickly.

"Well, not exactly, 'what's going on'," said Jesse. "But I know what Skalla's Son told the rest of the Sires before they came into the city."

"What??" asked the group.

"He went to meet up with someone just before they came into the city. Someone who wasn't a Whre," announced Jesse.

"You mean, Faayn did?" asked Jerome.

"Yeah!" exclaimed Jesse somewhat excited. "When he came back, he was telling the Sires that the day that he and his Brother Delan, and Delan's...girlfriend had planned for, was about to come to pass."

"Girlfriend??" asked the girls in unison.

"Wait! I don't remember anyone mentioning anything about a girlfriend being involved with Delan and Faayn," said Angi. "Do any of you?" she asked.

Everyone shook their heads indicating that they didn't.

"I thought it sounded as if it was only the two of them, and maybe a couple of the Sires that followed them," said Amanda.

"He called her, Lady G. or something like that," said Jesse as he threw out that little tidbit of information. He didn't think that it was important, but it was information.

"Well then, it would make sense that if he had a girlfriend who was working with him, she's probably one of the Sires that escaped with him," offered Angi.

"What else, Jesse?" asked Amanda as she tried to get as much information as she could.

Whatever they could glean from Jesse's brief contact with the Sire, would surely prove to be helpful to Paytric and the others in discovering what was really going on between the Whre and the Pre'.

What she hadn't noticed was the look on Cherese's face when Jesse mentioned the name of Delan's girlfriend. It was a look of recognition, almost. She wasn't quite sure, but for some reason the name, Lady G. felt familiar to her. And not in a good way either.

"He told the others that soon, with the help of some 'new' friends, the Whre and the Pre' were going to bring down the Gargoyles. And when they did, nothing could stop them."

"So Faayn and Delan must've had some sort of agreement with the Pre' to fight against the Gargoyles," stated Cherese. "Obviously, the same Pre' who helped him to escape from his Father's men."

"Yep! And it sounds like they're going to wage a full fledge war against Humans, starting with New York City," said Angi as she sat back down onto one of the chairs.

"Yeah!" exclaimed Jerome. "And it looks like we're smack dab in the middle of it! Again! It's like I said before. It's never a dull moment!"

As everyone started to talk amongst themselves, Cherese turned toward Amanda and noticed that she was quiet. She seemed as if her mind was working overtime as she slowly stood up and walked around the room. Cherese could tell that something was bothering her, and in true Amanda fashion, she was trying to sort it out.

"Amanda, you okay?" asked Cherese.

"Yeah!" she said slowly. "But something doesn't make sense."

"You got that right!" said Cherese knowing why she was feeling on edge, but curious as to what Amanda was referring to.

"It was something that Jesse said," answered Amanda she turned to Jesse and asked another question.

"Jesse. Was Faayn referring to the Pre' as being the 'new friends' that were going to help them fight the Gargoyles, or did it sound like he was referring to someone else?"

"What??" Whoa! What are you talking about, Amanda?" "Yeah! Someone else! Who, who else would be involved?"

"Guys!" cautioned Amanda as she looked at them intently. "The way that Jesse heard Faayn say it, it sounded as if he was saying that there're other players in the game. Someone who we don't know anything about!"

Turning back to Jesse, Amanda pressed her brother a little harder.

"How did he say it, Jesse?" she asked. "Can you remember the exact way that he said it?"

"Yeah!" answered Jesse, as he repeated what he had heard Faayn tell the Sires. "He said it exactly like that! 'With the help of some 'new' friends, the Whre and the Pre' were going to bring down the Gargoyles.' I remember because one of the other Sires asked the same question about these, friends."

"And what did Faayn say?" asked Cherese intently.

"Just that they had thousands," said Jesse slowly. "And I repeat, 'thousands' of new recruits to call on whenever they needed them."

"New recruits!!" someone in the group repeated.

"Oh, I don't like the sound of that one bit!" exclaimed Jerome as he looked around the room to see if the others were getting the same vibe as he was.

And as he looked into the faces of his friends, he realized that they had.

"Is he saying new recruits as in, 'newly vamped' Humans, or what?" asked Vi as an uneasy feeling began to rise in her gut.

"I have no idea!" exclaimed Amanda. "But we need to let Paytric and the others know about this right away."

"I think there's something else that Paytric and the others may need to know too," noted Cherese cryptically.

"Oh God! Don't tell us there's more!!" exclaimed Angi as she spoke from the chair she was sitting in.

"I'm afraid so, Angi," said Cherese as she spoke to the group. "I'm not a hundred percent sure, but my gut is telling me that Delan's girlfriend, the one that Jesse heard Faayn talk about. This… Lady G.! I'll bet you anything that she's not a Whre. And I'll even double down on that bet and go so far as to say, I bet this Lady G. is Givant!"

"Wait a minute!" exclaimed Jerome as he looked at Cherese. "You mean, you think that Delan's girlfriend is Givant, as in the Vamp who was threatening to snap your neck down in the Pre' caverns?" asked Jerome with such an incredulous tone, that his voice actually went up a couple of octaves. "That Givant!!!"

"One in the same!" answered Cherese. "And remember. Givant is the one that we know of that got away. And trust me! My gut is telling me that it's too much of a coincidence that Lady G. and Givant are not one in the same."

Everyone got quiet as they all gave Cherese a sidelong look. They knew that Cherese still had a 'bone to pick' with Givant. And given another chance, they knew that there was no way in hell that she would spare Givant a second time.

"Ohh Buddy!!!" exclaimed Thomas out loud as he observed from the sidelines.

He really didn't have a whole lot to add to the conversation as it went on around him. But there was one thing that he knew for sure. And that was that from what Cherese and Sean had disclosed about what had happened to them in the caverns of the Pre', this Givant was a true B… to the core. And if she was still out there, they truly had to be on their guard.

As Amanda quickly turned to Cherese, she asked, "You gonna be okay?"

"Yeah, Baby," added Jerome as he made it over to where she was standing. "How you doing?" he asked.

"Oh, I'm better than okay!" said Cherese as she smiled slightly.

Cherese was dwelling in her own space of personal satisfaction knowing that she was going to get another chance at Givant. And that felt good! Real good!

As Amanda threw Jerome a concerned, sidelong look, she nodded her head slightly, and cast her eyes in the direction of Cherese as if to say, 'Keep an eye out for her. This cannot be good.'

Nodding his head that he understood, Jerome quietly vowed to himself to watch over Cherese. He would not allow her to go to that dark and scary place that she had gone to when Sean had to bring her back. He would fight to keep her from ever going there again.

"Guys!" said Amanda. "I don't know who Faayn is referring to when he spoke about these 'new' recruits," she said quickly. "But if what Jesse says is true, and you add Givant in the mix. Then we may have a really bad situation on our hands. And if this comes down to a confrontation, Faayn and the Pre' can blind side the Gargoyles and the Warriors with these 'new' recruits, whoever they are. We need to warn them before they're lured into a trap. And if this, Givant is leading them, that makes this situation twice as bad."

"So, what do we do?" "Yeah!"

Everyone stood ready to do whatever it took.

Cherese said, "I'll get in touch with Granna, and see how soon she can get back here. I think we're gonna need her!"

Everyone nodded their agreement.

Cherese turned and gave Jerome a quick hug and a kiss on the cheek.

"I'll be back!" she said.

Before she could exit the great room through a magical threshold in search of her Grandmother, Jerome pulled her close.

"Are you sure that this stuff about Givant hasn't got you rattled?" he asked intently. "Cause I…"

"Jerome," interrupted Cherese. "I'm okay. I've got a grip on my anger for now!"

"For now?" he repeated.

"For now!" said Cherese. "I'm afraid that's the best that I can do. I can't make any guarantees for later."

"Then we'll deal with later when it comes, okay!"

"You got a deal," agreed Cherese.

Then she opened up a magical threshold, and in a whirlwind of magic, was gone.

"J.D." said Amanda. "We need you to let Paytric and the others know what we've found out. This must be that 'bad' feeling that Paytric was referring to before he left," relented Amanda as she turned to the others. "But I don't think he knew just how bad it was really going to get!"

With that, J.D. also disappeared through a magical threshold from the great room of the Sanctuary to seek out Paytric and the others.

"But we still don't know who these, new 'recruits' are," said Angi. "And we don't know 'where' they are either."

"But at least we know that they're out there," said Jerome. "And that means that we're one step closer to figuring this out than we were before."

"Yeah!" agreed Angi. "And at least we can warn the others!"

"You don't think that there're hordes of Humans out there, just walking the streets who've been turned by the Pre', do you?" asked Vi as she shuddered at the thought. "I mean, that would be awful!"

"Tell me about it!" agreed Jerome as he plopped down into one of the chairs in the great room.

Catherine, who had been listening intently from the backside of the chair she had landed on when Jesse inadvertently 'growled' at everyone, leaped onto the low coffee table in front of the couch. With her thick, black tail whisking from side to side she spoke to the group.

"I will continue to monitor the perimeters of the Sanctuary to make sure that we don't have any uninvited guests. It is highly unlikely anyone can get past the magical guards that have already been put in place. But it is better to be safe, than sorry."

"And I will remain and stand guard from inside the Sanctuary while we wait for the return of the others," said Gharvey.

"Thanks, Catherine, Gharvey. That would sure make us feel a whole lot better." said Amanda as she smiled at the unusually large, black cat and black Lab. They had both become like an aunts to everyone.

Nodding her head once, Catherine gingerly leaped off of the table onto the floor, and disappeared around the corner to do what she did best.

Protect those that she cared about.

Gharvey continued to stay close to Thomas and the others in the great room while they waited.

"So, what do we do now?" asked Jesse as he looked to the group for an answer. "Just wait?"

"Yeah, squirt. Just wait and pray that this doesn't come down to a fight," answered Amanda solemnly as she looked at her brother. "Because if it does come down to a fight, and these 'new recruits' are Humans, then a lot of innocent people are going to get hurt. And I can tell you, that's not going to sit well with a whole bunch of people I know. Not well at all!"

The group remained seated in the great room, silently contemplating the last couple of days they had gone through, and what the current turn of events meant. They were hoping to hear back from someone, anyone. And sooner rather than later would have been great as far as the group was concerned.

As Cherese went off in search of her Grandmother, J.D. went to find her sister, Laura. They both knew that time was of the essence, and they had very little of it to waste.

Paytric and Mrs. Whitehall, along with the others in their group, had materialized outside of a containment facility where the Wielders of Magic were holding E'nal and his two friends. They brought along Zachary Boyd, the old man that had originally warned Sean and J.D. about the Pre'.

Paytric figured that if E'nal wasn't forthcoming with information willingly, perhaps the Wau-doun could channel something off of him. Then again, he also had Mrs. Whitehall who could use magic if need be. He knew they may not have a second chance at getting the information that they needed, and it was better to be prepared for every foreseeable possibility.

The place they had transported to, was an old castle that looked and felt as if it had been torn right out of the pages of an old gothic novel. At first sight, you would have thought that you were in the middle of a medieval story, as the castle, perched high on the edges of a ragged cliff, rose upward to the darkened sky. And it appeared to be to set off unto itself with no surrounding land in sight, save the rocky island it rested upon.

The castle walls had been built with large, misshapen stones that were covered in damp, black moss, and they appeared to climb straight up toward the sky and disappear into the gray clouds hanging overhead. And as far as the visitors could tell, there were no windows of any kind visible on the bleak moss-covered walls. And at each corner of the castle was a turret that was comprised of the same stone as the walls were. They each faced a different direction and seemed to be on the lookout…for something.

And Paytric and the others could only imagine the worst.

As the wild waves crashed and pounded against the black rocks that surrounded the castle on all sides, the skies above were full of dark and menacing clouds as they billowed and slowly moved themselves across the horizon. The weather in this place was dreary to say the least, and it looked like a huge storm was beginning to brew in the distance.

After the travelers materialized, they quickly made their way into one of the arched, outdoor corridors made of stone. They were glad to be able to escape the blustering wind and the constant drizzle of cold rain as it pelted down on them from the angry skies above.

"Mrs. Whitehall!" called out Paytric as he ducked into the dark corridor with the others and shook the rain from his clothes. "What is this place?"

"It is a place that we Wielders of Magic have used from…time to time," mused Mrs. Whitehall with a hint of humor in her voice. "You know, for those situations where you need to put something, or someone, until you decide what is to be done with them."

"Ohhh!" exclaimed Jonathan Gates solemnly. "You mean like a prison!"

"Yes. Like a prison," acknowledged Mrs. Whitehall as she walked past the group and made her way down the outdoor corridor. "This way!" she said as she led the group to a large, oversized, arched door that was set back into one of the darkened recesses off of the outdoor hallway.

As she lifted the iron level up and pushed, the massive door opened up into a medium sized room with a large fireplace in the left corner and had a blazing fire roaring in its' hearth, and warm woven rugs laid on the floor in front of it. Along the walls were several chairs and a table set in the middle of the room.

"Come in, quickly!" exclaimed Mrs. Whitehall as she secured the door after everyone had entered the room. "You can get warm by the fireplace if you wish."

"Is this all, real…?" asked Jerome's mother as she looked around the room while she tried to warm her arms and hands by the fire. "I mean, this is magically created, right?"

"Oh, My Dear. Who is to say what is 'real' and what is not," answered Mrs. Whitehall. "Whether it is magically generated or created by ones' own mind. What is important, is that as long as the mind believes that it is real, that is all that counts."

"Oh, okay!" said Jerome's mother with a vacant tone, as she gave her friend, Lillian Gates, a sidelong look.

Then to her friend Jerome's mother asked, "Did you understand what she just said?"

"Yeah," said Lillian Gates as she smiled slightly. "I kind of get the gist of what she means. Basically, it doesn't matter how it's achieved, whether by magic or through one's own mind. As long as the end results are the same. It just depends on how you look at it."

"Gotcha!" exclaimed Jerome's mother.

She still wasn't a hundred percent sure if she could handle a lot of the things that the Watchers were a part of, but she knew she'd give it her best shot. And the idea of magic being as real as the creatures that wield it, was still beyond amazing to her. But fascinating all the same.

"Mrs. Whitehall," said Ziggy as he stepped up beside her. "Can I ask, where we are? Are we even still in our dimension?" asked Ziggy as his curiosity ate away at him.

"Let's just say that we are in a place where none voluntarily wish to be. It is a place where wicked dreams die along with the dreamer. And where hope that was lost, resides, for here it finds redemption in the punishment of those who dare exert their will onto the defenseless. We are within the creases of time and space, where evil dares not to venture, for fear of being contained, and lost forever. This is a place where one need not be for too long of a time. It can have a strange effect on you. Especially on Humans. Therefore, we will be quick about our business here!"

After everyone had warmed themselves, Mrs. Whitehall led the way to another door that was to the right of the entrance they had first come in through. As they passed the door, they could hear the howling of the wind as it swept through the open aired corridor outside as the storm seemed to intensify. And then they heard what sounded like pounding on the door from outside. as if the wind had substance, and was demanding to be allowed in.

Then they heard the sound again. But this time they knew it wasn't the wind pounding on the door. There was someone outside, knocking to come in.

As everyone looked uneasily at each other, they noticed that Mrs. Whitehall was smiling.

"It's alright!" she exclaimed. "it's only J.D."

"J.D.!" exclaimed everyone as they watched Mrs. Whitehall approach the door and unlock it.

As the force of the wind outside pushed the door open, J.D. rushed inside to get out of the storm.

"J.D. what's wrong?" asked Lillian Gates with a concerned look on her face. "Are the kids alright?"

"Is the Sanctuary still secure?" asked Paytric as he too stepped forward with a concerned look on his face.

"Everything is fine, don't worry," said J.D. as she set about to warm herself. "It's just that we found something out, and we thought that you should know about it as soon as possible."

After J.D. relayed to Paytric and the others what Jesse had discovered after making a connection with the Sire in the park, she opened up a magical threshold and quickly returned to the Sanctuary.

Realizing that this new information they had just received could be used as leverage when they spoke to E'nal, Paytric and Jonathan Gates quickly devised a plan on how they were going to get the information that they needed. And Zachary Boyd was the key to their plan.

After a brief discussion amongst themselves about the plan, Mrs. Whitehall then led the group to another arched doorway in the room that opened up into a darkened, narrow passageway. It had small, lighted fire pits situated along the upper parts of the wall to light the way for those that dared to venture further. The entire passageway, from the floor to the walls and even the ceiling above, were damp, and paved with some sort of smooth, dark stone that made the space feel even more closed in. And as a rigid chill crept along the floor and swirled about them, it felt almost as cold in the narrowness of the passage way they had entered, as it had felt outside.

Paytric followed behind Mrs. Whitehall as she disappeared into the darkness beyond the door, while Lillian and Jerome's mother entered next.

"Lillian!" exclaimed Jerome's mother as she hesitated at the entrance of the door. "I'm not sure I'm up for this!"

"I'm right here, Carolyn," said Lillian Gates with as much confidence as she could. "Just follow my lead. You'll be okay!"

Taking that leap of faith, Carolyn stepped into the passageway as Ziggy, Zachary Boyd and Jonathan Gates brought up the rear. And although it seemed as if they had been feeling their way through the dark, damp passageway for much longer than it had been, it had only been a few moments.

They found themselves stepping out into a three storied cavern that curved into a dark foreboding cathedral ceiling high above them. And for a moment, they all thought that they heard some sort of howling and shallow screams coming from the dark recesses that dotted the walls of the cavern. At least that's what they thought they had heard.

"What in the hell was that?" Screamed Jerome's mother as she jumped nearly two feet into the air.

"I'm with Carolyn on that one!" exclaimed Lillian Gates as she too began to look frantically around. "What was that?"

"That what you are hearing, are the echoes of the dammed and the demented," said Mrs. Whitehall as she walked forward into the center of the cavern. "They are just echoes and are harmless to us."

"Are you sure about that?" asked Paytric as every fiber in his Warrior body stood on edge as he gripped the hilt of his short sword.

Just feeling it in the palm of his hand, gave him comfort. He could not remember when he had felt such uneasiness, such dread. This was a place he did not wish to spend more time than was necessary.

"The creatures housed here can do no harm to us or to anyone else. The magical safeguards that are in place, are of the kind the world has never known before. The magic is so old, it has all but been forgotten. But so powerful, that it remains in tack even today."

"And what are those?" exclaimed Ziggy as he pointed up toward the ceiling of the large cavern.

What everyone saw were three figures flying overhead, circling far above them. They had enlarged heads with bulging eyes that were protrude from their eye sockets. And they could see strands of wispy hair as it flowed behind them as they twisted and turned in the air.

One had pointed, fang-like teeth jutting out from her mouth, while another had oversized teeth that seemed to be frozen in a perpetual smile. The third figure had what appeared to be live, writhing snakes protruding from her mouth as she and the other two circled above. Just below their heads, they didn't have a body to speak of other than ghostly tendrils that flayed behind them as they darted about, hovering just above the group.

"Those are the 'Ides of March', the three keepers of the Dark Castle," answered Mrs. Whitehall. "They are three Sisters who are doomed to remain here in this place, and on this forsaken rock for all time because of past deeds. Who better than they to guard such undesirables from the outside world?"

As the group stood and watched the three figures, Paytric was the first to speak.

"Then let us be about our business here and leave!" said Paytric as he continued to eye the 'Ides of March' and the dark recesses that surrounded them. He was not comfortable being in such a place as this for too long.

"E'nal, the one you seek is this way," stated Mrs. Whitehall as she made her way across the floor of the cavern to the other side.

The 'Ides of March' quickly followed the group from above as they kept a close eye on the visitors.

"WHO ARE THEY HERE TO SEE?" "WHO?" "WHO?" they whispered from above.

As Mrs. Whitehall stopped in front of one of the darkened recesses, she turned to Paytric and the others and spoke.

"I will bring him out of stasis so that you may speak to him. But he will not be able to do much more than that," said Mrs. Whitehall. "I trust that will be sufficient."

"That will be sufficient," answered Paytric as he held onto the hilt of his short sword, just in case.

"Mrs. Whitehall," said Jonathan Gates. "I assume that you keep them in stasis to control the situation with as few problems as possible."

"Yes, Jonathan," answered Mrs. Whitehall. "It is the most efficient and safest way to keep them contained."

Then she asked, "Are you ready?"

"We are ready!" exclaimed Paytric as he and Ziggy prepared themselves.

With a wave of her hand, Mrs. Whitehall cast a spell and lit the dark recess up with a dull, yellowish light exposing only the head and the shoulders of E'nal. At first it appeared as if he was seated in a pitch black room in a chair and staring straight ahead. Blankly, at nothing in particular.

Then Mrs. Whitehall murmured a few ancient words to a magical spell. Instantly, E'nal's eyes seemed to come to life as they began to look wildly around.

"This place he was in was unfamiliar to him," he thought. "As were the people standing in before of him.

"And why can't I move?" his mind screamed. "Where am I?"

It was then that he realized that he did recognize one of the people standing in front of him, just out of arms reach. It was the older woman standing in front of the others.

"Yes! He remembered her from the caverns," he thought to himself. "She was one of the Witches that had come to the rescue of the young fledgling Witch and her friend. She was one of the Wielders of Magic that it was his misfortune to have ever crossed paths with!"

"Why am I being held here?" he yelled out to Mrs. Whitehall. "And who are these 'Humans' you have brought with you?"

Yet as he spoke, he could feel a different kind of energy coming from the warrior-like being that stood next to the Witch. His energy was not Human, nor was it magical. It was an energy of the kind that he couldn't quite place, nor had ever felt before.

"Odd," he thought to himself. "Very odd!"

"They have come to ask you some questions, E'nal," stated Mrs. Whitehall as she stepped aside to allow Paytric to move forward.

"QUESTIONS?" "QUESTIONS?" repeated the three 'Ides of March' among themselves as they hovered above. "WHAT KIND OF QUESTIONS?"

"E'nal!" said Paytric in a authoritative voice. "I am Paytric of the Endeari Warriors!"

"And is that supposed to mean something to me?" quipped E'nal with attitude.

But in the back of his mind, he had remembered something that Carmine and Weasel had spoken to him about. Something about ancient Warriors and their vow to protect the Humans. Just like the Gargoyles.

"Fools they were!" thought E'nal to himself.

"Whether who I am means something to you or not, is not important," said Paytric. "What is important is the question I have for you."

"And what might that question be?" said E'nal, arrogantly.

So far, the plan was working. To keep E'nal occupied, giving Zchary Boyd the opportunity to 'channel' what images he could from him.

"What plans did you and the Whre have for the new recruits that have been enlisted?"

"What!!" exclaimed E'nal instinctively. "The Whre! The Pre' would never work with the Whre! The 'dogs' that they are!"

THE DOGS THAT THEY ARE!" whispered the 'Ides of March as they swirled about. **THE DOGS THAT THEY ARE!"**

"And I know nothing of these, 'new recruits' you speak of! Why would you ask such a thing?" yelled E'nal, incensed at such an assumption.

"WHY??" "WHY??" repeated the 'Ides of March as they mimicked E'nal.

"Do you deny that the Pre' have been planning something?"

"I will not deny nor confirm anything to you," stated E'nal as he glared at Paytric and the others.

"Well, it seems that some of your kind do not have such distain for working with the Whre as you do," stated Paytric simply. "Particularly someone called Lady G. as she is known to the Whre. I believe you know her as Givant."

"GIVANT!" "GIVANT!" "YES!" GIVANT!" "HE KNOWS WHO YOU SPEAK OF!"

"That is impossible!" exclaimed E'nal now wondering what this Warrior was up to.

E'nal knew that Givant was a loose cannon for sure, as well as being unbalanced. That's why he kept her on such a tight leash. But to go against her own kind and to work with the Whre.

"That is impossible!" screamed E'nal as he tried not to display any emotion for his captors to read. "She would not dare!"

"It would seem that this, Givant, has put her own agenda in motion behind your back," stated Jonathan Gates in a slightly taunting tone. "And she has plans to use your new recruits for her own purpose. Especially, with you now out of the way."

Paytric waited a few moments for E'nal to ponder what had been said, before he dropped the 'other shoe'.

When enough time had passed, he continued.

"And did you know that Givant and Skalla's oldest Son, Delan, had become more than co-conspirators? That they had become…involved with each other?"

"THEY BECAME LOVERS!" cried out one of the 'Ides of March. "LOVERS!" she screamed in her shrill voice as she dipped lower.

"You lie!! You Lie!!" screamed E'nal, as his face seemed to quiver at the thought. "No Pre' would ever enter into such a relationship with the Whre. Never, do you hear me? Never!!"

"NEVER!" "NEVER!" "NEVER!" screamed the 'Ides of March' together as they too appeared to get agitated along with E'nal.

He knew that they were searching for information by trying to bait him with lies about Givant and the Whre.

"But they had only touched the tip of the iceberg of what was really going on," thought E'nal to himself. "They would never know the whole truth about the 'Humans' who were marked. And even if they did find out what their plans were, when they did, it would be too late to do anything about it!"

Then Zachary Boyd stepped out of the shadows of the cavern where he had been quietly waiting. As he moved forward into what little light there was, it was obvious that he had been cleaned up, dressed in proper clothes and looked well despite the hardship he had been through the last few decades. And his demeanor was that of a reborn man. He had come back from the dark, shadowy existence he had been living in for decades. And now, for the first time in as many years, he truly felt like a man again.

Like the Wau-doun he had once been.

And as fate would have it, he now stood before his former tormentor, not afraid. And the tables had truly been reversed.

As he moved forward, E'nal recognized him immediately.

"You!" he exclaimed loudly, not believing his own eyes as he looked upon the old man. "Why is he here?" bellowed E'nal to the Warrior.

Although E'nal was aware that Zachary Boyd knew more than he should have about the Pre', he was never able to figure out just how he knew what he did. He never knew about Zachary Boyd's ability of 'channeling'. A residual gift from the Warriors' dimension Nor did he realize that he was using his gift at that very moment.

Then to Zachary Boyd, E'nal said, "Come to get your due have you, old man? Hah!" taunted the leader of the Pre' boldly. "Well, take a look! You may have stopped me! But none of you will not be able to stop what is coming! None of you, do you hear me?" he yelled. "You will no longer be able to protect the Humans that you and the Gargoyles so desperately care for!"

As Zachary Boyd stared at E'nal, he pitied him. Not only for his hatred for all those who were not as he and his kind were. But for the lengths his kind would go to, to make others bend to their will, or perish.

"Well, say something, old man!" exclaimed E'nal. "I know you have been waiting a long time for this, have you not?"

"SAY SOMETHING!" "SAY SOMETHING!" taunted the three sisters.

"Yes. I guess I do have something to say to you," said Zachary Boyd quietly. "But it is only one thing that I need to say to you, E'nal," said the reborn Wau-doun, in a voice that was barely above a whisper. "With the information that I have been able to 'channel' from you, the Warriors and the Gargoyles along with the rest of us, 'will' protect the Humans that you and your kind so desperately despise. And all I can do for you, is to pray."

"AHHH! PRAY FOR HIM!! PRAY FOR HIM!!" Screamed the 'Ides of March as they spun and twisted from up above.

Then turning to Paytric and the others, Zachary Boyd said, "I have all the information that we need. But we must hurry!"

"Good!" exclaimed Paytric. "Then let us leave this place."

As the Warrior and the others turned to take their leave, Mrs. Whitehall began to recast the magical spell that would return E'nal to stasis. Before she could finish, he called out to the Warrior.

"Wait!! How is it that you know?" he exclaimed. "Tell me! How can you know?"

Paytric stopped midstride and turned to face E'nal one last time.

"You will have plenty of time in this place of dread, to ponder that question, E'nal," said Paytric with no hint of emotion in his voice whatsoever. "Just know that your plan is about to be dismantled, and your kind will be 'cast' to the four winds, never to rise again. The Gargoyles will make sure of that!"

"AHHH! GARGOYLES! GARGOYLES!" screamed the 'Ides of March' as they tried to hide among the recesses of the cavern at the mere mention of the Gargoyles' name.

"It would seem that even in this dark and foreboding place, the Gargoyles were well known," thought Jonathan Gates as he kept his eye on the three sisters.

Paytric, having nothing more to say to the leader of the Pre', turned and made his way across the cavern to the exit door, as the others followed. Mrs. Whitehall continued with her spell despite the cries of E'nal.

"No! No! Stop!! Stop!!" he called out as the Ides of March swirled frantically about the cavern.

"NO! NO! STOP!! STOP!!" they called out as they mimicked him in their high-pitched voices. "HEE, HEE, HEE!! YOU ARE OURS FOREVER, DO YOU HEAR? FOREVER!!"

Finishing her spell, Mrs. Whitehall turned and joined the others as the 'Ides of March' continued to dart back and forth overhead. As E'nal's voice became quiet, his eyes dulled and the dim light in the recess faded to black.

As Mrs. Whitehall also left the cavern, she too was glad to leave the 'Ides of March' behind along with the dread of the 'Dark Castle'.

With no time to waste, the group made their way back through the narrow passageway leaving E'nal and the 'Ides of March behind and returned to the outer room. Within moments, Paytric had summoned a 'portal' that would return them to the great room of the Sanctuary. All were grateful to leave behind the Dark Castle, and the three Ides of March that were fated to forever watch over its' occupants.

Chapter VI

'Come One – Come All

Come Forth – Come Forward'

11:30pm

As the group exited the 'portal' into the great room of the Sanctuary, Paytric saw that Granna had returned along with the Gargoyles and Skalla and his men. Remy's group and the group that Kenadi had led were also there, waiting for him and the others to return. Even Sean had returned to the Sanctuary, much to J.D.'s delight.

"We believe we have found them!" stated Remy as he strode over to Paytric as he and the others exited the 'portal'. "There appears to be a large group gathering in the center of Central Park. For what reason, we are not sure."

"I believe we may have found the answer," stated Paytric as he glanced over to Zachary Boyd.

Then turning to face all those who had gathered in the great room of the Sanctuary, he made an introduction.

"To those of you who are not familiar with the man standing to my side, I would like to introduce him to you. His name is Zachary Boyd."

As Paytric paused for a minute, he turned to the man and placed his hand onto his shoulder.

"Zachary was a Wau-doun many, many…many years ago. He, along with other Wau-douns came to the Warrior's dimension for training so they could help to defend your world against those who would do harm to the Human race. While there, he had also developed an ability like some of you have. His is being the ability to 'channel' past experiences from those he is in close proximity to. He was lost to us, to the Watchers and to the Wau-douns a long time ago. But he has been found, and we welcome him back into the fold. And I understand that we have Sean and J. D. to thank for bringing him to us and protecting him from those that would do him harm."

As everyone turned toward Sean and J. D., and patted them on their backs to congratulate them, all the two could do was to give embarrassed smiles.

"Without the help of Zachary," continued Paytric. "We may not have been able to get the information that we needed from the leader of the Pre'."

"So what is their plan, Paytric?" asked Skalla as he stood with his men. "And what connection does the Pre' have with my Son, Faayn?"

He along with the others, all wanted to know exactly what they were up against. And more importantly, who. And Paytric knew that some of the information they had obtained might not be what Skalla wanted to hear. But it was what it was.

"I will let Zachary do the honors of explaining what the Pre' and the Whre are up to," said Paytric as he gave the floor to the Wau-doun.

As Zachary Boyd stepped forward, he was almost unrecognizable to the others. Was this the same old man who hadn't had a bath in who knows how long. The same one they had to literally drag to the Sanctuary for his own protection.

The man that now stood before them was of a very slender build, about five foot eleven, and looked to be about in his mid to late forties, with slightly graying hair at the temples. And although he was much older than what he appeared to be it was something that wasn't obvious to the naked eye.

"Wow!" exclaimed Sean as he looked at the Wau-doun as he stood next to Paytric. "Our friend sure cleans up good!"

"I'll say he does," agreed Cherese as she and the others were blown away by the transformation.

No one would ever have known that this was the same man they had met in the apartment only one day ago. No one!

Even Zachary Boyd himself was amazed at his own transformation when he got a look at himself after he was able to clean up and get a haircut and a shave. He had forgotten what he had looked like when he was an active Wau-doun. For him it felt good to be back. Real good!

Thanking Paytric, Zachary Boyd stepped forward and addressed the mixed group that stood before him. He could tell that some were Human and magical, while others were creatures of the night. Then there were the Warriors and the Gargoyles who were neither magical nor creatures of the night. Actually, he wasn't quite sure what category he'd put them into. But no matter. They all stood before him as one group, with the same purpose.

Protect those of this world.

And to himself he thought, "It felt good to be back in the game."

And when he spoke, his voice wasn't as gruff and harsh as it had been when he was found in the alley. The group noticed that his voice was actually very soft spoken.

"Thank you, Paytric," he said as he looked over the group before him. "It is good to be back. And thank you Sean and J.D. for believing me. I know I must've seemed to have been way out there. But you listened to me and help get word to the Warriors. And I truly thank you for that and for bringing me back home," he said with a slight twinkle in his eye.

And then turning to the situation at hand, Zachary Boyd proceeded to enlighten the group about the plans of the Pre'.

"As far as what the Pre' and the Whre are up to, I can only say that we have an unusual situation on our hands. Once I was able to get a good connection with E'nal, I saw what he and the Pre' have been up to," explained Zachary Boyd. "Basically, they've been recruiting, and recruiting heavily among the Human population."

"Wait a minute!" exclaimed Jonathan Gates. "You mean they've been 'turning' Humans to increase their ranks?"

"No, not turning them into Pre'," responded Zachary Boyd. "That would be too difficult and time consuming. They would have to take the time to teach those that they turn how to control themselves and their thirst. And with the numbers that they needed, it would attract too much attention, and take too long. No. What the Pre' have been doing is going out into the city and 'marking' the ones that they want to use."

"Zachary, what do you mean, 'marking' them?" asked Lillian Gates intently.

"What I mean is, they've been going to where large groups of Humans gather at night. At clubs, parties, malls. Anywhere they would not attract any undue attention to themselves. Once there, they would mix with the crowd as if they were one of them. At one point, each of the Pre' would select a Human that they were to 'mark'. Then they would somehow, scratch that person somewhere on their body with their index finger. Just enough to break the skin and transfer a toxin they had developed into their bloodstream.

"The toxin travels through the blood and settles in the part of the brain that regulates 'self-control', or your 'will power'. The person 'marked' for the most part, doesn't even realize it. This toxin that they have developed, provides a telepathic connection between the Humans that were chosen, and the Pre'. And as far as I can tell, the connection with the Humans chosen, is only useable when they are in an unconsciousness or semi-conscious state."

"You mean, like sleeping?" asked Paytric.

"Yes. Or if the person has had, let's say, too much to drink, and is in a kind of stupor where they are not in total control of themselves and are hovering at the brink of being unconscious," said the Wau-doun.

"And with the toxin in their system, the Pre' could 'summon' them whenever they wanted."

"So, they become like walking zombies?" asked Thomas from the couch where he was sitting with his parents and Jesse.

He wasn't sure he liked the idea of walking zombies. As a matter of fact, no one listening wanted to hear that.

"No, not walking zombies, Son," said Zachary Boyd to Thomas, making sure that he didn't mislead them with the information he was disclosing. "They're still very much alive, they're just in a deep sleep."

And then to the rest of the group he said, "And guys, this is the tricky part. And I'm not quite sure how we can handle this."

"Handle what?" asked Granna as she spoke for the first time.

"Whatever toxin they've devised, once injected into the bloodstream, it somehow gives the Pre' control over the subconscious part of that person. They are totally unaware of what is happening to them and are oblivious to what they are doing. Somehow their 'spirit', if that's what you want to call it, can be drawn out of their bodies while they are unconscious, and controlled."

"Are you trying to tell us that the Pre' have found a way to control the Human soul?"

"No, not their 'souls'," stated Zachary Boyd. "Their 'life-force', their 'essence'. And the Humans that they call forth, will appear as apparitions or phantoms to us, while their bodies are still asleep. The Pre' call them, 'spirit walkers'. And that's where we may have a problem."

"How do you fight an apparition?" said Remy after realizing what he had just heard.

"Yes," answered the Wau-doun. "How do you fight that which cannot be harmed by any weapon we may wield, possibly including magic. And especially apparitions that 'can' do harm to us if directed to."

"What??" "You gotta be kidding us??"

The response from the group listening was unanimous.

Thomas sunk back into the folds of the couch he was sitting on, not really wanting to revisit anything that had to do with the taking of 'life forces' and 'essences'. Even though it had been three years ago when the Dark Dimension had tried to take his 'life force', for Thomas that wasn't long enough to try and forget what had happened.

"I've had my fill of someone trying to take my 'essence', thank you very much!" exclaimed the voice in Thomas' head.

As the explanation of what the Pre' were up to sunk in, the group surrounding Zachary Boyd just sat in awe. They couldn't believe what they were hearing. The Pre' were drawing the 'life essences' from human bodies in the form of apparitions, while they were asleep to do their bidding.

"And if we do find a way to stop the, the 'spirit walkers'? asked Angie cautiously. "What happens to the Human part of them? Does their essence just return to their bodies…or what??"

"Yeah!!" "Yeah!!" exclaimed the group. "What happens to them?"

"From what I gleaned from E'nal, the Humans that are being used as 'spirit walkers' are expendable. If for some reason we do find a way to stop them, and they fall during the fight, their Human body also dies."

"Crap!!" exclaimed several people in the group.

As Warriors, Paytric and Remy along with Kenadi and Ziggy would stand and fight whatever came before them. But an apparition. How were they or the others expected to fight that which had no substance to it, therefore, could not be harmed? And if they could stop them, how could they justify bringing down Humans who were being controlled by the Pre' and were not aware of what they were doing?

"And I hate to be the bearer of more bad news," said Zachary Boyd solemnly. "But the Pre' themselves have far greater numbers than you were led to believe they had."

"How many more?" asked Paytric fearing the worst.

"Perhaps two hundred, maybe a little less."

"And how many of these, 'spirit walkers' do they have?" asked Jonathan Gates as he tried to get a feel for what they were truly up against.

Before Zachary Boyd could respond, Jesse and Thomas did the honors.

"Thousands!" exclaimed Jesse and Thomas together.

"Thousands!!" exclaimed the group as they turned toward the two teens.

"Yeah!" exclaimed Thomas and Jesse.

"Jesse made a connection with one of the Sires earlier in Central Park," said Amanda. "Sort of like the one you made with the Pre' leader, Mr. Boyd. What he saw was that the Pre' had 'marked' literally thousands of Humans."

The young man is right!" confirmed the Wau-doun. "They have thousands of Humans who have been 'marked' and are just waiting to be called upon."

"Then that must be who they are gathering in the middle of Central Park right now!" exclaimed Remy.

"So, it would seem that they have determined when and where this fight is going to take place," stated Paytric.

"And they know we must respond!" exclaimed Remy. "It would seem that this, Givant of the Pre', and Skalla's Son have planned their strategy well."

"Faayn?" exclaimed Skalla as he stepped forward toward Zachary Boyd, his steps unsteady.

This was the first he had heard of his son being part of what the Pre' were planning. As far as he was aware, his two sons were only guilty of breaking the Whre law by hunting within the city. But this! This was something different altogether.

"Faayn has been working with the Pre'? That cannot be!" exclaimed Skalla as he looked around.

Zachary Boyd looked at Skalla with sadness in his eyes. He was aware of the dislike the Whre and the Pre' had between each other. And he could see how this information had affected the Whre leader. But it was in fact, true.

"You are Faayn's Father and the leader of the Whre?" asked the Wau-doun.

"I am leader of the Whre. But I no longer have a Son!" stated Skalla sadly. "I no longer have any Sons! Delan, my oldest was 'felled' when he went against my decree. And Faayn has been disowned by me and the Brood for his actions. But I cannot believe that he would join the ranks of the Pre' and go against his own kind! For what reason?"

Then it dawned on Skalla.

"Is that why the Pre' attacked us in the tunnels and helped Faayn escape?" he asked. "Because he has been working with them all along?"

Then Skalla paused.

"And Delan. I assume that he was part of this too?" he asked.

"Yes. Apparently, they have been planning this for some time now," explained Zachary Boyd as he tried to ease the pain of the Whre leader. "All along, Givant was planning to undermine the Pre' leaders when the time came. She had the help of your two Sons, and they felt that they would have better odds if they joined forces to get rid of the Gargoyles."

Zachary Boyd didn't feel that divulging the fact that Skalla' oldest son, Delan and Givant had entered into a relationship was necessary information that needed to be relayed at this time. He could see that the Whre leader already had a great deal to absorb.

"The young!" he continued. "They are impatient, and always feel that they know what is best. But in some respect, they have shown us one thing that cannot be denied," stated the Wau-doun.

"And what might that be, pray tell?" asked Skalla still reeling from what he had heard.

"That the Pre' and the Whre can put aside their differences and work together if need be. Granted, this is not what we would like to see bring your two groups together. But it is something."

"So, what they are planning to do is to break the pact between the Gargoyles, the Whre and the Pre' by drawing the Gargoyles into a battle where the winner reaps the prize," stated Jonathan Gates. "And they seem to feel they will have the upper hand against the Gargoyles, because they will not rise up against any Human."

"Yes." Confirmed Zachary Boyd. "This Givant and Skalla's two Sons, felt that their kind was meant to rule over humans. And in their minds there is no middle ground. For them, it's all or nothing."

"Then it will be nothing that they gain!" exclaimed Paytric as he stepped forward. "The pact was established to allow the Pre' and the Whre to co-exist alongside the Humans. Not to be able to hunt and feed on them, nor to rule over them."

"And we, the Gargoyles will not allow the Pre' to escape punishment for what they have tried to do in the past, nor for what they plan to do today," said Irina in her shallow voice. "They shall see no mercy from my kind!"

As Paytric looked over the group that had gathered in the great room of the Sanctuary, he knew that this was not going to end well. This was not just a battle they were going to have fight against the Pre' and the Sires that followed Faayn. It was also a battle they were going to have to engage in against the Humans that the Pre' had turned into 'spirit walkers'. It was going to be a battle against those that they were sworn to protect.

And he had no idea how they were going to get around it.

As everyone began to talk among themselves, Granna approached the Warriors and Zachary Boyd as they stood in the front of the room.

"As the fates would have it,' she said. "I believe that I may have a solution to the problem of the 'spirit walkers'. But I need to confer with my friend. The one that I went to recruit."

"You think that he can help, Granna?" asked Paytric intently.

At this point, Paytric would take any help offered that might increase their chances of success.

"Yes. I believe he can," confirmed Granna. "But as I had mentioned before. There are those that may have issues with him, and may find it difficult being around him. But I'm sure we can find a way to work around that."

"Work around what?" asked Lillian Gates as she and Thomas' father joined them.

"It would seem that the friend Granna went to recruit may be able to help us deal with the Pre' and their 'spirit walkers'."

"Really!" exclaimed Jonathan Gates. "I'm game for any help we can get! I wasn't particularly looking forward to battling thousands of 'Human' apparitions controlled by the Pre', that's for sure."

Then he asked, "By the way, who are we talking about?"

Chapter VII

The Infamous Barnabas Bane

After a brief explanation by Cherese's grandmother of who she was referring to, she paused to get the reaction of her friends. She knew she was taking a gamble on this, but it appeared to be their only hope.

The look on Thomas' parents' faces as well as Zachary Boyd's said it all.

"You, you gotta be kidding me!" exclaimed Jonathan Gates as he instinctively took a step backwards. "I thought that he was just an urban legend, you know, not real. Fairytales and such that were told to us when we were kids! And now you're telling us he's real?" As he spoke, his face began to flush and perspiration began to form across his forehead.

Granna knew that he, like many others were going to have very strong feelings about who she was planning to bring into the group. She just hoped they could get past it.

"Jonathan!" exclaimed Lillian Gates quietly as she turned to face her husband. "Jonathan, listen to me!"

As she spoke, she placed both of her hands on his chest as if to quiet him.

"We've got to be able to put some things aside that we've experienced in order to achieve the greater good, right? Right?"

As she looked up into his face, Lillian Gates was trying to reassure her husband that everything was going to be alright. She knew about some of the bad experiences Jonathan had as a child. Some of them terrifying. But he had to leave those feelings behind and accept this, if they were going to be successful.

"I, I guess!" agreed Jonathan Gates reluctantly. "If you will excuse me, I ahh…need to get some air. Excuse me!"

With that, Jonathan Gates quickly left the great room with Lillian following on his heels. He didn't dare to look up. If he had, many of the group would have seen the expression of total fear that was written across his face. And he couldn't allow them to see his fear. Not at such a crucial moment.

Perplexed, Paytric and Remy looked at each other with confused glances. They didn't understand why this particular magical creature brought forth such an emotional reaction. Especially from a grown man.

As a matter of fact, they really didn't know anything about the Human fairytale that involved someone called the 'Boogey Man'.

"Who is this, 'Boogey Man' that you speak of?" asked Paytric quietly. "And why did Jonathan react in such a way as he did when you mentioned his name?"

"Actually Paytric, many children and adults throughout Human history have had an experience or two with the 'Boogey Man'," explained Granna. "Some may have had more frightening experiences than others, like Jonathan apparently has had. But he's an apparition, if you will, that parents would sometimes use to scare their children into doing what they should."

"They would scare their children?" asked Remy, not understanding the methods that humans used to teach their offspring. "For what purpose?"

"Well, for example, they might say something like, 'If you don't do this or that, the 'Boogey Man' is going to get you!' Things like that," explained Granna. "And in order to not have the 'Boogey Man' come to you in the middle of the night while you're sleeping, kids usually buckled down and did what they were supposed to. I agree, it may not be the most practical way to get your children to do what they should. But he has been part of our culture for as long as can be remembered. And not to mention, in cultures throughout the entire world."

As a child, even Zachary Boyd knew that he too had nightmares of the 'Boogey Man' from time to time. But as he grew older he left those childish things behind him. Or so he had thought. Now he had come to learn that they weren't just scary tales told by his parents, or the imaginative dreams of a child. They were in fact, real.

The 'Boogey Man' was real!

"And he's a friend of yours?" asked Zachary Boyd as he also stood in shock after hearing what he had.

"Yes, he is a friend," said Granna. "And before I introduce him, I need everyone to try and understand that he is who he is, and he presents no true malice or cruel intentions to anyone."

On second thought, Zachary Boyd wasn't sure if he was going to be okay with this. This was something that he truly had to take time to process and wrap his mind around.

"Then let us proceed," said Paytric as he moved away from the group and once again went to stand in front of everyone gathered in the Sanctuary. "Time is truly of the essence, and people will have to put aside any misgivings they may have for the present. Agreed?"

"Agreed!" confirmed Granna as she turned and stood with Paytric.

As Paytric stood in front of the group ready to explain what the plan was, he looked across the room and noticed that Jonathan Gates and returned after his abrupt departure. He now looked a bit more calmer than he had when he left, to the obvious relief of Lillian.

"It would seem that the Pre', along with several of the Whre have decided to challenge not only the Gargoyles, but us and the magical community as well," stated Paytric as he addressed everyone. "While it is a challenge we do not take lightly, we do have a concern."

Paytric paused for a moment, and then continued.

"The concern we have, is that the Pre' have devised a way to use Humans in their bid to challenge the Gargoyles. They have put them in middle of this confrontation, and that is what we are concerned about. Granna has information on how we may be able to sidestep their use of Humans in this situation. If so, it will clear a path for us to deal with the Pre' and the Whre. So, I will let her explain to you just what the plan is."

As everyone got settled in, Granna took the floor.

They were all hoping that there was another way to resolve this situation other than having to fight Humans as well as the Pre' and the Whre. That option didn't sit well with any of them.

"I'll keep it brief and simple," started Cherese's grandmother in her usual exact tone.

"The magical creature that I had referred to earlier has agreed to help us," she stated. "As a matter of fact, he was delighted to have been asked. He is hoping to possibly show another side of himself that you will appreciate. But as I had mentioned before, some of you, perhaps all of you may have some unresolved issues with him. I am asking that you put those issues aside and concentrate on the situation that is before us. With that being said, I want to introduce you to someone who I have known to be a friend for as long as I can remember."

As Cherese stood with the rest of the group, she was holding her breath, waiting for the reaction of those around her. From what Granna had told her about this friend, she was able to deduce exactly who it was. And after she realized it, she knew that his presence would make her uncomfortable. She only hoped that the others would fare better with his introduction, than she was doing at the moment.

"Everyone!" announced Granna as she stepped aside. "I would like to introduce you to Barnabas Bane."

From behind Granna, a whirlwind of gray shadows began to stir and churn until it revealed the figure of a short, very stout, round man standing in the middle of its mists. As the mist faded away, it revealed the mysterious, Barnabas Bane.

Lillian and Jonathan Gates as well as Cherese were surprised at his appearance. They weren't sure what they had expected, but not this. He was about five feet nine inches tall, was bald, and was dressed in a gray pinstriped suit with a soft gray colored shirt. He looked…normal. But then again looking around, so did everyone else in the group. Whether they were Human, magical or Warrior. Everyone looked normal. Everyone, that is except for the Gargoyles.

It was at that point that Cherese felt a little embarrassed.

She herself was a Witch! A real, bona fide Witch! And her kind as well as all of the other magical creatures standing there, had been depicted at one time or another throughout history, as being scary, terrible creatures of the night.

"And that just wasn't true!" thought Cherese to herself, as she felt more and more ashamed of the way she had reacted. "It wasn't true!"

As she looked down at the floor to hide her obvious embarrassment, she thought to herself.

"I can't have that kind of attitude. I have to give others a chance as I would like them to give me," she thought.

Jonathan Gates had returned with his wife as he shifted his stance uncomfortably, keeping his distance from the new arrival. It was still going to take a lot for him to get beyond this, but he knew he was going to have to try. There was something at stake here that was more important than his childhood fears. And he was going to have to let go of them if he was going to be of any practical use.

And this was just something that he was going to have to remember.

As Barnabas Bane stepped forward, even he seemed as if he was a little nervous. He nodded his head in acknowledgment to the group and then turned to Cherese's grandmother.

"Have you told them?" he asked quietly as he eyed her intently.

"Only a few know who you are, Barnabas!" she stated simply. "I thought it best that the rest see you as you are, not as each of them remembers you. This will help to dispel any past perceptions they may have of you. Besides, everyone here is willing to work with each other as one for the common cause," she said. "That includes working with you!"

"Thank you, Constance," acknowledged Barnabas humbly as he turned to look over the group that had gathered. "I hope so!"

"Trust me," said Cherese's grandmother. "We are ushering in a new day where the magical community and Humans can coexist together. And if I may say so myself, we've made a good start."

"So, it would seem," stated Barnabas as he noted that besides Humans and Witches, there were Banshees present as well as Whre and Gargoyles.

"An odd mixture of creatures to say the least," he thought to himself as he also noted the presence of the Warriors. "Truly an odd mixture."

"Might I ask, exactly who you are?" called out Jerome's father, as he stood with some of his retired buddies that were from is old 'Special Opts' unit. They were now some of the newly recruited Waudouns that had been working with Mrs. and Mr. Gates and the Watchers.

Breathing in deeply, Barnabas Bane took a step forward.

"I am known by many different names, in many different cultures," he said quietly. "I have been called El Coco, Babau, the Sack Man. But I believe that when you were children, you knew me best by one name. You would've called me, the 'Boogey Man'."

When he finished speaking, there was complete silence in the room.

Eyes just stared blankly ahead, and mouths hung open as the understanding of what the new arrival had said was still being absorbed by those listening. No one could even find their voice to utter a word. The air in the entire room had been sucked out, and all that was left was a stifling silence that hung in its place. It was as if there were a 'white elephant' in the room, and no one could find the ability to acknowledge it.

Then from the crowd someone asked, "Wha…..what did he say? I thought I heard him say…"

"The Boogey Man!!" said someone else as they finished the sentence. "He…he said…the Boogey Man!!"

Then Jerome chimed in.

"You don't mean, the Boogey Man, Boogey Man? Do you??"

He tried to laugh it off as he spoke, but for some reason it didn't come out right. His laugh sounded more like a terrified admission on his part that he had heard correctly.

Finally, Cherese found the courage to speak up.

"Guys! I'd be lying if I said that I wasn't somewhat bothered by this," said Cherese as she stepped forward. "When I was a kid, I had some pretty scary visions of the…Boogey Man!"

As she spoke, she glanced quickly at Barnabas Bane as he stood at the front of the room, and then looked away.

"But as kids we all had issues with a magical creature at one time or another in the past. We came to know them one way, through stories and fairytales that were told to us. But today we've come to find out that they're all not that way. I'm not that way, and neither is my Grandmother or her Sisters. And hey! We're Witches! And you know how we have been viewed not only today, but in the past."

As Cherese's grandmother stood by and listened to her granddaughter speak, she felt the pride swell within her. Cherese had truly grown to be a mature young woman. And she was voicing her tolerance of others who were different than she was.

"Cherese is right!" said Mrs. Gates as she stood next to her husband. "Any fears or misgivings you have concerning Mr. Bane here, have to be put aside if we are going to work together."

"Agreed, Lillian," said Granna. "If there is anyone who truly feels that this is going to present a problem for them, we will understand if you choose not stand with us."

For a brief moment, everyone shifted their positions, considering their options. Some even cleared their throats, but no one made a move to leave.

Granna, seeing that no one was going to back out, silently praised everyone for not disappointing her, or the magical community. It was truly a turning point for Humans and those of the magical community.

"Then it is settled!" announced Paytric as he began to lay out the plan to everyone. "We move forward," he said. "More than likely, Givant and Faayn will surround themselves and the other Pre' with the 'spirit walkers' that have been created. That means we will have to deal with them first. Because this is something that we would like to avoid, I understand that Barnabas Bane may hold the solution to our problem."

Taking his cue, Barnabas Bane bowed slightly, and thanked the Warrior as he once again turned to face the group in the great room of the Sanctuary.

"I too, will keep it short and to the point," he stated. "What we will be facing will be the spirits or the essences of the Humans that the Pre' control. And because they control them in their unconscious state, that is where I do, what I do, best."

Barnabas paused for a moment, then continued.

"I will be able to reach them while they are asleep and tap into the fears and anxieties they have hidden away in the dark recesses of their mind. I will take that which makes them have nightmares and increase it ten-fold upon them."

"Man!" exclaimed Thomas as he leaned over and whispered to Jesse. "That's gonna be one heck of a nightmare he's gonna give 'em," he said as he sat on the couch listening to Barnabas Bane.

"You got that right!" agreed Jesse as he continued to listen.

They couldn't believe that they were actually in the presence of, of the Boogey Man! While it was awesome in one way to them both, it was also kind of scary.

And then from the other side of the room came a question.

"I'm sorry, but giving them a nightmare! How does that help us?" asked one of the Wau-douns standing with Jerome's father.

It was Cherese's grandmother who answered.

"What usually happens when you have a nightmare?" she asked to no one in particular.

At first no one responded. Most were still processing the explanation of how Barnabas Bane, aka the Boogey Man, did what he did.

Then it was Jesse who realized what Granna was referring to.

"You wake up!!" he exclaimed out loud as he sat forward. "You wake up!! At least, I do!" he said.

"That's right, Jesse!" confirmed Granna. "You wake up! Once Barnabas takes whatever fears they may have and turns them into a nightmare, they will wake up! And once they are awake, the Pre' will no longer have control over them because they are no longer in an unconscious state."

"And one by one, as each Human wakes up," said Barnabas Bane. "Each of the apparitions that have been created will disappear, clearing the way for you to deal with the Pre' and the Whre. I will take away their, 'ace in the hole', if you will."

As everyone sat processing what they had just heard from Barnabas Bane, another question was asked from the group.

"How are you going to be able to reach all of them at one time? How is that possible?"

"Trust me!" answered Barnabas Bane in a slow and deliberate manner as he turned toward the person who had asked the question. "It is what I do! And I do it very well, Jonathan."

Hearing Barnabas Bane address him by name, caused Jonathan Gates to stiffen as he tried to retreat from his stare. Even Lillian Gates had a look of surprise on her face when she heard Barnabas Bane mention her husbands' name.

"How is that he knows my name?" Jonathan asked as he glanced over at his wife with a questioning look. "That's, why that's impossible!"

"I never forget the names of those I have visited," said Barnabas Bane simply. "Never!"

"Any other questions?" asked Paytric, anxious to move forward with renewed hope of having a way to fight the Pre' and their new army.

When there appeared to be no further questions, Payric continued.

"Once Barnabas has eliminated the 'spirit walkers', the Gargoyles will take the lead and deal with the Pre'," stated Paytric. "The majority of the Gargoyles will attack from above, which will give them the advantage, and will keep the Pre' busy. The few Whre that have joined them, will be scouted out and dealt with. Skalla and his men are the only ones who can identify who the Sires are before they transform. And believe me. When they do transform, they can move fast and have enormous strength."

Turning to the leader of the Whre, Paytric asked, "Is there anything we may need to know about what to expect from the Sires, Skalla?"

Skalla, leader of the Whre stepped forward and spoke.

"Only that the Sires will not do a frontal attack if they can help it. If they can use any trees or bushes to conceal themselves in, they will," stated Skalla. "A surprise assault always give the attacker the advantage. The men I brought with me will scout them out first so we will know exactly where they are before they transform. Then we'll take it from there."

"Good!" said Paytric as he saw their plan falling into place.

"The rest of us will be the second line of defense. Particularly make sure that if any of the Pre' get by the Gargoyles, or any of the Sires get by Skalla and his men, they do not get far. Use whatever means you have to stop them. Their purpose is to eliminate the Gargoyles so they can have free reign. We cannot lose this confrontation and allow it to spill over into the Human population. If it does, it will be a slaughter."

Then another question came from one of the Wau-douns standing with Jerome's father.

"How are we going to bring them down if the Whre' can only be stopped by silver, and the Pre' by a wooden stake?" he asked. "Even if we had tons of wooden stakes or silver bullets, how are we going to get a good fix on them if they're that fast and that strong? It's hard enough to hit a moving target, much less to try and hit it in the heart! That's going to be tough."

"You're right!" agreed Paytric. "It will be tough. It would be great to be able to get at them while they are at their weakest which is when they are Human, before they transform. But the odds of that are astronomical. They will be poised and ready to transform and attack at a moments' notice."

"So how do we get to them?" the Wau-doun asked.

"Before they were Whre or Pre', they were in fact Human," stated Paytric. "We are hoping that when Barnabas works his magic, it will also affect the Whre and the Pre'."

The reaction from everyone was immediate.

"What!!" "What do you mean?" "Yeah! They're not Human!"

"No, they may not be Human anymore," stated Barnabas Bane. "But there's always that part of them that was 'Human' and still remembers me, for I remember each and every one of them. I will take that memory and make them relive the most terrifying fears they have ever had and exploit it times ten. If I can get to them before they transform, what I will make them experience will surely cause them to become confused and disorientated with the fear and the terror that I will instill in them."

"And that is when we strike!" exclaimed Paytric.

"If you cannot deliver a clear blow to the heart," cautioned Zachary Boyd. "You take their heads. Plain and simple. It's the only way."

"That is why we will be in teams of three or more," announced Paytric. "Each team make sure that you have someone with them that can wield magic or an ability. This is truly going to be a fight that can turn messy. Watch your backs out there, and watch out for each other," encouraged Paytric. "Neither Givant nor Faayn will give us a second chance at this. We must get it right the first time and eliminate this threat once and for all."

As he spoke, the Gargoyles quickly departed, leaving Irina and several of her kind behind. She knew that if there were no Gargoyles with Paytric and the others when they approached where the Pre' were gathering in Central Park, it would look suspicious.

As Granna and Paytric watched from the front of the room, the rest of the group in the Sanctuary began to form their teams and prepare themselves.

It was time!

Immediately, Mrs. Gates pulled both Thomas and Jesse aside. They were not going to be able eo accompany everyone else to Central Park but were going to remain at the Sanctuary with her and Jerome's mother, Carolyn.

"What!!" "No fair, Mom!!" "Yeah! We're old enough!!"

"I'm not discussing this with you, Thomas and Jesse," exclaimed Lillian Gates. "You both are still too young and haven't had enough training with your abilities to be thrust into a battle. So, the answer is, No!"

The two teens mounted their protest in hopes of changing Thomas' mother's mind. But she was adamant. There was no way she was going to send her teenage son, or her best friends' son into a battle against the Whre or the Pre'. Three years ago, when the kids helped to fight the Dark Dimension, there were different circumstances that were involved.

Not only had Thomas been kidnapped by the Dark Dimension, but before a rescue could be mounted, they had also kidnapped Jesse. And with everything that had happened, there was no way she or anyone else was going to keep Amanda or any of the others out of the fight to get them back. They were older and more experienced. But this time was different, and nothing the two teens tried to say was going to change Thomas' mother's mind. Even the fact that they had been practicing with their newfound abilities didn't change her decision.

They were not going! And that was final!

So, Thomas and Jesse, along with Gharvey, Catherine and Mus and Scrat, who had somehow gotten out of the bedroom, sat on one of the couches in the great room as everyone else prepared themselves. And to their anguish, all they could do was watch as the teams began to form.

Angi and Ziggy paired themselves as a team, while J.D. and Sean did the same, as did Amanda and Jonathan Gates.

Laura grouped with Zachary Boyd, while Cherese, Jerome and Jerome's father, Reginald made up the fourth team. Remy, Kenadi and the Witches all made up the remaining teams. Then, one of Jerome's fathers' retired 'Special Opts' buddies were delegated to each of the teams.

Irina, Barnabas Bane and Skalla would stand with Paytric and Granna as they prepared to be the first to approach the clearing in the middle of Central Park where the Pre' and the Whre had gathered.

Although there was little hope that either Givant or Faayn were in the mood to talk, it was a chance that they were willing to take. If they were not willing to back down, at least it would give Skalla and his men the chance to scout out the Sires, while the Gargoyles prepared themselves to attack from above.

"We must be prepared for anything!" thought Paytric to himself as he turned to the newly formed teams.

"If we cannot talk them out of their current course of action, then we must be prepared to defend those that we are sworn to protect!" stated Paytric. "And remember, no one is to make a move until signaled to do so. Once Barnabas has done what he does best, and the Humans that the Pre' control are dispelled, we will give them one more chance to stand down. If they do not relinquish…we have a couple of surprises in store for them that they will not be expecting."

As Paytric looked over the group that stood before him, ready to do what was needed of them, he prayed that a fight could be avoided at all costs. But if a fight could not be avoided, he knew that they all were prepared to do had to be done.

And he prayed that the Creator was with them and would grant them success.

As everyone stood ready to leave, they nervously gave slight smiles and nods of encouragement to each other, praying that a battle could be avoided.

Jerome hugged both his mother and father. Then he looked at his father and kidded with him.

"You watch your back out there, Pops! Okay!"

"And you, too, Son!" replied Reginald Parker as he smiled broadly.

This moment was all a little too reminiscent of what they had gone through three years ago back in Hampton when they had to face the Dark Dimension. But it was what it was. And in the true fashion of a Wau-doun, it was once again time for Jerome and his father to defend their world.

Carolyn Parker took in a deep breath and said to both her husband and son, "You both watch yourselves out there, you understand me!" she said. "I won't take it kindly if anything happened to either of you, so…don't make me have to get ugly!"

And then smiling nervously, she said, "You know, I…I don't think that I'll ever get used to this. Never!"

Reaching over and lightly planting a kiss on his wife's lips, Reginald Parker smiled and gave her a wink.

"I know. But God willing and creeks don't rise, we'll be back!" he said as they hugged one more time.

Jesse moved himself off of the couch and approached Amanda and Angi as they hugged each other.

"Mandi," said Jesse quietly as Amanda turned toward him.

"Please be careful, okay!" he said in a serious tone.

And then in a more kidding tone of voice he said, "You know Mom and Dad will kill you if you're not, right?"

Laughing lightly, Amanda pulled Jessed toward her and gave him an endearing hug.

"Don't worry squirt," she said. "I have every intention of being careful. Besides, we all have to be alright, don't we girls?"

As Amanda spoke, she turned toward Angi, Vi and Cherese and gave them a broad smile as they all nodded their heads and smiled back. If Jesse didn't know any better, it looked as if they all had some kind of secret between them.

"Not like that would be out of the ordinary for his sister and her friends," thought Jesse to himself.

But if he didn't know any better, this was different.

So Jesse figured he'd ask. All they could do was to ignore him and say he was imaging things.

So, he asked.

"What ah…what's up, guys?" he asked as Thomas joined them.

At first, the girls gave each other a coy look as if to say, "Whaat?" "What do you mean?"

Then after a few moments of playful banter back and forth, Amanda finally broke down and explained it to Jesse and to Thomas.

"We…girls, have decided that life is too short. That you have to live it while it's before you, because you may not get the chance to go back. And despite what some people say, in some instances, it can be too late!"

"Okaaay," said Jesse slowly, not sure what his sister was talking about.

"Amanda, just tell him!" exclaimed Angie, excited to let someone in on their secret.

"Tell me what?" asked Jesse as he eyed his sister.

"Yeah!" chimed in Thomas. "What gives?"

"Okay," started Amanda as she took a deep breath. "Paytric and Jules almost waited too long. But the fates were with them, and they were rejoined after almost a hundred years," said Amanda. "We, meaning Angi, Vi, Cherese and I, have decided to take the next step. We're not going to wait any longer. After all of this is over, we're going to marry our betroths as soon as we get back. But don't tell Mom yet!" exclaimed Amanda.

Just hearing herself say it out loud, sent excited chills down Amanda's back as she let out a little squeal.

The other girls joined Amanda as they did a little girlfriend dance among themselves as the idea of finally marrying their betroths sunk in.

"I can't believe it!" exclaimed Angi.

"Neither can I!" said Vi as she looked ahead to being married to Ziggy.

It felt so right to her!

Jesse and Thomas were so stunned that their mouths just fell open and hung there.

When Jesse finally found his voice, he blurted out, "Marry, as in marry and move away to the Warriors' dimension, marry?"

He couldn't believe it!

It was hard enough to realize that growing up meant, that eventually you grow up and away from your friends, and your family. When Amanda and the others moved to New York City that was hard enough to get used to. But Amanda was still somewhat close, and she was still his sister. But

Jesse knew that once Amanda and the others married their Warrior betroths, that meant that they would join them in the Warriors' dimension and start their own lives and their own families.

He didn't want to be a baby about it and appear to be selfish, but somewhere in the back of his mind, he felt as if he was losing her as his sister. She was going to become a wife, and he would lose her as his sister.

"Heck!" his mind screamed out to him. "We just barely discovered that we like each other!"

Then his mind did a retraction and he corrected himself.

"No!" he thought to himself. "I love my Sister, and I'm not sure I'm ready to lose her just yet!"

As he tried to fight back the tears and hide just how emotional he was about the announcement, he realized he wasn't doing such a great job of it.

Amanda saw Jesse as he stepped back and noticed the tears as they started to form in his eyes.

"Jesse!" exclaimed Amanda softly as she walked up to him. "Jesse. I want you to be happy for me!" she said. "Please tell me those are tears of joy. 'Cause if they're not, I don't what I'd do!"

"But," stammered Jesse as he fought to keep the tears from falling. "But what about me? I barely got to see you when you moved here to New York City. After you get married, you'll be going back to the Warriors' dimension, and I'll probably never get to see you then!"

"Jesse…!" said Amanda as she tried to hug her little brother again.

But Jesse wouldn't have it!

He pulled away as he took a step backwards and shrugged off her intended hug.

Then in a quiet voice he whispered softly, "You'll get married and have kids of your own," he said. "And you'll forget about me. And then we'll never see each other. I know it!"

Not realizing how Jesse had felt about her going away to New York City, Amanda was stunned by her little brother's reaction.

Over the last three years, they had grown closer than anyone could have guessed they would've gotten. She didn't know that Jesse had felt she had abandoned him when she and the others moved to New York City. And now with her most recent announcement, it made it more difficult for him to accept her decision to finally marry Jason and move to the Warriors' dimension.

But that was always the plan. She thought that Jesse understood that.

Before Amanda could console Jesse any further, Paytric announced that it was time to leave to take up their positions.

Others standing around, gave their congratulations to the girls and to Ziggy and Jerome, and then made ready to depart. They could see that Jesse wasn't taking the news well, but they also knew that it was something he was going to have to accept. People move on with their lives. That's just the way it was. And it didn't necessarily mean that they left those who were in their lives behind.

Amanda turned to Jesse before she had to leave.

"Jesse!" she said in a pleading tone. "We'll talk when all of this is over. Okay squirt?"

It had been her own endearing name for him for as long as she could remember. Even before they grew to like each other as siblings.

And then out of left field Jesse blurted out, "Don't call me that!" as he briskly turned and walked away.

"Only my Sister who cares about me can call me that!" he said in an angry tone. "You don't care about me, and you're not my Sister! If you were, you wouldn't plan to leave!"

It was Amanda's turn to be stunned by Jesse's response as he lashed out at her.

"Jesse!" she pleaded.

Amanda couldn't believe the pain she felt at that very moment.

"Com'on Amanda," said Angi as she put her hand on her friends' shoulder. "He's just upset right now! Let him calm down."

Amanda reluctantly turned and followed the group as they made their way to the portal that the Warriors had opened up. She felt bad leaving Jesse with the feeling that she was somehow 'deserting' him.

"That's not how it was at all!" she exclaimed to herself. "Not at all! She loved Jesse."

As Mrs. Gates and Jerome's mother stood at the portal opening, they wished everyone well as each of the group entered the portal opening. Jerome's mother gave both her husband and her son a long endearing hug before they too, stepped through the opening.

As Amanda approached the portal, Mrs. Gates stopped her. She gently put her arm around Amanda's shoulder and spoke to her.

"He'll be alright, Amanda," she said quietly. "It's just one of the changes that kids go through at this time in their lives. The older sibling leaves home and goes out into the world to start their own lives. And sometimes the younger sibling feels as if they're being left behind. Don't worry," she said. "We'll look out for him. You just watch out for yourself and the others out there. You understand?"

Amanda nodded her head in acknowledgement. She was still in shock by Jesse's reaction.

She took one last look over her shoulder at Jesse before she stepped up into the opening of the portal. Above everything else, she knew she had to be focused and ready once she stepped out onto what could very possibly be a battlefield in the middle of Central Park.

But that didn't make leaving Jesse in the state that he was, any easier.

As Angi followed behind Amanda, Jonathan Gates brought up the rear. He stopped and gave his wife a hug and kissed her lightly.

"You watch your back out there, Mister!" she said jokingly.

"Will do!" he said softly as he gave her a slight smile and then turned to follow the others into the portal.

At least this time he knew that Thomas was safe in the Sanctuary with Lillian, and not in any danger. And with that worry off of the table, he felt he could deal with what lay ahead of him without concerns for his family.

As the last of the group left, the humming of the portal grew faint and then faded away, Lillian Gates and Carolyn stood in the middle of the room silently saying a prayer that those they loved would return to them safe and sound.

Jesse had plopped himself back down onto the couch and slumped there feeling confused and mixed up. He didn't know why he had said what he did to Amanda. But after he saw how what he had said hurt her, he began to regret his outburst.

It had all got to be just a little too much for him, and he had lashed out in the only way that he could. And now he was feeling bad that it was Amanda that got the brunt of his emotional outburst. He knew all along that this day was going to come. He just hadn't expected it to be so soon.

"Man, did I mess up!" shouted the voice in Jesse's head as he continued to slump on the couch.

And now to top of everything else, he had hurt Amanda.

Before Jesse knew it, Thomas had plopped himself down next to him and proceeded to try and cheer him up.

"Hey Jess!" he said. "You've always got me! I mean, I know it's not the same as having your Sister around, but hey. I'll always be here. For true," confirmed Thomas in his and Jesse's own private saying they had established between themselves years before.

"Yeah, I guess," said Jesse as he shrugged his shoulders, trying to reel in the emotions that he had lost control of earlier.

And then to his surprise, someone else sat down on the other side of him. When he and Thomas looked over, they were surprised to see Vi sitting there.

"Hey guys!" she said as she settled herself into the cushions of the couch. "Mind if I join you?"

With everything that had happened, they hadn't noticed that Vi didn't leave with the others.

"You're not going with the others?" asked Thomas as he looked over at her with a surprised look on his face.

"Yeah!" chimed in Jesse. "Did they make you stay behind, too?"

Vi shook her head.

"No. I just know what my strengths are," she said simply. "And while I'm not a fighter like Angi and

Amanda are, I have an ability that's only useful if I have access to techy stuff. You know, computers, modems, satellites. That kind of stuff," she quipped. "And I don't think I'd find much of that out in the middle of Central Park. So I hope you don't mind if I stay here and help hold down the fort with you guys?"

"We don't mind, Vi," answered Thomas as he too leaned back into the cushions of the couch.

"Yeah, why not," agreed Jesse, still feeling embarrassed by the way he had acted.

And then he asked her, "I acted kinda stupid with Amanda, didn't I?"

"I wouldn't say stupid, Jesse. Maybe a little overemotional," she said. "But not stupid. Besides, think about it. You'll be able to visit her in the Warriors' dimension whenever you want. And that'd be cool, wouldn't it?"

"I guess," agreed Jesse realizing that he did kind of overreact after hearing Amanda's announcement.

The more he thought about it, he realized there were going to be some perks to Amanda being in the Warrior's dimension. And with him and Thomas being older, they were going to be able to participate with the Watchers even more. Including going back and forth to train in the Warriors' dimension.

As the trio sat on the couch with their menagerie of magical creatures gathered around them, Lillian Gates and Jerome's mother couldn't help but to feel sorry for them. There they were. Gharvey was laying at Thomas' feet, while Catherine had curled herself up on the back of one of the couch's cushions. Mus and Scrat were burrowed into the cushions of the couch on the other side of Vi, and they all looked as if they had lost their only friend.

The two mothers felt so bad for them, that they announced that they were going to prepare some snacks for the group in hopes that it would kind of cheer them up and soften the blow of them not being included.

After the two mothers had left out of the great room, Jesse sat forward.

"I've got to let Amanda know that I'm sorry about the way I acted," said Jesse mournfully. "I can't let her think that I hate her or that I'm not happy for her," exclaimed Jesse as he stood up. "I can't! I've got to get outta here!"

"You're gonna do what??" exclaimed Vi not believing what she had just heard Jesse say. "You can't Jesse!"

Yeah!" chimed in Thomas. "We're supposed to stay here!"

"Besides," added Vi. "We can't just go running out there and, and…and!"

Vi was so stymied by Jesse's declaration, she couldn't even finish her sentence.

"Why not?" cried Jesse. "Guys, this is something I've gotta do! I'm not asking you to come with me. Just cover for me, okay!"

Catherine stood up on the back of the couch and joined in the conversation.

"Master Jesse!" she exclaimed. "They are right! You should reconsider what you are planning to do. Think of the danger you will be putting yourself in."

"Yeah!" agreed Thomas.

And then Thomas added, "Besides Jesse. How you gonna get otta here? I mean, they've got this place locked down tight!"

Jesse's shoulder fell as he realized that what Thomas was saying was probably true. Then he had a thought. Glancing over at Catherine, Jesse smiled slightly as a mischief look sparked in his eyes.

"You could get me out of the Sanctuary, couldn't you, Catherine?" he asked.

Catherine stood up on the back of the couch.

"Jesse, even if my magic could somehow get past the magical barriers that have been set up around the Sanctuary, you don't know 'where' in Central Park they've gone," stated Catherine as her thick black tail swished behind her. "How would you find them?"

"Yeah!" exclaimed Thomas. "And isn't Central Park as big as a small city?" asked Thomas to no one in particular. It was just something that he had remembered someone saying at one time.

"Yeah, it is!" confirmed Vi as she too stood up. "Jesse, this is crazy!"

Jesse turned to face Vi and spoke in a calm voice.

"Vi! If your last words to Ziggy was something that you really didn't mean, and then he had to go off somewhere where he could truly be in danger. How would you feel?" asked Jesse with as much sincerity as he could. "If you had a chance to take it back, even a crazy, slim chance. Would you take it?"

"No fair, Jess!" exclaimed Thomas. "This is a whole different situation."

And then to Thomas' surprise, Vi agreed with Jesse.

"No, Thomas. He's right!" said Vi.

"What!!" cried Thomas not believing what he was hearing.

"He's right!" said Vi. "If I had said something to Ziggy that I really didn't mean, and I didn't get a chance to at least smooth it over before he left. I'd regret it. Especially if I had an opportunity to talk to him before something happened, and I didn't take it."

And then to Jesse she said, "Yeah, Jesse. I'd take the chance!"

Then Vi leaned into Jesse and said softly, "But you know I can't let you go alone, don't you?"

"Whaaat!!!" cried Thomas as he looked back and forth between the two of them. "You both are crazy!"

"Well, if you're going, Jess, so are we!!" chimed in Mus.

"Yeah, buddie," said Scrat. "We're with you all the way!"

Mus and Scrat felt that they had already missed out on a lot of the action already. And they weren't about to miss out on this if they could help it.

Then, both Vi and Jesse looked at Thomas.

"What??" exclaimed Thomas as he tried not to be pulled into doing something stupid.

"Thomas, we could sure use you, Catherine and Gharvey," said Vi.

"Yeah, Thomas," said Jesse now beginning to feel confident about his decision. "If you guys came, we'd have our own magical protection with us. And don't forget about your birth parents!" exclaimed Jesse before he caught himself.

"His 'birth parents'?," said Vi as she looked at both Jesse and Thomas with a questioning look on her face . "But…three years ago in Hampton, didn't Thomas' birth parents…"

"They did!!" exclaimed Jesse quickly as he corrected himself before Vi could finish her sentence. "They are!! They're…gone!!" said Jesse. "But ahhh….they're with him in spirit. Right, Thomas!" said Jesse as he tried to sidestep the hole he had started to dig for himself.

Thomas panicked as he looked back and forth between Jesse and Vi.

He looked like a deer caught in headlights as he just nodded head quickly, agreeing to whatever Jesse had said. He couldn't help the expression that spread across his face as his eyes bugged out and his mouth dropped as he heard Jesse almost spill the beans about his 'birth parents'.

Jesse had never found himself doing as much 'back peddling' as he was doing at that very moment. He had to say something before Vi figured out that Thomas' birth parents were still earthbound and hadn't passed on like everyone had thought.

"Especially, Mr. and Mrs. Gates," thought Jesse to himself.

"Ahhh! Okay." said Vi as she eyed the two teens suspiciously.

She didn't know what was going on, but her gut told her there was more going on than they were letting on. But that was going to have to be something left for later.

"Master Thomas," said Catherine as she quietly changed the subject. "I believe the phrase goes, 'the ball is in your court' now. Are we to join them or not?"

Thomas paused for a few seconds grateful for the distraction.

He knew that this was a bad idea, but it was something that his best friend felt he had to do. And that was good enough for him.

"Well, I guess I'm just as crazy as the two of you are." relented Thomas as he let out the breath he had been holding for the last couple of minutes. "We're in!"

"Yesss!" exclaimed Jesse as he felt exhilarated having Thomas with them.

Not wasting any time, Jesse quickly turned to Catherine.

"Catherine! If you can get us out of the Sanctuary, that'll be a start," said Jesse as he looked back over his shoulder.

He didn't want either Thomas or Jerome's mother to came back into the room before they had a chance to sneak out.

"I'll try, Master Jesse," said Catherine as she leaped off of the couch and onto the large table in front of the fireplace. "But remember, the magical barriers they've place around the Sanctuary are powerful. This might be a rough ride."

"We'll take whatever you can give us, Catherine," said Jesse. "But whatever you're going to do, you'd better do it fast before Thomas' Mom comes back."

"Alright everyone," announced Catherine. "I'm not sure where we'll end up, but at least it'll be outside of the Sanctuary. As soon as my magic pokes through the barriers, and you see the threshold open up, get through it as fast as you can. I'm not sure how long my magic will be able to keep it open."

"We have faith in you Auntie," encouraged Thomas as he and the others stood back to give Catherine room to work her magic.

As Catherine stood in the middle of the table, her thick tail swished back and forth and then contorted into the shape of a question mark. Her blue eyes turned darker and darker as she concentrated and focused all of her magic on breaking down one small part of the barrier that was surrounding the Sanctuary.

The part of the barrier that was in the great room where they were standing.

As Catherine concentrated, the tip of her tail began to quiver as streams of multicolored magic shot out and hit the area in front of them. Suddenly, an opening appeared in front of the fireplace in the great room of the Sanctuary. At first it was like a dime sized, multicolored pinwheel spinning faster and faster as it hung suspended in midair. The more Catherine concentrated, the larger the opening became until it was almost three feet across.

"Quickly!" yelled Catherine as she struggled to keep the threshold open. "Jump!! I cannot hold it open for too long! The magic surrounding the Sanctuary is powerful and is resisting me!"

Without any hesitation, Jesse dived through the threshold head- first, followed by Vi.

"Oh God! Oh God! Oh God!" exclaimed Vi as she followed on Jesse's heels. "I hope we land somewhere soft!" she called out as she disappeared into the opening.

"You and me both!" called out Thomas as he followed Vi, and just prayed as he dove in headfirst.

Then Gharvey leaped into the opening behind Thomas. Catherine called out to Mus and Scrat as she leapt off of the table and into the threshold.

"Quickly, before it closes!" she called out as she too disappeared.

"Move your furry butt, Scrat!" yelled Mus as he scurried off of the couch and onto the table and then followed Catherine just as the threshold began to close. "Hurry!!"

"I'm a comin'!" responded Scrat as he scampered behind Mus, and just made it through the opening before it closed completely.

Just as Scrat nosedived his way into the opening, Thomas' mother came from around the corner. All Lillian Gates had time to do was to open her mouth and scream her son's name as she saw Scrat's rear end almost get caught on the Sanctuary side of the threshold as it closed with a loud, "POP!!!

"Thomas!!"

And then it was gone, along with Thomas and the others.

Jerome's mother, hearing Lillian Gates scream, came running from the other room. Not knowing what to expect when she got there, on the way to the great room Carolyn picked up the nearest thing that could be used as a weapon.

"Lillian!! Lillian!!" cried Carolyn as she rounded the corner wielding her makeshift weapon. "What is it?? Girl!! What's going on?"

All Lillian Gates could do was to let out an exasperated breath and drop her head onto her chest.

"Thomas and Jesse were going to be the death of her yet!" she thought to herself as she just stood there looking at an empty couch.

Then Carolyn looked over to the couch where Thomas, Jesse and Vi had been sitting only moments before.

"Where'd they go?" was Carolyn's first question.

And then in the same breath she exclaimed, "Ahh! Don't tell me!!"

"Yep! They're gone!" answered Lillian Gates as she turned on her heel and left the great room exclaiming loudly, "I'm gonna kill 'em!! I'm gonna kill 'em both!! And those rodents, too!!" she yelled.

Seeing that there was no threat, Carolyn dropped her upraised arm and just shook her head.

"Oh Buddy!! There's going to be hell to pay now!" exclaimed Jerome's mother as she turned to follow behind her friend who was still yelling at the top of her voice.

Then Jerome's mother stopped and took a good look at the decorative vase she had swiped off of the credenza to use as a weapon as she ran into the great room.

"Hmmm! This is kinda nice!" she stated to herself as she turned the vase over in her hands. "I wonder who did their decorating?" said Jerome's mother as she continued out of the great room and disappeared around the corner still eying the decorative vase.

Chapter VIII

The Battle for Central Park

1am

As the full moon sat in the blue, black sky high above the city that never sleeps, it formed a backdrop for its majesty as the lights of New York City shined below it. The light snow that had fallen earlier, wrapped the bare trees in Central Park in a coat of white fluff as they were about to witness the worlds of Ancient Magic and Humans collide once again.

In the middle of a small clearing in a secluded area of Central Park, swirling sounds of the opening of a threshold began to echo in the night. At first, a small, dime sized spinning pinwheel appeared in the middle of the clearing a few feet above the snow-covered ground. As the sound grew louder, so did the opening of the magic threshold that Catherine had created.

Then without warning, one figure popped out of the center of the threshold, then another and yet another. As the figures fell out of the opening, they found themselves sprawling in the snow a heap on top of each other. A large black Lab leaped out of the opening next, and then a rather large black cat with unusually blue eyes joined them.

Unlike the others, Catherine landed gently on all fours into the soft carpet of snow that had just fallen. Then, just as the threshold began to shrink and disappear, two small figures were thrust out of its opening with such force, they actually flew over the heads of the others that had exited before them.

"Ahhhhhh!!!" screamed the first hairy figure as it flew through the air and landed in a snowdrift few feet from where Jesse and the others had ended up.

And then no more than a second later, Jesse and the others heard another scream.

"Whooooaaaa!!!"

A second figure had followed the first one, as it too, 'flew through the air with the greatest of ease'. As the second figure landed in the snowdrift next to the first one, it made a loud, 'Pooof' sound as it sunk into the soft snow.

Then just as abruptly as it had appeared, the magical threshold quickly disappeared with a loud, 'POP'!!!

Lifting his head up out of the snow he had landed in, Thomas spit out the cold confection that had filled his mouth and looked over at Vi who was sprawled out on her back.

"Well, Vi," he said in a matter-of-fact tone. "You got your soft landing."

Hearing Thomas' voice, Vi sat straight up and looked somewhat disoriented. Her hair was disheveled and seemed to be going in every direction possible, all at the same time. As she shook the snow out of her hair and looked around, she realized that Thomas was right.

Although she had hoped for a soft landing, this wasn't exactly what she had meant.

"Thank you???" she said in a confused voice.

"Is everyone okay?" called out Jesse as he raised himself up onto his knees and looked around.

"I'm good! I think!" answered Thomas.

"I think I am too," said Vi as she continued to shake the snow off of her. And like any other girl would do, she tried to smooth her hair back down so it at least looked presentable.

"Mus? Scrat?" called out Jesse as he strained to see any sign of movement from the snowdrift that they had landed in. "You guys okay?" he asked.

"Sure! We're fine!" exclaimed Mus as he poked his head up out of the snow. "That is if you enjoy feeling like you've been shot out of a cannon!!" screamed the rodent. "What was that?"

"Well, Catherine did say it might be a rough ride," stated Jesse as he went to stand up, and then reached down to help Vi. "At least she got us out of the Sanctuary."

And it was then that Jesse and the others realized something else. In their haste to sneak out of the Sanctuary before they got caught, none of them had thought to bring a coat, gloves or boots.

Nothing!

And in the middle of Winter in New York City, it wasn't just cold! It was freezing!

As Thomas also got to his feet, he realized that he didn't see Catherine.

"Auntie!" called out Thomas as he stumbled and turned to his right.

That was when Thomas saw both Catherine and Gharvey standing in the snow just beyond where he and the others had landed.

"There you two are!" exclaimed Thomas as he tried to grin without shivering. "Good work, Auntie!" said Thomas. "You got us out!"

As Jesse turned toward the two, he noticed that something was wrong!

Catherine and Gharvey were standing motionless in the snow together, and were intently staring behind where Thomas, Jesse and Vi were standing.

"Wha...what's wrong, Auntie?" asked Thomas as he too noticed that something wasn't quite right.

"Nephew!" said Catherine carefully, as she and Gharvey continued to stare past them. "It would seem that perhaps we have jumped 'into' the frying pan!"

"The what...?" asked Thomas.

"Yeah! What are you staring at?" chimed in Jesse as both he and Thomas slowly turned in the direction that Catherine and Gharvey were looking.

That was when both Thomas and Jesse froze and almost stopped breathing.

Vi wasn't paying much attention to what Thomas or Jesse were talking about. She was still trying to brush as much of the freezing snow as she could out of her hair and off of her sweater and pants.

"This is just great!" exclaimed Vi with a tone of irritation to her voice. "I'm not really a fan of snow, you know!" she said as she bent over and continued to brush the snow off of her pants. "It's cold!!"

"Vi!" said Thomas slowly, trying not to alarm her. "Vi, please stop talking."

"What!!!" exclaimed Vi in a high-pitched voice as she jerked herself up into a standing position and faced Thomas, who was standing next to her. "Did you just tell me to, 'Shut up!' Thomas?"

"Yes, please!" answered Thomas quietly as he continued to stare straight ahead of him.

"Just wait til I tell your Mother, Thomas!" fumed Vi. "She will not be happy with you, I can tell you that!"

As Vi continued to rant, she noticed that neither Thomas nor Jesse were paying any attention to her.

"Are you listening to me?" asked Vi as she turned to her left to see what had caught the attention of the two teens.

Vi looked once to her left, and quickly did a double take as she saw what everyone else had seen.

And in the proper fashion of a real girl, Vi froze like a statue as her mouth dropped open, her eyes bugged out, and she hunched her shoulders as she dropped her arms to her side.

And at the same time, Vi let out a loud, high pitched scream as her mind tried to comprehend what she was seeing.

"Ahh…..!!!!!"

Hearing her high-pitched scream as it started to echo into the night, Thomas quickly reached over and covered Vi's mouth with his hand to cut her off. And before he could turn to say anything to her, he saw her eyes roll back, and he felt her body tense up as she fell back into the snow.

At first Thomas didn't know what had happened to her.

Then as Vi landed in the snow with a soft thud, he realized that she had fainted.

"Such a girl!!" exclaimed Mus as he chuckled at Vi.

And then he turned in the direction that the others were looking, and asked, "Hey! What'd she see anyway?"

Scrat had already seen what the others had, and quickly dived back into the soft snow. He had decided that for the time being, coming out of the snowdrift that he and Mus had fallen into was not a particularly good idea. After Mus turned and looked, he too joined Scrat without any hesitation.

Thomas tried to stand as still as he could, hoping he didn't join Vi on the ground.

"Jesse??" whispered Thomas softly as he tried not to move his head. "Do you see what I see?"

"Uhmm! I...I guess!" stammered Jesse not sure what to make of what he saw coming toward them.

In the darkness, off in the distance, it looked like several figures were moving toward them. But there was something off about what they were seeing. Although there was fresh fallen, white snow on the ground all around them, the ground around the figures moving toward them wasn't white at all.

As a matter of fact, the ground surrounding the figures coming in their direction, looked like a carpet of rolling blackness as it seemed to heave up and down in a waves. It was as if the ground was swelling up and down and was in constant motion. The blackness contrasted against the snow-covered ground that was elsewhere.

"Auntie! What do we do?" whispered Thomas helplessly as his muscles began to tense up and cramp.

He was so scared, he wasn't even sure he could move if he had to.

"When I say so, I need you to hit the ground!" said Catherine tensely. "Do not hesitate, Nephew! Jesse!" warned Catherine as she slowly moved herself into position.

"Now!!"

As quickly as they could, both Thomas and Jesse hit the ground. At the same time, Gharvey uttered a low warning growl and bared her teeth as Catherine arched her tail and took aim. Instantly, a shot of magical energy emitted from the tip of her tail and flew straight for the unknown, upright figure approaching them.

As the blast of magical energy shot out from Catherine's tail, it arched itself and staggered through the air as it aimed straight for the figure.

The figure closest to them made a movement to the side, and with one sweep of his arm, a long sliver like staff seemed to appear out of nowhere. And just as the magical blast reached him, he spun the staff with such speed that it reflected Catherine's magic, and in a flash, it absorbed the energy.

As Catherine quickly took aim again, from out of the darkness, a voice called out.

"Hold Witch!! We are not your enemy!!"

The figure nearest to them stepped closer and held up his hand as a sigh that he was not a threat to them.

As Thomas and Jesse lifted their heads, they immediately recognized the man as one of the Sentinels who stood guard outside of the Lexington.

"Wait Auntie!!" yelled Thomas as he called out just as Catherine was about to throw another magical blast. "He's one of the Gargoyles' Sentinels!"

And sure enough.

As the man stepped into the shimmering light of the full moon, he was still wearing his dark royal blue jacket. Gone was the derby hat, that they all wore, but Thomas and Jesse recognized him nonetheless. As he trudged over the snow-covered ground toward them, he called out once again.

"What are you kids doing here?" asked the Sentinel as he stopped only a few feet from them. "Do the others know you are here?"

As he stood in front of the two teens, the slow rolling darkness behind him also seemed to stop moving forward, but it was still rolling in an odd up and down motion.

As both Thomas and Jesse slowly got to their feet, the Sentinel caught the guilty looks that had spread across their faces as Catherine and Gharvey joined them.

"You are not supposed to be here, are you?" asked the Sentinel as he intently searched their faces.

"Maybe not!" blurted out Jesse quickly. "But Central Park is still a public place, right?"

Then turning to Thomas looking for some kind of support, he repeated, "Right?"

"Right!" agreed Thomas as he shoved his hands deeper into his pockets trying and get some kind of feeling back in them. "Right!"

He had been in too much snow this night and was beginning to feel its effect. His teeth had begun to shiver and his knees were beginning to quiver.

"It was cold out here!" his mind screamed.

"You all need to leave this place, now!" said the Sentinel sternly as he looked over at the prone figure of Vi.

She was still out for the count and hadn't budged an inch.

"And you need to look after her," suggested the Sentinel as he moved past Thomas and Jesse. "This is no place for you."

"But…but…!" stammered Jesse as he caught up with the Sentinel. "Maybe we can help!"

As the Sentinel turned to face the young teen to reprimand him and the others again for leaving the Sanctuary without permission, one of the other Sentinels that were with him called out.

"There is no time!" he said quickly. "We have the signal to make our approach! It has begun!"

"What's begun?" asked Jesse as he could feel the intensity in the air increase. "What?"

"The battle!" announced the Sentinel. "The battle begins if Paytric and Irina cannot dissuade the Pre' and the Whre from going forth with their plan."

With no time left to try and further discourage the young group from staying, the Sentinel turned to Catherine and spoke quickly.

"Witch! Whatever powers you have, prepare yourself to use them to protect those that are with you! We are a surprise element that neither the Whre nor the Pre' are expecting. If we do go into battle against them, it will get bad. Do you understand?"

"I understand," acknowledged Catherine as she nodded her head.

"Good!" said the Sentinel as he motioned to the others behind him with a wave of his hand. "We move into position. May the Creator be with us all this night!"

As the Sentinel and the others with him strode past Catherine and the two teens, they made their way to move further into the park. They and the darkness that they had brought with them, trudged into the pale light of the moon as it cast down onto the fresh, fallen snow. It was then that Jesse and the others saw exactly what the darkness was, and what had caused the odd movements within it.

Surrounding the handful of Sentinels were hundreds upon hundreds of small, dark, grayish black creatures. As they moved forward, the teens saw that they were all different. Some of them had small wings perched on their backs, while others had ridges rising along their backside and up and down their limbs. And as they moved along the ground, they used their arms and legs to drag their short, squat bodies forward which accounted for the bobbing up and down motion. And none of them could have been any more than one and a half to two feet high.

As Jesse and Thomas moved out of their way as they scurried past, Jesse couldn't help to wonder, "How were these small creatures expected to be a surprise element against the Pre' and the Whre?"

"What are they, Auntie?" asked Thomas as he watched the creatures follow behind the Sentinels as they made their way to their appointed spot.

"If I am not mistaken, Nephew," said Catherine. "I believe they are called, 'Goyles'."

"Goyles??" asked Thomas and Jesse together as they watched them roll past them.

"Yes," confirmed Catherine. "They are the Gargoyles' young. Very few if anyone ever gets a chance to see them that young. They are very well protected, and watched over," continued Catherine. "And do not let their size fool you. They can be very quick! And when they are that young, they do one thing and one thing only. They eat! And as I recall, the Gargoyles' young are known to be extremely ravenous at that age, until they learn to control their hunger."

"What??" exclaimed Thomas and Jesse at the same time.

Fully understanding what Catherine meant, without any hesitation, Thomas and Jesse quickly moved themselves further away from the horde of mini Gargoyles as they continued to roll past them.

"Just in case some of them hadn't eaten yet," thought Jesse as both he and Thomas kept a sharp eye out. "You never know!"

Just as the last of the 'Goyles' had past, they heard a low moan come from behind them. With everything that had happened, they had totally forgotten about Vi.

"Vi!!" screamed Jesse as he turned to check on his friend. "Oh my God!" he exclaimed. "We forgot all about her!!"

"Is she okay?" asked Thomas as he helped Jesse get her to a standing position and dust the snow off of her.

"Vi!! Vi!!" exclaimed Jesse. "You okay?"

As Vi tried to steady herself, she felt disoriented as she looked back and forth between the two teens supporting her.

"Wha…what happened?" she asked.

And then she mumbled something else that neither Thomas nor Jesse could make out, and then a second later, she had remembered what she saw before she had fainted.

"Ahhh!! They're coming!" she screamed as she tried to turn and run in the other direction. "They're coming!!"

"No Vi! No!" exclaimed Jesse as he caught her before she could make a run for it. "It's alright!" he said. "They're gone! They're gone!"

"What was that??" she asked as she continued to wildly look around her.

"We'll explain later," said Jesse as he turned her in the direction that the Sentinels had gone and proceeded to lead her. "But right now, we need to go!"

Then Jesse looked back over his shoulder and called to Thomas.

"Com'on Thomas, we've got to catch up!"

"No!" exclaimed Thomas. "I can't go any further! It's too cold!"

He was shivering so badly he couldn't even talk without his teeth clicking together.

"Auntie! Please!" Thomas said. "We need to get warm, here!"

"Oh Nephew!" exclaimed Catherine. "I am so sorry!"

Without hesitation, Catherine arched her tail and let go a magical spell that in an instant had clothed everyone in warm and dry coats, boots, hats, and gloves. She had even draped Gharvey in an extra warm coat and doggie booties that wouldn't constrict her movements.

Everyone was more than grateful for the warm, snug clothing that they had been fitted for.

"Finally, I can feel my feet and hands!!" exclaimed Thomas as he pulled the warm garments that his Aunt Catherine had provided for them tightly around his body.

And from the snowdrift that Mus and Scrat had ducked back into, they heard a loud, gleeful yell.

"Now that's what I'm talkin' about!" yelled Mus as he got a good look at the tiny, fur lined coats and boots that Catherine had magically spun up for him and Scrat.

"Com'on guys," called out Jesse as even he had begun to get the feeling back in his hands and feet. "We've got to catch up!"

The small group made their way across the snow-covered ground in the middle of Central as they followed behind the Sentinels and the 'Goyles'. And as they trudged over the light, snow covered ground, Thomas and Jesse explained everything that they had been told about the 'Goyles' by Catherine, to Vi. And although they couldn't tell her much more than what had been told to them, it was enough to settle her nerves about what she had seen before she fainted.

Then Thomas looked over to Jesse.

"Just how are you planning to get to Amanda, Jess?" he asked. "I mean with everything that's going on, it's going to be kinda hard."

"I was thinking about that," admitted Jesse as he moved through the park with the others. "I think I'm going to try and open a 'mind portal' with her," he said carefully. "Kinda like the one I opened with you when I was in the Warriors' dimension three years ago. But I think when I try and do it, I have to be fairly close to the person I'm trying to contact."

"How close do you have to be?" asked Thomas hoping that they didn't have to actually get into the middle of the battle for him to contact Amanda.

"That's just it. I don't know," answered Jesse as honestly as he could. "I'm just going to have to start trying to contact her and see what happens. I haven't been practicing much with people, so…I don't know how it's going to go. But I've got to try."

"Well, after Amanda kills you and probably me for sneaking out of the Sanctuary, I'm sure she'll appreciate it," said Thomas.

"Yeah!" agreed Jesse as he gave a little laugh. "As will your Mom and Dad."

"Oh God! I forgot!" exclaimed Thomas as he came to a dead stop.

He tried not to think about what his mother and father would do when they learned that he and Jesse had snuck out.

"You know I'm dead, right?" stated Thomas as he turned to Jesse.

"Well then, before I forget, Thomas," said Jesse in the most sincere way that he could. "Thanks for coming with me," he said. "I really appreciate it."

"For true?" asked Thomas of his best friend.

"For true," answered Jesse back as he slapped Thomas on his back.

Just then, Vi who was a few feet in front of them stopped abruptly.

"Guys!" she exclaimed softly. "Look!"

The Sentinels and the 'Goyles' had stopped just inside of a tree line that edged along the backside of a raised mound. The mound was surrounding what looked like an area that was used as a baseball diamond. Even though they were still a distance away, they could see that the Pre' had gathered on top of the mound and were all facing in the direction overlooking the baseball diamond itself.

As the Pre' on the mound looked across the field to the opposite side of the diamond, a portal had just opened up. And exiting from its opening was Paytric and Granna, along with Irina and two Gargoyles, and Barnabas Bane and Skalla.

As they all stepped out of the portal, the group slowly moved themselves forward across the semi-dark baseball diamond. Once they got halfway across the field to the mound, they stopped.

Stepping out from the middle of the Pre' that had gathered on the mound, was Givant and Faayn.

Seeing his son on the mound with the Pre' caused Skalla pain. He took in a deep breath and tried to control the emotions that were churning inside of him.

"My Son has not only betrayed his kind, but his own Father," thought Skalla to himself.

He wondered where he had gone wrong. What he could have done with his sons that would have made a difference. Now he had no sons to speak of, and the continued existence of the Whre was teetering in the balance of what transpired here this night.

For the second time, Skalla truly questioned his ability to lead his kind.

As the Givant and Faayn stood on the mound looking out over the field, Paytric could tell that they were trying to assess who was going to make the next move.

Paytric only hoped that he and the others could provide enough of a distraction to keep them occupied. They had to keep the Pre' and the Whre from realizing that there were others that were moving into place right under their very eyes behind a magical cloak of invisibility, and that the Sentinels, along with the 'Goyles', were preparing to attack from the rear, if things didn't go as planned.

Hopefully, it wouldn't come to that. But they had to prepare for every possibility.

And unknown to the others that stood with Paytric, there was one more surprise element he had to throw into the mix, if it truly came down to a battle and they needed the extra support.

"When it comes to a fight, I do not like to be at a disadvantage," thought Paytric to himself as he moved himself away from the group, and further out into the opened field to stand alone.

"Givant of the Pre'!" called out Paytric as he stopped his approach. "Faayn of the Whre! Being here is breaking the pact set in place hundreds of years ago by the leaders of your kind. What say you?"

Givant smirked slightly, and then stepped forward.

"We say that we no longer wish to be under the boot heel of the Gargoyles!" stated Givant loudly as she glanced over to Irina and smirked again. "We say that it is time that we make our own destiny as the creatures of the night that we are! We are Pre'!" exclaimed Givant defiantly.

"And we are Whre!" shouted Faayn as he raised his arms up, just as rebellious. "And as creatures of the night, we were meant to 'feed' on Humans! And we will no longer allow the Gargoyles to force us to go against our nature!"

The Pre' surrounding them on the mound all began to yell and cheer in agreement as they too raised their arms in defiance. As they jumped up and down, Paytric could see that their thunderous shouts and yells were a sign that they were being whipped into a frenzy before they attacked.

"Givant, Faayn! Do not force a battle that you cannot win!" stated Paytric. "We ask you one more time! Stand down! This will end badly for you and your kind if you do not!"

The smirk on Givant's face disappeared as she moved herself forward.

"And we have taken a pledge amongst ourselves!" yelled Givant back. "For one of our kind, it will end tonight. One way or another!" said Givant arrogantly. "And by the looks of the 'rag-tag' group you have brought with you, you are no match for us!"

Everyone could see that Givant was high on her own adrenaline, and seemingly drunk with power.

As Sean stood on the left side of the field, waiting behind one of the magical cloaks provided by the Wielders of Magic, he saw the same look in Givant's eyes that he had seen when he and Cherese were in the caverns of the Pre'. Except this time, he could see that she had really gone over the deep end.

"This 'Bitch' is crazy!!" thought Sean to himself as he watched with J.D. the others from the left side of the field. "I mean, she's really gone off her rocker!"

And then he remembered what E'nal had told him about Givant before they were rescued. The reason why he said he kept her on such a 'short leash'.

"According to E'nal, Givant was a beautiful, tormented, psychopath," thought Sean to himself.

And Sean could see exactly what he had meant.

Her eyes were glassed over, and her breathing was becoming rapid. The intense hatred she had bottled up for centuries, not only for Humans, but for the Gargoyles as well, had finally surged to the surface and spilled over. She couldn't see or feel anything but the hate she felt inside. And all of that had blinded her to anything else. She was overconfident of herself and what she thought was an invincible plan.

As Paytric stood out in the opened field, he also noticed that Givant's demeanor was seemingly beginning to deteriorate right before his eyes. He could see that she was not showing signs of being a good leader but was exhibiting signs of being overly sure of herself.

He thought back to when he was in training in the Warriors' dimension with his teacher, Shiro. The one thing Shiro had always taught him from the very beginning 'was to never underestimate your enemy'. Never. You do the best that you can, but never be overconfident.

He remembered Shiro standing before him and the other young Warriors on the training fields. booming at the top of his voice as he spoke.

"Always remember! No matter how well laid your plans may be, there is always someone else, who with a little more creativity can unravel that which you have put forth. And no matter how good you 'think' you are, there is always someone that is just a little better! And that is all it takes for you to be brought down."

Paytric smiled slightly as the memories from long ago flooded his thoughts. He only hoped that he didn't have to call on his teacher this night if this turned into a full-fledged battle.

"But time would tell," he thought to himself. "Time will tell!"

Then Paytric was brought back to the present when he heard Givant call out to him again.

"You are pathetic, Warrior!" she screamed. "You protect the Humans and yet they could care less about you. If you presented yourself to the real world, they would scoff at you. Well, let me show you how these Humans should be handled," said Givant as she reached into the crowd that had surrounded her.

She had grabbed a hold of someone standing beside her and pulled them out into the open so everyone could see.

It was a young, dark-haired woman who looked to be about in her early twenties. She was dressed in the usual party clothes for a Saturday night in New York City, and her hands had been bound in front of her, while her mouth was gagged.

She didn't know what was happening, and was looking wildly around, while trying to break free as she screamed into her bindings, pleading for someone to help her. Even from where he was standing, Paytric could see the fear and total terror in the young woman's eyes as could the others behind him.

"They are cattle to us!" said Givant as she pulled the young woman in front of her.

As Givant held the woman tightly with one arm, she reached around and ripped the gag away from the young woman's mouth with her other hand. In that same instant, the young woman's scream echoed through the night air.

"Help Me! Please, help meee!!" she screamed at the top of her voice.

But it was to no avail.

It all happened in a matter of seconds.

Even before Granna could step forward and blast a surge of magical energy toward the mound to try and save the girl, Givant had jerked the young woman's head to the side exposing her neck.

"This is what Humans are for!" yelled Givant as she transformed, and in the same instant, buried her fangs deep into the young woman's neck as she drank.

"Nooo!!" screamed Granna as she and the others witnessed the young woman's life as it slowly ebbed out of her body. As her body jerked and heaved, in total disregard, Givant continued to drink her blood until the young woman's eyes had faded to dark.

"No, Granna!" exclaimed Paytric as he caught Cherese' grandmother before she could move further toward the mound.

And then looking back at Irina, he reiterated as he saw her also move forward.

"No, Irina!" he said quickly. "There was no helping her! We couldn't have known! "It's too late for her," he said solemnly. "It's too late! But we must stick to the plan, or all is doomed!"

As Granna and Irina relinquished, they heard the crowd on the mound cheered at the senseless killing they had just witnessed. To those standing with Paytric, a sense of helplessness swept over them.

Even Paytric didn't see that coming.

As the young woman's body hung limp in Givant's arms, she continued to drink until she had drained the last drop of blood from her. Then Givant slowly lifted her head up and smiled through her blood-stained lips, exposing her fangs as she let the body fall to the ground in a lifeless heap.

"They are nothing but food for our kind!" exclaimed Givant as she licked any errant blood droplets from her face that she had missed. "And even with your magical friends, you couldn't save her," taunted Givant as she smirked. "Such a shame!" she said as she stepped over the body of the young woman she had just drained and stood before the crowd.

"You couldn't save one woman!" she exclaimed. "What makes you think that you can save the rest of the Humans from us?" she asked. "You see, we know your weakness," she said. "It is the very ones that you protect. And we will use them to bring you down."

As Givant spoke, she walked back and forth in front of the crowd on top of the mound, inciting them more and more.

"Bring it on!" she screamed at the small group standing before her. "Bring it on!"

"We have something for you, Warrior!" she screamed as he pointed to Paytric. "And for you, Witch!" she yelled as she pointed to Cherese's grandmother.

And then as Givant stood on the snow-covered mound, she looked over at Irina and smiled fully at her.

And for you, Irina!" she said with the most hateful tone she could. "Come! Come and taste my flesh like you and your kind did of my beloved, Delan. Come, if you dare, Gargoyle!!" she taunted. "We especially have something for you! You and your kind will pay for his death!"

Then Givant strode back over to Faayn and smiled.

"Skalla, even your Son has turned against you!" stated Givant. "How does that feel?"

Paytric quickly looked over at Skalla and cautioned him.

"Control, Skalla!" he said. "She is trying to bait you."

"Yes. I know, Paytric!" replied Skalla as he stepped forward. "I know!"

And then to Givant, Skalla said, "I do not know who you are, Pre'. But I can see that you are one twisted soul. I feel sorry for you, and for those who follow you. Including my Son, Faayn."

Faayn quickly stepped forward and spoke to his father.

"Do not feel sorry for me, Father!" he said. "I have tasted more Human flesh and blood this night than I have ever tasted before. It is enticing, and I will not give it up, do you hear! I would rather die!"

"Then so be it!" said Skalla as he slowly stepped back. "Then so be it!"

It was then that Paytric and the others realized that there was no way they were going to be able to diffuse this situation peacefully. The Pre' and the Whre on the mound had passed beyond the point of no return.

There was no room for any further negotiations.

It was what it was!

~~~~~~~~

From behind the mound, as the Sentinels stood ready, waiting for the signal to advance forward, they heard whopping and hollering coming from the Pre' and the Whre. They were reacting to something that had happened in front of them.

"What happened?" exclaimed Thomas as he tried to stretch himself to see.

"I dunno!" answered Jesse as he shrugged his shoulders. "I can't see anything!"

Other than what they were hearing, they couldn't see a thing!

None on the mound knew what waited behind them in the dense trees. The wind was blowing in their direction from across the open field. And as fate would have it, that kept the scent of the Gargoyles' young hidden from detection.

"A good advantage," thought the lead Sentinel as he waited with the others. "A very good advantage."

As the group behind the mound continued to observe from their hiding place, Gharvey heard a slight rustling in the bushes to the left of where the Sentinels and the others were waiting. She wasn't sure at first. But when her ears picked up the almost indistinguishable sounds of an animal slowly padding its way through the snow toward them, she paused.

"Catherine!" whispered Gharvey, trying not to raise unwarranted concern. "To our left!" she said. "Do you hear it?"

Catherine simply nodded her head once.

She was already ahead one step ahead. She had already positioned her tail so that it was aiming in the direction of a group of low-lying bushes.

Then from the mound in front of them, came another burst of yells.

At the same time a dark, low crouching figure had separated itself from the bushes to the groups' left, and advanced. It was one of the Where Sires that had been also hiding in the tree line, waiting to initiate a surprise attack. It had picked up the scent of the Sentinels and the Gargoyles' young when the wind had shifted briefly.

As the Sire leaped out of the bushes, it caught everyone off guard, except for Gharvey and Catherine. As it planted in front of them, it's head dropped below its shoulders and its tail swung from side to side as it let out a low growl and started to move toward them.

"It's a Wolf!" It's a Wolf!" "It's a Wolf!" screamed Mus and Scrat as they scampered into the bushes to the right.

But before any of the Sentinels could swing their sliver staffs into position, or even Catherine could dispatch a volley of magical blasts directed at the Sire, another Sire had appeared further to their left.

"It's another one!" cried Thomas as he and Vi tried to back up as fast as they could.

And before they knew it, the second Sire had let out a vicious growl, and in two bounds, it leapt across the frozen ground toward the first Sire. As it landed on the back of its' brother, the second Sire literally tore into

the hide of the first one. As the two rolled onto the ground thrashing the light snow into the air around them, they ripped and tore into each other.

Confused, and not really understanding what was happening, Thomas and the others backed further out of the way of the two battling wolfs to wait for the outcome. The Sentinels continued to keep a close eye on the Gargoyles' young, making sure they kept them under control until it was time to release them.

Within a few minutes it was over.

The second Sire had successfully overpowered the first one. And then it looked over to Jesse.

It started to limp toward him but was only able to take a couple of steps before it too collapsed onto the soft, snow-covered ground with a whimper.

Jesse found himself compelled as he moved himself over to the fallen wolf.

"Jesse!!" exclaimed Thomas. "What are you doing?"

"It's not dead, Jesse!" cried Vi as she feared the worst.

"Son...!" started one of the Sentinels.

But before any of them could finish their warnings, Jesse had already slid himself over the frozen ground to the wolf's side.

"But I know this wolf," said Jesse softly as he reached the Sire's side. "This is the wolf from the Lexington," said Jesse as he turned back to Thomas and Vi. "You know, Thomas. The one from the elevator."

"Oh!" exclaimed Thomas. "You mean, the one that you were able to persuade not to eat us alive?" asked Thomas from a distance. "That wolf!"

Ignoring the sarcasm in Thomas' voice, Jesse returned his attention to the hurt animal. It tried to lift its head to acknowledge Jesse, but found its strength ebbing as the animal dropped its head back onto the ground.

"Protect!" said the wolf softly to Jesse's mind. "Protect!"

"Yes! You did protect me. Thank you!" said Jesse as he tried to comfort the animal. "But don't move! You're hurt pretty bad!"

Then turning to Catherine, Jesse pleaded.

"Catherine! Please help him! You can do something, can't you?" he said. "It saved us! We've got to try and do something."

"I'll try, Jesse," said Catherine as she stepped forward and began to murmur a spell under her breath, trying to heal some of the more serious wounds that the animal had.

When she had done all that she could, Catherine had Jesse stand back as she placed the animal in a stasis envelope to protect it from the cold while it healed. Then with a flip of her tail and another magical spell, she transported the animal, while still inside of the envelope, back to the Den of the Whre, where its own kind could take care of it while it recovered.

And then with another flip of her tail, Catherine disposed of the first Sires' body in a flash of magical energy.

Watching from the sidelines, the Sentinel observed Catherine's handiwork. Then he looked over at her.

"You are truly worth keeping close, Witch!" said the lead Sentinel. "They call you, Catherine?" he asked.

"Yes! That is my name," answered Thomas' Aunt.

"Well then, Catherine," he said with a slight smile. "Welcome. Perhaps I need to keep you closer than first thought."

"Perhaps you do!" responded Catherine with a coy flip of her tail and a slight tilting of her head.

Then catching herself, Catherine thought to herself, "Nooo! I did not just flirt with him! Did I? That cannot be! I am a…! And he is a…! Besides, it has been so long since I have even felt anything like that!"

But Catherine wasn't the only one to notice that she had flirted with the Sentinel.

"Auntie!" exclaimed Thomas as he, Jesse and Vi stood nearby, observing what had just seemingly transpired.

Then, turning his attention back to what was going happening on top of the mound, the Sentinel said, "Be ready to watch over your wards when the time comes. When it happens, it will happen fast."

"I will be ready," confirmed Catherine, feeling a little gitty and embarrassed at the same time, as she made a point to avoid the stares that she was getting from her Nephew and his friends.

"So will we!" "Yeah!" exclaimed Thomas and Jesse in unison as they both eyed the Sentinel with sidelong glances.

Then leaning over to Thomas, Jesse whispered, "Did he just make a pass at Catherine?"

"Yesss, he did!!" exclaimed Thomas trying not to get overly worked up over it. "And, 'Oh my God!' She flirted back!"

And not being one to miss out on anything, Vi leaned in and said with a smile, "Yes. Yes, she did!"

Then, before Thomas could even throw Vi an irritated look, they heard Givant address Paytric and the others again.

"We will finish the job that we started a hundred years ago, Irina!" yelled Givant. "But this time we will not fail! With my new army, we will wipe you and your kind, off the face of the Earth!" she ranted. "Meet my new soldiers!"

As she spoke, eerie, ghostlike figures began to materialize in the sky and around the mound. As they did, some drifted across the flat area of the park as they hovered a few feet above the snow-covered ground. Others floated through the bare branches of the desolate trees and the low-lying bushes as they joined the others surrounding the mound.

At first, there were only a few dozen. But then hundreds upon hundreds of them began to materialize as the flat area around the mound became clustered with the phantom like apparitions. None of them seemed to have any real form or substance other than the hazy, vaporous part that appeared underneath their heads. And the area where their heads would have been, was what appeared to be a distorted, engorged image of the face of the human the apparition was embodying.

Thomas, Jesse, and Vi watched from tree line below, as the apparitions floated over where the Gargoyles' young were hidden. The Sentinels prayed that their presence would remain hidden until the signal was given. But as luck was with them as none of the ghostly figures even took note of the group below them. They just instinctively made their way to the place where they had been summoned.

As Givant stood on the mound, she spread her arms out as if to welcome and embrace the apparitions as they made their way to her.

"Look!" she yelled out. "Look upon the Humans that you so dearly protect! We control them now! And you and your magical friends can do nothing about it!"

As Paytric, and the others slowly backed away from the mound and the increasing number of ghostly figures that had gathered, he looked toward Barnabas Bane.

Before Paytric could even speak, Barnabas had squared his shoulders and lifted his head up and took in a deep breath.

"I believe that it is time for me to do, what I do best," he said as he returned Paytric's glance. Yes?"

"Yes, Barnabas," answered Paytric solemnly as he realized that there was no way either Givant or Faayn were going to listen to reason. "It is time!"

"Then I am off," said Barnabas as he turned to Paytric. "You will know it is time to give the signal to the others when the apparitions begin to dissipate. That should allow the Gargoyles open access to those on the mound."

Without another word, he took in another deep breath and closed his eyes. And in an instant, the well fitted, gray stripped suit that he wore, seemed to deflate and fold in onto itself as Barnabas Bane, the man, disappeared. And as the empty suit fell to the ground, all that remained was the pure essence that was, truly Barnabas Bane.

Writhing and coiling out of the fine, silk threads of the suit, was the same dark, grayish mist they had seen him appear out of when he was first introduced to everyone in the Sanctuary. But this time, the mist that was Barnabas Bane, slowly crept along the snow-covered ground as it began to make its way to the mound.

And from up above, what appeared to be a rolling bank of dark, winter storm clouds began to develop over the tops of the trees in the distance. As it slowly moved itself across the sky, it covered the flat area of the park as it billowed and swelled and grew in intensity as it headed for the mound.

"Granna!" exclaimed Paytric as he looked up. "What is happening?"

"It is Barnabas Bane, doing what he does best," answered Granna. "He's such a showman!" said Granna proudly. "Get ready! He is about to make his presence known."

The Pre' on the mound, also took note of the odd storm that seemed to come out of nowhere as it rolled toward the open field. They could tell it didn't have the feel of any kind of storm they had ever felt before.

And they were right!

"Your magic doesn't scare us!" called out Givant as she looked toward the changing sky.

"Come Warrior, Witch, and Gargoyle!" she said. "You want us? Come and get us! That is, if you don't mind going through a few of your Human pets to do so! You see, the 'spirit walkers' will fight to the death if we tell them to. And when they do, there their Human bodies will cease to exist. Will you let that happen?"

As she spoke, neither Givant nor Faayn had taken note of the grayish mist that was creeping its way along the ground toward them. They both were too occupied with keeping the Pre' on the mound stirred up.

And then they felt it!

All of them on the mound felt it at the same time!

At first it was a sense of 'uneasiness' that seemed to invade their minds and slowly creep its way into their very being. Odd! It seemed to cause them for just a second to feel, apprehensive. Maybe a little frightened.

"But of what am I frightened of?" each of them asked themselves as they nervously looked around.

Then, as each of the Pre' on the mound began to feel their own personal sense of dread growing within them, they noticed that the low lying, grayish mist had not only eased itself up onto the mound, but it had slowly crept up upon them. It began to wrap and coil itself around each of the Pre', caressing them as if they were children.

"What is it?" "What's happening?" "Get it off me!!"

The Pre' on the mound began to panic as they screamed out.

As the mist edged its way upward, some even tried to swipe away at it with their hands. Before they realized what was happening, the gray mist had coiled and encircled each of them. And then it seemed to move with intent, as it quickly adhered itself to their faces as it wrapped itself around them. As they struggled trying to tear at the gray shroud covering their faces, they began to find themselves almost suffocating beneath it.

And then they heard it!

A soft-spoken voice inside the hidden recesses of their mind.

"I am the sum of all of your fears...your doubts...the secret misgivings you try to suppress!

I am the one behind the thin veil of horror that seeks you out in the darkness of the night! That separates you from all that you know, so that you are...alone!

I am the one you try to escape from...again...and again...and again! But there is no escape. For I am always with you, as are your innermost fears! And you know what fears I speak of!

For I know you...!

Come to me. For I am...the Boogey Man..."

All of the Pre' on the mound, including Givant and Faayn, struggled as they attempted to transform before whatever small part of their humanity that was left, could be compromised.

At the same time from up above, the dark, rolling cloud bank had reached the mound.

As it began to engulf each of the apparitions that had appeared, they began to writher and twist in midair as Barnabas Bane spoke to each of them. As he made them experience that which they feared the most. That, which Barnabas Bane was making them experience, times ten.

Their already distorted faces had become more and more twisted as they tried to break free of the fear that overwhelmed them. The fear that consumed them. Their screams and shrieks began to echo throughout the night like that of a wounded animal being torn apart from the inside out. It was a harried sight as the apparitions darted back and forth over the mound as they sought some kind of refuge. Some even dived into the surrounding trees to escape.

But there was no escape from Barnabas Bane.

He would not allow it! Not until the hold the Pre' had over the Humans they had marked had been completely severed.

As the apparitions dived down to try and escape, some of them ended up colliding with some of the Pre' or Humans that were on the ground as they tried to get out of their way. It was a sight to see as the ghostly figures screaming, flung themselves through the air and then, "Pouf!'

They'd slam into a solid body!

And then just for a second or two, the two were as one as the misty haze of the phantom engulfed them both, creating a 'ghostly' halo around them. And then after a few seconds, the apparition realizing there was nowhere to hide, quickly disengaged itself from its Human host, and again tried to flee.

Thomas, Jesse and Vi ducked and tried to cover their ears as the apparitions wailed and howled about them.

And all over New York City and the surrounding areas, Humans who had been 'marked' were being jolted out of a deeper than normal sleep, screaming and shrieking into the darkness. They were being awakened from what they would testify to as being, the worst nightmare they had ever experienced in their entire lives.

Some of the screaming of those being jolted awake, was so horrific, so terrifying, that calls began to flood into Police stations around the city as people panicked. They were reporting what they thought were possible beatings, and in some cases, what sounded like animal attacks from inside of homes and apartment buildings.

"But that can't be!" thought many of the callers. But if not that, then what were they hearing?

It was an epidemic in the city.

And in Central Park, one by one, the apparitions floating over the mound began to lose their form and began to dissipate as Humans in the city began to wake up from their drug induced sleep.

Givant looked wildly around as she saw her new army being dismantled before her very eyes. She realized that somehow, Irina and the others had found a way to force the Humans awake before she could utilize them.

"Noooo!!!" screamed Givant at the top of her voice as she transformed. The others on the mound followed suit as they tried to shake off the influence of Barnabas Bane.

Faayn, standing on the mound, quickly shook off the words of the voice he had heard in the deep recesses of his mind. Even his worse fears only fed his deranged persona.

He welcomed them!

He transformed and leapt in one bound, off of the raised area as he sought out his father. Landing on all fours, not far from where Paytric and the others had moved to, he reared back and stood to his full height.

As he threw his head back, he let go a howl giving the signal to the other Whre hidden in the trees and bushes to attack! The Whre responded to the call as their growls joined Faayn's as they separated themselves from the shadow of the trees and moved in for the kill!

But the Sires that had followed Faayn were young.

They had not yet learned all that a Whre needed to know about hunting, stalking and lying in wait for their prey. Especially, if it was your own kind that you were hunting. But the older Whre that Skalla had brought with him, did.

Unbeknownst to each of the young Sires hidden in the trees and bushes surrounding the field, they themselves had already been hunted and staked out by the older Whre of their den. They were lying in wait for the young Sires as they crept out of their hiding places.

So sure of their plan. So sure of themselves.

As Faayn waited for the surprise attack that was supposed to catch his father and the others in the cross-fire, he listened. It was then that he heard vicious growls and the sounds of fighting coming from the wooded area surrounding the flat area of the field. His whole body began to tremble with rage as he heard the yelps and the cries of the Sires. He knew in an instant what his father had done. The young Sires that had followed him were now engaged in the fight for their very lives against their own kind. And it was unlikely that any of them would survive if they did not submit, and yield to defeat.

Enraged beyond anything he had ever felt before, Faayn spun himself around to glare at Skalla. As he drew back his trembling lips, revealing his dagger like fangs, he took the stance of challenge, prepared to meet his father head on.

He would not submit!

"Face me, Father! As a Whre!" he shouted. "Let us end this now, once and for all! Only one of us can survive this night!"

Skalla, knowing that his son was right, accepted his challenge and quickly transformed. And in one leap he landed in the middle of the field and stood at his full height before his son and the others.

"So be it, Faayn!" exclaimed Skalla solemnly as he towered over his son. "So be it!"

Paytric and Granna quickly gave the signal to the others who were hidden behind the magical barriers, that it was time!

"Prepare!!!" yelled Paytric as he drew is short sword.

 He and the others were to back up the Gargoyles if any of the Pre' on the mound, or any of the Whre in the trees and the bushes got past the line of defense that had been set up. They had to be prepared to stop them at all costs.

Appeared out of thin air along the left side of the field, Witches, Watchers, and Wau-douns. and Banshees appeared along the right side of the field from behind their magical barrier, as did Zachary Boyd. Also, from the right side of the field the other teams disengaged themselves from behind the magical barrier and approached the mound.

Cherese, Jerome, and Jerome's father, Reginald, appeared on the right side of Granna and Paytric, while Remy and Mrs. Whitehall, Kenadi and the Wielder's of Magic' sister appeared on their left side.

Seeing that his father had laid a trap for him, Faayn became blinded by his fury. Snapping and growling, he charged at his father trying to go for his jugular. Skalla, standing his ground, drew his massive right arm back and easily swept Faayn off of his feet, and sent him flying back across the field from which he had come. And in two leaps and bounds, Skalla had reached his son's side and pinned him beneath him on the snow-covered ground.

"You would make me rip you apart?" yelled Skalla as he glared down at his son, not wanting to do what Faayn was forcing him to do.

"Yes, Father!" snarled Faayn back, as he struggled to free himself. "You will either let me go, and forever know that you unleashed a monster upon the world. Or you will kill me and live with the knowledge that you had to rip apart your own Son! Your own flesh and blood!"

As Faayn spoke, he thrashed about trying to remove himself from under his father's weight. He swiped at Skalla with his claws and ripped open a gash along his left side.

"Grrrrrrrrrhhhhh!" howled Skalla as the pain from his son's attack coursed throughout his body.

Ignoring the pain and the open wound, Skalla continued to contain his son. He found himself hesitating doing what he knew he must!

He could not!

Granna, seeing the pain on Skalla's face as he hovered over his son, and seeing him hesitate destroying his last offspring, made a decision and cast a spell.

In an instant, Faayn disappeared from beneath his father as a magical threshold opened, and he fell through it as a surge of energy engulfed him. And then the threshold was gone. Granna had transported him to the Dark Castle, and forever to the care of the 'Ides of March'.

"Faayn!!" screamed Skalla as his mind tried to comprehend what had just happened.

Looking wildly around for an answer, Skalla's eyes rested on Cherese' grandmother as she stood watching him from a short distance away.

"It is for the best, Skalla," whispered Granna as her heart broke for him. "It is for the best!"

Knowing what Granna meant, Skalla's whole body began to shake as he threw back his head and let go a mournful, grief- stricken howl to the sky above as heart broke into a million pieces.

After Faayn had transformed and charged the field to face his father, Givant continued to look to the skies as she witnessed the ghostly phantoms, she had depended on to keep the Gargoyles at bay, disappear, one by one. She yelled at the remaining Pre' to attack. She knew that without the phantoms as a 'buffer', the Gargoyles would surely seek out their revenge on the remaining Pre'.

And she was right!

As the screams of the phantoms became fewer and fewer, they themselves began to disappear from the embrace of the dark, menacing clouds above that was Barnabas Bane. They had been freed! And one by one, as they faded into nothingness from the sky above, larger, darker figures appeared to take their places.

The Gargoyles were coming!

From the dense tree line behind the mound, the signal had been heard.

"Alla-mah! Seytoush! Lapoora!"

As the lead Sentinel began to speak unfamiliar words to the 'Goyles', he pointed his silver staff toward the mound and those standing upon it. The Gargoyles' young had been unleashed and given permission to feed upon the Pre'. And none would be spared from their attack.

As the 'Goyles' thundered out of the tree line and headed for the mound, they moved with exceptional speed. They literally covered the distance between the tree line and the mound within seconds, and then engulfed the slightly raised area with their mass of scurrying, dark bodies.

Just as the Pre' had begun to cast off the whisperings of Barnabas Bane, and the gray mist that had encompassed them, they heard a rumbling sound coming from behind them. As they turned, they could only stare in disbelief. Many of them were so stunned as they took in the sight of what was surging toward them, they didn't have time to escape off of the hill.

For those, it was already too late!

The 'Goyles' engulfed the mound and brought down any Pre' that remained on the hill as they began to feed. Those who had recovered from the sight, and tried to transport themselves away, found that half-way into the process, they were literally ripped back and pulled down into the mass of hungry, ravenous bodies. All that could be seen from the flat area of the field where Paytric and the others were standing, were the arms of the Pre' who had been caught by the 'Goyles', as they were dragged down into the dark mass on the mound and devoured.

And the screams of the Pre' took the place of those of the phantoms, as the Gargoyles' young fed.

Granna turned her head, not bearing to watch.

"It did not have to come to this," she thought to herself as a sadness sweep over her. "It did not have to come to this!"

And then as she looked up, she saw that Irina and the two Gargoyles that had been with her, had already taken flight to join the rest of their kind. With vengeance they were already in pursuit of any of the Pre' who may have escaped off of the mound.

As the Gargoyles darkened the sky above, they relentlessly went after the Pre, as they dived at those who were on the flat area of the field. Before they could even get their bearings, the Gargoyles had swept them up into the air as they dangled helplessly, while they clawed and snapped at their captors. They tried as best they could to break the hold of the Gargoyle that held them.

But it was to no avail.

Givant was one of those who had fled out into the open field, just before the 'Goyles' swarmed onto the mound. As she materialized on the flat area of the field, she quickly ducked and dodged around those trying to evade being picked off by the Gargoyles. Just as she turned and tried to make a run for the safety of the trees along the right side of the field, she saw a shadow quickly move in front of her. And a second later, she felt her neck being grabbed and held by the strong and unyielding hand…of Irina.

"Givant!" whispered the leader of the Gargoyles in her raspy, shallow voice. "We meet again! Why in such a hurry?"

As Irina spoke, she had easily lifted Givant up off of the ground and held her at least three feet in the air. Givant struggled to catch her breath as she tried to scratch and claw at Irina. No matter how much she snarled and hissed, Irina's grip only tightened more around her neck, as she squeezed harder.

"Do not worry," said Irina as she brought Givant's face even with hers as she glared at her while keeping her at arms' length. "I will not let you suffocate. That would be too easy of a death for you."

"I am not afraid of you, Gargoyle!" yelled Givant as her breathing became more and more constricted. "Or what you may do to me! I thrive on pain and torture," she said. "I live for it!!"

But Irina could see a flicker of fear in Givant's eyes as she spoke. Just a flicker. And that was enough satisfaction for her to know that she had her just where she wanted her.

Irina half smiled as she prepared to take flight with Givant still held tightly in her grip.

"Then I will not disappoint you," she whispered.

But before Irina could unfold her wings from underneath her cloak and take to the skies, Cherese had suddenly appeared by her side.

"She is mine!" exclaimed Cherese as she stared down the leader of the Gargoyles.

Cherese still had a serious bone to pick with Givant. And she wasn't about to let what she had tried to do to her in the caverns, go without some kind of pay back!

As Irina swung around to face Cherese, she yelled.

"Be gone, Witch!! This one will pay for what she and her kind have tried to do," stated Irina. "Not only for tonight, but what her and her masters collaborated to do over a hundred years ago with the Dark Dimension," she said. "They would poison my kind and have us dissolve into nothing but dust. She will pay for everything!"

"You see…" said Irina as she turned to face Givant once again. "She is the one who initiated the plan to work with the Dark Dimension, over a hundred years ago. A plan to deploy a toxin amongst my kind. A toxin that infected one Gargoyle, who unknowingly, would pass the contagion on to all others.

"She and her lover were the ones who brought the Pre' into an alliance with the Dark Dimension that almost spelled our doom. And if it had not been for the Warriors helping us to overcome the effects of the toxin, and allowing us to revive ourselves in their dimension, we would have surely perished."

"Sooo!" rasped Givant as she struggled for air. "That is where your kind disappeared to!"

"Yes, Givant!" responded Irina. "But we are back, now! And it is time to pay for your deeds."

As Cherese stood listening, she could see that Irina and her kind had more of a reason to be the ones to deal with Givant than she did.

But Cherese wasn't giving up that easily.

"I need a little satisfaction, here!" exclaimed Cherese' as she glanced towards Givant. "I'm just sayin…!"

Then Cherese asked a question of Irina.

"If I relinquish her to you, do you promise to add onto her pain, a little 'somethin, somethin' for me?"

Hearing Cherese's request, Givant snarled and hissed.

"I promise you that she will suffer and endure the pain of every atrocity that she has ever devised for punishment, throughout all time," said Irina.

And then turning to Cherese with a slight smile, Irina added, "You know, we Gargoyles hail from before the time of man," she said proudly. "But I have found that some of the more…interesting forms of punishment have come from the time of the Ancient Egyptians. They…were masters!"

"Then, Irina," said Cherese with a satisfied look as she glanced back at Givant. "I have no regrets. She's yours!"

No sooner had Cherese finished speaking, did Irina unfurl her wings and take flight into the sky above, with Givant securely held within her grip. And what added to her satisfaction, was hearing Givant shrieking at the thought of what awaited her at the hands of the Gargoyles as Irina carried her away.

Cherese knew she should feel some kind of remorse for the thoughts she had about Givant. But all she could feel was pity for those like Givant and Faayn, and Faayn's brother, Delan. Pity for those who lived in their own twisted reality, and would try to enforce it onto others, no matter what.

She knew in the end, that there was no hope for them.

As Paytric and Granna looked upon the scene taking place before them, they saw Gargoyle after Gargoyle take flight with one or more of the Pre' they had captured, twisting in their grip. But they could also see that even with the number of Gargoyles attacking from above, it still wasn't going to be enough to stop the rest of the Pre' that were left.

There were still about a hundred or more left to be dealt with. And they knew that they couldn't depend on the Sentinels who were controlling the 'Goyles', for back-up. They had to keep a tight rein on the Gargoyles' young while they fed. And then they were going to have to try to restraint and harness them for their own safety.

Many of the Pre' that had escaped off of the mound, were trying to get away from the attack of the Gargoyles from above. But they didn't expect there was a secondary line of defense waiting for them. In their attempt to try and transport themselves out of the park and away from the carnage before them, they found that a magical barrier had been placed around the area they were in by the Wielders of Magic.

As the hundred or so remaining Pre' tried again and again to bombard the magical barrier to escape, to their dismay, it held fast. As they stood snarling and hissing at the perimeter of the magical barrier that surrounded the mound and the field, it was then that they realized their situation.

They were unable to escape.

And they knew that if any of the Gargoyles got a hold of them, none would survive. They were going to make sure that the Pre' paid for what their kind had caused the Gargoyles to endure and suffer over the last hundred years. And the Pre' knew that the only way now, was that they were going to have to fight their way out or die trying!

So, the Pre' that were left, turned to face their enemy.

As they barred their fangs and prepared to attack, they did not care if they were Warrior, Witch, Gargoyle or Human. They were going to take down as many of the small group that stood before them as they could, before they themselves fell.

And that was a promise!

As Skalla recovered from witnessing his own son being condemned to an eternity of imprisonment, he took his place next to Paytric and Granna. He knew that they and the others were prepared to face off with the remaining of the Pre'. And he was prepared to finish what he and the other Whre had set out to do.

The near one hundred Pre' that were left, re-grouped and formed a semi-circle on the flat area of the field with their backs to the magical force field that had been erected. As they eyed the small group standing before them, they began to smirk and snicker among themselves.

They knew that even with magic, there was little chance that the small group before them would be able to stop all of the Pre' that remained. The realization of the odds ironically shifting in their favor, gave the Pre' renewed confidence and arrogance.

"Is this all you have to face us!" cried out one of the Pre' from the field as he slowly moved forward. "The Gargoyles have done their damage, true!" he said. "But now they leave you to deal with what is left. And even with your magical friends, you cannot take us all!"

As the Pre' slowly moved toward the small group, he continued to taunt and goad them. The other Pre', following his lead, also began to move forward.

"You are going to die this night!" exclaimed the Pre' as he edged his kind forward. "But before you die, you will know that 'we' the Pre', have survived all you had to give. And yet, it still was not enough to stop us!"

Trying not to let the goading of the Pre' get to her, Amanda looked nervously around. She could tell by the look on everyone's face that what the Pre' was saying was true. Even with the magic they had backing them up, the sheer numbers of the Pre' that were left told the story.

As she stood next to Jonathan Gates, he could see her fear trying to take over. He placed his hand on her shoulder and quickly spoke to her.

"Courage, Amanda!" he said quietly. You are not alone! Remember that!" he said. "Look to your right and see!"

As Amanda leaned forward a little and glanced to the right, she saw what Thomas' father meant. Standing just to her right were Jerome and his father and his 'Special Opt' buddies, along with the Banshees and Zachary Boyd. The Witches and the Warriors had also stepped forward as they all stood with Paytric,

Granna and Skalla as they were prepared to stop the Pre' at all costs.

And further down to the left was the rest of the magical creatures that stood once again with Humans to defend against a common enemy. Just seeing them all standing shoulder to shoulder gave her the renewed strength and the courage that she needed, as she took in a deep breath and prepared herself.

"At least Jesse, Thomas and Vi were okay," she thought to herself as a sadness swept over her. She realized that after tonight, the chances that she may never see them again were all too real.

Then from the far right of where the group stood, a lone figure stepped out of the shadows.

As the figure drew close, Jerome breathed a sigh of relief. It was Cherese.

He noticed that she had abruptly disappeared when she spotted Irina take off after Givant as she tried to escape. Although he wasn't sure where she went, or why. He was relieved to see that she had returned and was alright. He just hoped that any issues she and Irina had with Givant had been resolved. One way or another.

As the group stood on the field waiting for the Pre' to make their next move, they all knew that they were about to face what was truly going to be, an all out fight to the death. The Pre' would have it no other way.

As they stood ready, Paytric stepped forward and addressed the Pre' one last time.

"Stand down now or know that your kind will be annihilated this night!"

Amanda and the others nervously stood their ground, while they waited for Paytric's signal, as the Pre' slowly closed the distance between them. The Pre' continued to smirk at the Warriors' overconfidence in himself and those with him.

"By you and what army?" cried out the Pre' who had taken the lead as he began to jog toward the small group that stood in front of them.

"Attack!!!" yelled the lead Pre' as he and the others moved forward with their fangs and claws exposed, ready to do battle.

"This army!" exclaimed Paytric loudly as he reached over and pressed several points on the tattoo embedded into his left arm and gave the signal.

Instantly, a 'portal' of massive size appeared behind Paytric and those that stood with him. It stretched the full width of the field they were standing on and reached three stories high above them. And out of its opening stepped Jules' father, Shiro, and a hundred plus Warriors that followed behind him.

And from the upper part of the 'portal', one Bird of Prey after another exploded from the opening, until ten of the strongest birds the Warriors had with their riders straddling them, hovered above the field, and the Pre'.

The appearance of the 'portal' caused everyone standing with Paytric to duck and hit the ground. Everyone except for Kenadi, Remy and Granna.

They were the only ones that knew of Paytric's backup plan.

The Pre' that had started to advance forward, found themselves stopped dead in their tracks as they took in the sight that appeared before them. As they eyed the multitude of Warriors that had emerged from the 'portal', they were led by Shiro, Jules' father. And as their Birds of Prey hovered high above them, they knew it was over.

In that moment, the last of the Pre' knew that it had to be all or nothing for them.

It was then that they realized what the only thing left for them to do was. There would be no escape or redemption for them as they all moved forward and made a suicidal charge at the Warriors that stood before them.

And as the multitude of Warriors and Birds of Prey surged forward to meet the Pre' in battle, the Witches and the Banshees along with the 'Humans' joined them. They had left Paytric and his Warriors with no other option, as they moved in to exact the 'true death' for the remaining of the Pre'.

"Take their heads or their hearts!" shouted Paytric as he drew his sword and charged forward.

~~~~~~~~~

On the backside of the mound, Thomas, Jesse and Vi were just beginning to recover from the Phantoms and their fight to escape the influence of Barnabas Bane.

"Oh My God!" exclaimed Vi as she lifted her head up from the prone position in the snow, she once again found herself in. "What was that?"

The Sentinels had released the 'Goyles' right after Vi and the others had witnessed the Phantoms as they tried to evade Barnabas Bane. They tried to escape by diving through the trees while some of them even tried to hide temporarily, by joining bodies with some of the Pre' and even a couple of the Sentinels before they were forced out.

And that in itself, was a sight to see that none of them would ever forget.

Vi didn't think she would ever be able to get rid of the eerie sight of the Phantoms shrieking and screaming as they fled from Barnabas Bane. And then she had the misfortune to look up right after the Sentinels had released the 'Goyles', as they proceeded to devour any Pre' that were on the mound.

"Ugghhhh!!" said Vi as she almost lost it. Not wanting to see, she covered her eyes and kept her head buried in the snow.

After the 'Goyles' were released, no one behind the mound could see much of what was going on in the area in front. From where they were, all they could see were the Gargoyles as they swept through the sky and swooped down, snapping up the Pre' right off of the field as they tried to run. And then they heard their screams as they were dragged into the night sky above and quickly disappeared.

After a while, they couldn't hear anything from the area in front of the mound.

"Hey guys!" called out Vi softly, as she remained under the park bench she had found cover under. "Do you think it's safe to go out?"

"Go out there!!" exclaimed Mus as he and Scrat remained hidden in the snow drift. "Girl! Are you crazy?" he said. "There's no telling what else might be out there!"

As Mus and Scrat ducked back into the snowdrift, Jesse answered Vi in a more calmer manner.

"I hate to say it Vi, but he might be right," said Jesse as he and Thomas continued to remain hidden in a clump of bushes they had ducked into.

Neither of them were quite ready to give up their hiding spot and step out into the open just yet. Especially, not after what they had just seen.

"Okay, okay!! Let's give it a few more minutes, Vi!" offered Jesse. "Then…well, then we can see."

"Hey, I'm good, guys!" answered Vi back. "Don't worry about me! I'm good right where I am! Yep! I could stay here all night if I had to. Trust me!"

As Vi continued to camouflage herself under the bench the best that she could, she thought for a minute that she heard voices. The more that she listened, she was positive that she was hearing voices coming from the area from in front of the mound.

Before she could turn herself around under the bench to try and get Thomas and Jesse's attention, an extremely loud sound boomed through the air.

"What was that?" screamed Vi as she looked around.

"Vi!" called out Jesse. "You okay?"

"I'm fine!" answered Vi back. "But what was that sound?" she asked. "It nearly blew my eardrums out!"

"If I didn't know any better," said Jesse carefully. "It sounded like a 'portal' opening."

"A 'portal'!" exclaimed Thomas as he too tried to shake off the effects of the sound. "Well, if it was it had to be a mighty big 'portal'!"

"Tell me about it!" said Jesse as he moved himself out from the protection of the bushes he and Thomas had been hiding in, and made his way over to where Vi was.

"Hey, Jesse! Where you goin'?" called out Thomas as he watched his best friend scamper across the snow covered ground to where Vi was.

"Can you see anything from here?" asked Jesse as he joined Vi under the bench.

"No! But I could have sworn that I heard voices speaking to each other just before that sonic boom hit," said Vi. "You think it was a 'portal' that opened?" asked Vi as she looked in the direction that the sound had come from."

"Yeah! I'm almost sure of it!" said Jesse. "But I don't think that I've ever heard an opening that sounded that loud before."

"But, but only the Warriors use 'portals'," whispered Vi.

"I know," exclaimed Jesse. "Which means that something really big is happening over there! We've got to get a look and see."

"Jesse, I don't think…"

Before Vi could finish her sentence, Jesse had left from underneath the bench, and was already making his way to the bank of trees that was a little way down and to the left of the mound. He tried to stay as low as he could as he made his way around to the left side.

As he peered through the trees and looked onto the open field, he saw what it was that had made the loud booming sound only moments ago.

"I knew it!" exclaimed Jesse to himself.

He had been right! It was the sound of a 'portal' that they had heard. And standing in front of it was Paytric and the others.

But as he looked at its size, his mind couldn't fathom what he was seeing. This 'portal' was larger than any he had ever seen before. It was even larger than the one the Warriors had opened up three years ago back in Hampton when they had fought the Dark Dimension.

"What's he doing?" yelled Thomas, as he slid to a stop underneath the bench that Jesse had just left from and joined Vi.

"He said he was going to get a look at what was going on over there," answered Vi. "I don't know Thomas. I'm getting a really bad feeling about this."

"You and me both!" exclaimed Thomas. "Stay here!" he said as he went to followed Jesse. "Somebody's gotta watch his back!"

"But...!" exclaimed Vi as once again, she had been left quite rudely before she could even finish her sentence. "Damm it! You guys, stop doing that!"

As Jesse watched from the tree line, he saw something that he would never forget, for as long as he lived.

As the Pre' faced the opening of the 'portal', hundreds of Warriors stepped out from its opening, prepared for battle. And from up above, Warrior Birds of Prey flew out and hovered above the field, and the Pre'.

Ready to attack!

It was a stalemate, and the Pre' were greatly outnumbered. The next move was on them.

And then it happened before anyone had realized it. The Pre' had all but charged at the Warriors with bloodthirsty yells, despite being outnumbered.

They were committing suicide!

Jesse's mouth dropped as he witnessed the charge.

And then in that same instant, he witnessed something else that caused him to move away from the tree line and make a mad, run for it. As he ran, he yelled at Thomas.

"Run, Thomas!! Run!!" screamed Jesse at the top of his voice as he ran.

Thomas, needing not further encouragement, quickly turned around and headed back in the direction of the bench where Vi was still hiding. He didn't know what Jesse had seen, but he took it on pure faith that running was the thing to do.

But Jesse knew what it was that had caused him to turn tail and retrace his steps in double time.

Not all of the Pre' had decided that charging head-first into a swarm of Ancient Warriors was the way to end it. Several of them had decided at the last minute, that they wanted to live. And it was those few who Jesse saw making their way toward him, fast, as the other Pre' charged into battle.

As Jesse and Thomas ran from the field and the fighting taking place there, they could hear blasts of magical energy as they streaked through the air, and the sounds of battle cries, as the Warriors and their friends collided with the Pre'. Over the treetops, they could see the flashes of light and smell the burning of trees as the battle went into full swing.

The first Pre' who was in front, zeroed in on Jesse, as he tried to run him down. The second Pre' made a b-line to the left and ran after Thomas as he raced back to the bench.

The Pre' chasing Thomas was on him just as he reached the bench. And before he knew it, Thomas felt his legs being swept out from underneath him, as his face hit the ground, hard. All Thomas remembered hearing was a high pitched, blood curdling scream from Vi, calling his name as she saw him go down.

"Thomasss!!!"

The Pre' tracking Thomas, had flipped him over onto his back, and in one motion, drew back his lips, and bared his fangs as he went for the jugular. In that same moment, Gharvey had leaped across the bench that Vi was still hiding under, and lunged at the Pre' straddling Thomas.

Snarling and growling, Gharvey knocked the Pre' onto his back as she tore into him. As Gharvey and the Pre' tussled on the ground, a surge of magical energy appeared in the ground beneath them. A 'portal' had somehow opened up in the ground, and literally sucked the Pre' into the opening. As it quickly slammed shut, they heard Gharvey yelp loudly as it just missed taking her with it by mere inches.

Thomas sat half-way up and looked around himself, slightly disoriented.

When he realized that the Pre' was gone, he looked over to Catherine and said, "Thanks, Auntie!"

Vi and Catherine rushed over the snow-covered ground to where Thomas was sitting. Catherine gave him a curious look.

"I...did not do that, Thomas!" exclaimed Catherine as she stared at him intently. "I believe that at last, you are beginning to channel your Mother's abilities!" she said proudly. "She was the only one I knew of who could actually open a 'portal' to another dimension with only the power of her mind. As you just did!"

"I..I did?" asked Thomas.

"Yes, Thomas. You did!"

"Oh! Coool!!" said Thomas as his eyes rolled up, and he fell back onto the ground, and was out for the count. It had been a 'hell' of a weekend for him.

The Pre' following Jesse, had caught up with him and had grabbed him by the neck. He pushed him up against the invisible barrier that the Wielders of Magic had put in place and yelled at him.

"Let me out!" he screamed at Jesse. "Drop the force field and let me out or die!"

"I...I can't!" exclaimed Jesse as he struggled in the grip of the Pre' as he felt his neck giving in to the pressure. "I don't know how!"

"Then die, Human!"

As the Pre' bared his fangs and jerked Jesse's head to the side exposing his neck, Jesse quickly grabbed his arm. He desperately prayed that he could persuade the Pre' not to rip out his jugular and suck his blood.

As his mind yelled at the Pre' to 'let him go', Jesse thought to himself, "I really do not want to go out like that! All that blood! My blood! And the pain!" screamed the voice in his head. "Really! Do not like the pain!"

For a moment, the Pre' hesitated as the look in his eyes went vacant, as he tried to silence the voice he was hearing in his head.

It was speaking to him...but that was impossible.

But the confusion the Pre' was experiencing, only lasted for a second or two. It was then that Jesse saw the fury and the hate flash back into his eyes, and he knew that he was in trouble.

"It's not working!" thought Jesse as he panicked and the Pre' tightened his grip on his neck. "It's not working, and I'm a 'freakin' goner!"

Jesse screamed just as the Pre' tilted his head and went in for the 'kill'. And then for a second, just a split second, Jesse thought he heard someone whisper his name. At the same time, an enormous shadow passed over them, darkening the area around them.

"Jesseeee!!!"

And then, as if the Pre' were nothing but a ragdoll, he was snatched from in front of Jesse by a tremendous force, and dragged into the night sky, just as the shadow above them moved away. The Pre' himself being dragged off was so taken by surprise, that all he had time to do was to let out a single, high-pitched yelp. And then he was gone.

Jesse felt himself slide down the face of the barrier, and slump onto the ground, as Vi and Thomas ran to his side, with Catherine and Gharvey following close behind.

"Jesse!" exclaimed Thomas. "Are you alright? Please be alright!"

"Jesse! Wake up! Wake up!" cried Vi as she shook him.

"Auntie! Is he alright?" pleaded Thomas as he looked to Catherine. "Is he gonna to be alright?"

"He has a few broken bones and some bruises," said Catherine as she looked Jesse over. But he's going to be fine, Thomas."

"Good! Good!" exclaimed Thomas feeling relieved.

Then to Vi he said, "Did you see what happened to the Pre'?" asked Thomas as he looked at Vi. "I mean... one minute he was in front of Jesse, trying to bite him, and the next minute, he was being yanked into the air, and he was just....gone!"

Vi just shook her head and sighed. She couldn't answer Thomas' question, because she didn't know the answer. Everything happened so fast she didn't know what to think. And for the time being, she didn't want to try and figure it out.

Jesse moaned as he began to regain consciousness and looked at his friends through bleary eyes. He was sure his eyes were bloodshot, because everything he saw had a reddish hue to it. After a few minutes he looked around and said one word.

"Pauly!!"

Neither Vi nor Thomas knew what to do. They were so scared out of their wits while trying to watch each other's back and avoid being killed, they weren't sure what they had seen. They definitely weren't sure that what had taken the Pre' that had attacked Jesse, was Pauly. All they saw was an enormous shadow overhead, and then the Pre' was gone.

"Way too big to be Pauly!" thought Vi to herself. "Way too big!!"

But Jesse continued to look to the dark sky above, searching for his Bird of Prey.

As the small group gathered around Jesse, they tried to comfort him the best they could. They could still see flashes of magical energy and fire, as they reflected over the tops of the trees as the sounds of the battle on the field continued. For a while, they could hear the screams of the Banshees as they mixed in with the shrieks of the Pre', unfortunate enough to be caught in their path.

And then within moments, the sounds subsided, and then it became quiet. The still, tranquility of winter was once again present in the air of Central Park.

"Wait! Listen. Is it over?" asked Vi as she looked over toward the tree line surrounding the field where the battle had taken place. Even though they were only about a half a city block away, they still couldn't see was happening.

Vi prayed that everyone was alright.

"Heck!" she thought to herself. "I've got wedding plans to make!"

And she wasn't about to let anything keep her from walking down the aisle with Ziggy. That was, not if she could help it!

As they waited for some kind of word from the others, a gust of wind had kicked up, and started to blow the light snow that had fallen. At first, the snow rose up and lightly danced in the wind as it made circles and patterns in midair. And then as the snow lightly settled back down onto the ground, it was then that Jesse saw it!

The outline of a large figure with outstretched wings to either side was visible within the settling snow. As it made a gentle landing onto the ground, its wings slowly moved back and forth, as the soft snow swirled and flurried around it.

Jesse looked up and found himself grinning from ear to ear as he recognized him immediately.

"Pauly!!" he exclaimed softly.

Both Vi and Thomas quickly turned as they saw Jesse's Bird of Prey, Pauly, slowly trudge toward them.

"Pauly!" exclaimed Vi and Thomas together, totally taken aback at how big he had gotten.

She knew it had been almost three years since they had all seen him when he was a 'fledgling', but he had gotten 'huge'. He had become one of the most beautiful, and large Birds of Prey they could recall ever seeing.

As Pauly moved in close to Jesse, he nudged his head toward him, and started to make deep, gurgling sounds in his throat. He was happy to see Jesse and his friends again.

Although he was hurting, Jesse lunged forward, and tried to wrap his arms around Pauly's neck and squeezed, giving him the biggest hug he could muster.

"I missed you, Pauly!" cried Jesse as he hung onto his neck. "I've missed you so much!"

"And I've missed you, Jesse. I told you I would be with you always. Are you alright?" asked Pauly.

Nodding his head that he was, Jesse still couldn't believe his eyes. For that matter, neither could Vi or Thomas.

After the battle in Hampton three years ago, it was agreed that Jesse and Thomas would finish high school, and then a discussion about returning to the Warriors' dimension would be had. And Pauly would return to the Warriors' dimension to continue his training as a Bird of Prey amongst his own kind.

To assure that there was no sidetracking Pauly and his training, Jesse hadn't seen him since then. It had been a long time, but it was good for Jesse to see his friend again.

Then they heard someone calling from the tree line as they made their way toward them.

"Squirt!! Squirt!!" It was Amanda as she quickly made her way to where Jesse and the others were.

When she stopped in front of them, gasping for air, she looked to her left.

"Pauly??" she exclaimed not believing her eyes. "Is that you?"

Equally glad to see her, Pauly gently nudged Amanda with his head as he greeted her.

"It's him, Amanda!" confirmed Jesse as couldn't stop smiling. "Isn't it great?"

Acknowledging that it was good to see Pauly again, Amanda turned to Jesse.

"The Sentinel told me you guys were here!" said Amanda as she looked suspiciously her brother. "What are you doing here?" she exclaimed as she gave them all the sternest look she could. "You know you could have been killed! What were you guys thinking?"

"Sorry, Amanda." "Yeah!" apologized Vi and Thomas together.

"It's my fault, Amanda," admitted Jesse quietly. "I had to let you know that I wasn't really mad at you for deciding to get married and going to live in the Warriors' dimension. And I didn't really mean all those things that I said. I'm happy for you. Really, I am!"

Jesse paused for a minute as he readjusted the way he was sitting, and then continued.

"And I kinda persuaded them to come with me so I could tell you. I didn't want you to go into a fight thinking that I didn't care about you. Sometimes you don't get the chance to take things that you say back. I guess it wasn't such a great idea after all, huh!"

"No, not really!" said Amanda as she half smiled at her brother. "Actually, it was a really stupid idea," she said as she looked at all of them. "Are you guys alright?"

"A little bruised up," said Vi as she smiled. "But I think we'll survive. Everyone else, are they okay?" asked Vi cautiously, not wanting to hear that any of their friends had fallen during the battle that had just taken place. Particularly, Ziggy.

"We're all okay, Vi. Thank God!"

"Jesse," said Amanda as she knelt down in front of her brother.

"I already knew that you didn't mean all those things that you said. It's okay!" said Amanda as she shrugged her shoulders. "No matter what. I'll always love you, you 'numskull'. After all, you are my little Brother. And it kinda comes with the territory."

"Thanks, Sis!"

"You're welcome," said Amanda. Then she looked in the direction of Pauly.

"Isn't he beautiful!" said Jesse as Pauly nuzzled a little closer for another scratch behind the ear.

"And big!!" stated Amanda. "Did not know he was going to get that big."

"Yeah! He was awesome!" chimed in Vi as she, Jesse and Thomas all began to relay to Amanda how Pauly rescued Jesse.

"And guys!" exclaimed Thomas, excited to share his news. "I opened up a 'portal' to another dimension and sent one of the Pre' right into it."

"You did not!!" "No way!!" exclaimed everyone in unison.

"Where did you send him to?" asked Vi just a little curious.

"Well, that's the thing," said Thomas as he looked a little uneasy. "I'm not quite sure. You know I was kinda 'freaking' out when I thought that I was going to be somebody's dinner! All I remember thinking was, he was as bad as the 'minions' from the Dark Dimension. And the next thing I know…a 'portal' opened up and he was gone!"

"You didn't, Thomas!" exclaimed Jesse as he just stared at his best friend as it dawned on him 'where' Thomas more than likely sent the Pre'.

"I think he did!" said Amanda with a slight smirk. "Well, good riddance! The Pre', the Dark Dimension. I think they both deserve each other. But I would have loved to have seen the look on the Pre's face when he realized 'where' he ended up."

"Yeah! That would've been a picture worth a 'thousand' words!" noted Vi.

"Com'on, guys!" said Amanda as she helped Jesse up. "Let's get outta here! Granna said that with the display of fireworks from the magic that was used during the fight, the Police are sure to be here any minute now. It's almost certain that it was seen from all over the city. Her Sisters are making sure that there's nothing left on the field to give the authorities a whole lot to go on."

"That's fine by me!" exclaimed Vi after realizing that leaving Central Park and heading back someplace that wasn't so cold or dangerous, was just what she needed. "I'm ready anytime!"

"Me, too!" joined in Thomas as he and Vi held onto each other as they started to walk. Then he called out to Pauly. "Hey 'big' guy! How's about a ride?"

More than willing, Pauly knelt down, folding his two front legs underneath him, and allowed everyone to board him. And then with quick turn, he began to walk the short distance to the tree line, and the safety of the 'portal'.

~~~~~~~~~~

Central Park -3:30am-

As the New York City fire trucks blared onto the scene with their lights flashing and their sirens blowing, they joined the numerous Police cars and investigators as they milled around the baseball field. They weren't exactly sure what had happened, but fire stations all over the city had been bombarded with alarming calls from New Yorkers.

They all reported seeing some sort of fire raging in the middle of Central Park. And because they also saw what appeared to be minor explosions erupting all over the place, everyone was called to the scene. Even the FBI showed up.

As officials from the various agencies huddled in their own groups, they tried to figure out what had happened. Basically, all they could do was shake their heads in total disbelief at what they saw. No one had a clue. And if they did, they weren't saying.

The entire baseball field and most of the surrounding trees had all been charred. It was as if someone had taken an enormous blow torch and lit up the entire area. Nothing had been spared. And then there were various sized depressions all over the ground. One of the investigators said that it reminded him of something he had seen during the war. He could only describe them as similar to mortar 'pot marks' resulting from missile strikes.

"But that was crazy!" he thought to himself. "Who'd be stupid enough to bring those kinds of weapons into the city, much less into Central Park and fire them."

It didn't make any sense to him or to any of the other investigators who were on site.

"Well, what do you think happened here, Sarge?" asked one of the patrolmen as he stood with his supervisor looking over the open field.

"Don't know! I really don't know!" he said with a tone to his voice that sounded as if he wasn't sure if he really wanted to find out.

"But one thing I have figured out!" he said in a matter-of-fact tone. "I don't know if it's the stars and the moon, or 'hell' just me! But somethin' weird has been going on in this city that's been sending chills down my spine for a while now. Somethin' that I can't explain. Hell!" he exclaimed. "Somethin' that nobody can explain. And over the last couple of days, it's been getting worse."

"You talkin' about the calls we got earlier?" asked the rookie. "About all of the screaming and yellin' folks were doing. They all said they were all having some sort of massive nightmare."

"Yeah, well. It's not only that," cited the Sergeant. "It's also the reports we've been getting about some of the homeless people who've been disappearing without a trace, and the large dogs, or whatever people have been seeing roaming around here in Central Park," said the officer with a tone of frustration. "And what about the remains we found in the park over by the Lexington. So far all they've come up with is that there were Human and wolf DNA present. And if that's not some kind of crazy, I don't know what is."

As the Sergeant hesitated, he took a sip of his coffee and glanced over at the patrolman standing next to him.

"And what about the call our guys got about that apartment on the skirts of the financial district. You know the one where all of the windows were supposedly blown out. And our guys said they thought there was something, but...they weren't sure. Even though the residents reported hearing all kinds of things going on inside, when they got there, nothing! I just don't know, Son," said the officer to the rookie. "Were they able to get any kind of forensics from the ashes left behind?" he asked.

"Not yet, Sarge. I'll go and see if they've come up with anything yet."

"You do that, Son!" said the seasoned officer as he watched the young rookie make his way back across the field and disappear into the crowd that was milling around the crime scene.

The Sergeant knew he wasn't in the mood for more weird answers. He had been on the force for over thirty five years. And until just recently, he had begun to question if maybe it wasn't time for him to call it quits.

He had always been a good cop. A fair cop to everyone. Never once took a bribe no matter what the situation. He always looked out for the 'average Joe' and made sure he got a fair shake in the system. That's just the way he was.

"But too many things, too many weird things had been happening lately in the city that he loved so dearly," he thought to himself.

And what made it worst, was that it seemed that every time he asked too many questions, he was shut down without an explanation. He felt as if he was being dismissed, and it was him who was imagining the unexplained things that were going on.

"Ahhh!" he exclaimed out loud as he felt himself become frustrated.

He tossed his cup of coffee still half full into one of the trash cans, and began to pace while he waited for the rookie to return.

"Although his gut told him different, maybe he 'was' making a 'mountain out of a mole hill'," he thought.

And then from behind him, he was startled by a woman's voice."

"Kind of irritating, isn't it?" the voice said in a matter of fact tone. "You know you're not crazy, but somehow the pieces just don't quite seem to come together."

Turning, he came face to face with a slender built woman with high cheek bones, and medium length dark brown hair. As she stood behind him, she too was looking out onto the burnt field. From what he could tell, she looked to be about in her mid-thirties.

"I'm sorry Miss," he said in his authoritative voice. "This area is off limits. No press, no questions! You'll have to leave."

"No problem, Officer," she said as she reached into the pocket of her dark blue, Navy peacoat and pulled something out. As she flashed her own badge at him, she said, "I quite agree with you."

"Oh, I'm sorry, Miss," apologized the Sergeant. "I didn't mean no disrespect!"

"None taken!"

"So many young ones now," he thought to himself as he returned his attention to the scene in front of him. "And there seemed to be more and more women coming into the ranks. Times had truly changed. And this made him question even more, whether it was time for him to leave the job he loved behind and retire."

"Can I ask you something?" said the woman bluntly, as she stepped up next to him.

"Sure…" he said cautiously, as he gave her a sidelong glance.

"Do you believe the stories that have been released to cover up all of the bizarre things that have been happening in the city lately? Or do you think there's more to what's really going on?"

Surprised at the directness of her question, the Sergeant just shrugged his shoulders.

"Hey. Who am I to question the 'big brass', right?" he said. If he did have any doubts, he'd keep them to himself. "Now, if you'll excuse me," he said. "I've got to check on my men."

As the Sergeant made his way back across the opened field, he had that 'gut' feeling again. Not about what had happened on the field, but about the female officer he had just been speaking with. He couldn't put his finger on it, but there was something 'odd' about her.

Against his better judgment, he stopped midstride and turned around to get another look at her. When he turned around, she was just staring after him, and had a slight smile on her face, as if she knew what he was thinking.

"Be seeing you, Sarge!" she called out to him.

And then she turned on her heel and made her way to the open door of a waiting black SUV with blacked out windows. He had noticed it was parked behind them with its motor running all the while they were talking.

As she stepped into the SUV, she looked at him again.

"You and I both know there's more to this than meets the eye," she said frankly. "And it's not the 'natural' kind of explanation we've been getting!"

"Well, you know what they say, right!" said the Sergeant with a sarcastic tone. "Curiosity killed the cat."

"Yeah! But satisfaction brought him back!" she said to him, just as sarcastic. "Be the cop you've always been, Sarge," she said. "Follow your gut. That's what I'm gonna do!"

As she stepped into the SUV and closed the door, the driver drove off. She had left the Sergeant with a feeling he couldn't shake. A feeling in his gut that for some strange reason, he would be seeing her again. And his gut was never wrong! That was for sure.

"Until then", he mused to himself. "This, like all of the other strange occurrences that had happened, would probably be explained away without even giving it a second thought."

"Ahhh, Hell!" he exclaimed to himself.

He loved this city. But sometimes, it was the kind of love affair that could drive a man to drink.

"As a matter of fact," he thought to himself. "A drink sounded like a good idea right about now."

As the Sergeant continued across the field, he shoved his hands into his pockets to ward off the cold, and started to whistle his favorite tune as he went. An odd rustling in the trees just to his right caused him to abruptly stop whistling and slow his stride. As he slowly moved one foot in front of the other, he glanced to the group of trees to his right.

"What was that?" he quickly thought to himself as stopped dead in his tracks and squinted his eyes so he could see better into the dark.

Even though they had set up the same kind of lights on the field that construction companies used so they could work at night, they didn't quite light up the trees along the side.

He thought, and he knows it sounded crazy. But he thought that he saw a large, cloaked figure hanging in one of the charred trees along the side of the field. But when he took a second look, there didn't seem to be anything there.

"Ahhh!" said the Sarge as he shook his head again and kept walking. "I'm beginning to let these weird things get to me," he said. "I think I need that drink sooner rather than later!"

With that thought in mind, he went about the business of wrapping up the crime scene so he could in fact get himself a drink. As a matter of fact, he was going to have several drinks. He owed it to himself.

~~~~~~~~

As the black SUV made its way away from Central Park, the detective sitting in the back seat was on her cell phone.

"John!" she said. "I need a favor. A big favor!"

"What is it this time, Frankie?" replied the voice on the other end of the line.

"I need you to see if any of the satellites we've got up in the air were positioned anywhere over New York about two hours ago. Particularly over Central Park."

"I'll check," said the disembodied voice. "But what the heck are you looking for this time?"

"Something that's out of the 'natural' realm of explanations," she said cryptically.

"What!!??"

"Never mind! Just call me when you're ready to send me the feed. Okay!"

"Sure thing!"

As the detective ended the call, she leaned back into the leather appointed seats inside of the SUV and looked at her watch. It was just about a half a minute away from 4am.

"I should be getting a call in a few…"

Before the detective could finish her thought, her cell phone rang.

"Hello! Yes. I think we may have something. I'll let you know as soon as I check out a satellite feed that's being sent to me."

She paused for a minute as she listened intently, and then said, "Right!" before also ending that call.

"Where to next?" asked her driver as he looked over his shoulder.

"Take me where they have beer and the best Philly Cheese Steaks in the City," said the detective as she relaxed in the comfortable leather seats in back, and closed her eyes contemplating what was next.

Then she thought about the officer she had been trailing ever since she was put on this assignment.

"Sarge! You and I will be seeing a whole lot of each other," she said softly to herself as she closed her eyes. "I hope you're up for it!"

As the black SUV slowly made its way through the streets of New York City, it passed by The Lexington on the far side of Central Park. Its' yellow headlights bathed the now almost empty streets in their glow as it sped away.

And unknown to the detective inside of the SUV, sitting high above the street on top of The Lexington building, several pairs of glowing red eyes were silently watching the path the vehicle below them took.

 Just as she had been on the heels of the Sarge all along, the Gargoyles had been on hers.

Chapter IX

Return to the Warriors' Dimension

The sky above was a crystalline blue as white billowy shaped clouds passed overhead in no particular hurry. They hovered over the lush green valleys and flowered plains of the Warriors' homeland as they slowly moved across the sky.

But below the tranquil sky, everything was in a bustle.

Beautiful flowers of every color, shape and size, were being gathered and arranged on the plateau. While on the multi-tiered outcroppings surrounding the main plateau on three sides, colorful carpets and overstuffed pillows were being laid out for the guests.

There was a wedding to prepare for.

Actually, there were several weddings. And never before in the Warriors' dimension had there ever been such an occasion. One wedding was always something to celebrate. But multiple weddings?

Who would've guessed?

There were going to be several weddings that night, and the air was alive with excitement as everyone went about their duties, as they prepared for the big event. Everyone was on a high alert because this was truly an event to rejoice about.

And the people of the Warriors' dimension were proud to be the hosts of such an occasion.

Out on the plateau below, Paytric and Remy walked with the grooms-to-be as they made sure that everything was perfect before the ceremony. And that among other things was something that Amanda and the other betroths had to get used to. In the Warriors' dimension, the grooms were the ones who made all of the wedding preparations, much unlike how it was in their world.

But that didn't matter.

The guys had Paytric and Remy to help them, as well as a very pregnant Jules and Haley. They all knew that the wedding was going to be, as Jerome put it, 'Off the hook!!' And as far as the girls were concerned, as long as they got their man in the end, it didn't matter who did the planning. They were all beyond ready for this to happen.

As the two Warriors walked with the guys, Paytric stopped in the middle of the plateau, and pointed in the direction toward the tiered outcroppings gracing the backside of the plateau.

"Your betroths will come from that direction," he said. "And they will approach each of their appointed spots just there, as the sun begins to set."

As he spoke, he walked to where the grooms were to stand.

"And here is where each of you will stand, awaiting their arrival."

"Man! I cannot believe that I'm getting married tonight!" exclaimed Jerome as he was beginning to get just a little nervous.

Not only was this a big step for him, but for all of the others, too!

"Trust in what you feel in your heart and soul for your betroth, Jerome," said Remy, as he placed his hand onto Jerome's shoulder. "That is all you need. That is all that any of you need," he said as he looked over at the others. "Everything else will fall into place as if it was meant to be."

"So, how is married life treating you guys?" asked Ziggy, as he looked at the two men he admired the most. "I mean, I've never seen either of you look happier or more content than you do right now."

"It is a wonderful life to have the ones you love and care about more than anything, around you," stated Paytric as he laughed, and his eyes seemed to gleam with unbridled joy. "It makes life worth living. As you all will come to experience."

 Paytric had truly done a 360 since the first time they had met him. He was no longer the hulking, brooding Warrior they used to know. Since he and Jules had been reunited after being apart for hundred years, he had truly changed. They themselves had 'joined' with each other in a double ceremony along with Remy and his betroth, Haley.

And now both he and Remy were fathers with their own young sons. Paytric's son's was named Caleb, while Remy's son was named Jaydin. And now, Jules and Paytric were expecting their second child, and it was a girl! And they found that being joined and having children of their own, made them different men altogether. They both had someone to pass on their wisdom to, about life, about being a Warrior and being true to oneself and those that you care about. And they both had a mate that would be by their side, always.

And they were happy!

"Come!" said Paytric to the young men who were about to take the next step that would change their lives forever. "It is customary for the friends of the grooms to break bread and to drink with them before they are joined with their betroths. Remy and I have had a groom's meal readied for you. Your fathers await you. And then when we finish, we will help you prepare yourselves."

As Jerome walked away from the plateau with the others, he stepped up next to Paytric..

"Yo, Paytric!" he exclaimed. "You think you might have anything that has a little kick to it! You know, something to kinda calm the nerves?" asked Jerome as he gave a nervous laugh. "Cause Man, I think I may need it!"

As everyone laughed to shake off their own nervousness about their upcoming nuptials, Paytric laughed along with them, and assured Jerome that he was sure he would be able to accommodate him.

While the men went about their pre-nuptial activities, the women had already sat down to their meal inside of one of the larger, carved out rooms set deep inside of the mountain. Not only were the girls' mothers there, but so was Channa and Granna along with her Wielder of Magic sisters. Laura, Jules and Haley had also joined them as they celebrated the upcoming event.

None of them could believe how quickly the guys had pulled everything together for the ceremony. They were told to relax and be pampered, for it was truly their day. And when the time came, all they had to do was to put on their dresses and walk out onto the plateau to meet their betroths.

It was the day that most women looked forward to all of their lives. To be joined with the one who had their heart and soul, and promised to forever be by their side as they built a life together.

Who could ask for anything more.

"I'm liking the way they do things here in this dimension," said Cherese as she beamed from ear to ear.

"You and me both," chimed in Amanda and Angi in unison as they both giggled with anticipation. They were beyond excited that they were all going to be wed together.

As Mrs. Gates, along with Jesse's and Amanda's mother, milled around a food ladened table with the other mothers, one of the first of several, of the, 'knock you off your feet' surprises of the day happened. J.D. had floated into the room with an expression on her face that said she was in 'seventh heaven'.

As everyone looked up and saw the expression on her face, they knew something had happened. And then when she lifted her arm up and proudly showed off her own betrothed bracelet, everyone in the room screamed and immediately rushed over to her. Her big sister, Laura found that she was almost beside herself with happiness.

"Her little Sister had become betrothed to Sean!" Laura thought as she hugged J.D. tightly.

She had hoped that somewhere along this journey, that perhaps her sister J.D. would find some kind of happiness. They were the last of the Banshees, and their kind had been alone in a world that for so long had forgotten about them.

And now her prayers had been answered.

"Oh God, J.D.," exclaimed Vi as she too hugged her friend. "I'm so happy for you and Sean!"

J.D. hadn't expected this of Sean. She was happy the way things were and hadn't put any kind pressure on him. But she had to admit she was curious about this ritual where you committed yourself, body and soul, to someone in a ceremony in front of hundreds of people that you knew.

But when Sean had returned from the meeting he was supposed to have with his agent, she noticed something about him seemed, different. He was actually nervous at times. Now J.D. knew why, and she couldn't have been happier. With or without the ceremony, she would have been delighted to spend the rest of her existence with Sean, if he'd have her.

And then J.D. revealed the rest of her surprise.

She and Sean were going to be joined together along with the rest of them in the ceremony that was going to take place in only a few hours!

This day couldn't have gotten any better as their excitement filled the air and echoed throughout the room and down the carved out halls of the mountain.

Still on a high from recent events, they all sat down to eat as everyone talked among themselves, wondering what the grooms had come up with for the wedding ceremony.

The anticipation was killing them.

Kenadi took her mother, Channa and her betroth, Obra's mother around to introduce them to the rest of her friends and their mothers. J.D. and her sister, Laura spent time conversing with both Ziggy's and Sean's mother. At first, the mothers were somewhat standoffish, and not sure of exactly what was expected of them. But after a while, they warmed up after realizing they were there to celebrate the same happy occasion that had brought them all together.

Amanda and Jesse's mother couldn't contain herself as she and Jerome's mother, Carolyn and Vi's mother went from one group to the next, chatting away as they went. In the end, they spent most of the meal with Jason and Galen's mothers, exchanging humorous stories about their children as they reminisced.

All of the mothers of the Brides and the Grooms from the Human dimension, were in awe as they tried to take it all in. The fact that Magic really did exist, as did those that wield it, was something that they all had to come to grips with three years ago. But now, to actually be in another dimension and to be able to see how the Warriors and their people lived was, overwhelming. Unimaginable.

But awesome at the same time.

Never, in any of their wildest dreams, had they thought they would find themselves in another dimension, much less attending their children's wedding there.

Who would've thought it possible?

As everyone ate and chatted among themselves, Cherese approached her grandmother and looked at her intently.

"Cherese," said Granna as she reached for her. "Are you happy child?" she asked.

"Yes, Granna, I am!" responded Cherese as she began to tear up. "I don't think that I have ever been happier in my life. Jerome is all that I've ever dreamed of."

"I know, child," said Granna. "I know."

Drawing her granddaughter to her, Granna held her for a moment, and then her body abruptly stiffened. As she pulled back from Cherese and looked her up and down, Cherese just smiled.

"Cherese!" exclaimed Granna as she looked her granddaughter. "What is this? I…I…don't understand. How could I not have known?"

"Because I used a 'concealment' spell when I found out, Granna,' said Cherese simply. "I just needed time to get used to the idea myself," said the fledgling Witch as she carefully watched the expression on her grandmother's face change as she realized that Cherese was with child.

"The first child born into a new generation of Wielders of Magic," said Granna softly.

"Are you happy about it, Granna?" she asked. "It wasn't planned, but I had hoped it would happen eventually."

"Oh, Cherese!" exclaimed her grandmother as she hugged her again. "How could I not be happy?"

And then Cherese' grandmother asked.

"Am I the first to know?"

"Who else would I tell first?" said Cherese as she felt a sense of relief flood over her. "I wanted to wait to tell Jerome. You know, with everything that been going on."

"And just when do you plan to tell him?" asked her grandmother as she looked at Cherese intently.

"Trust me, Granna," said Cherese. "I know the perfect time to tell him that he's going to be a father. I just hope that he doesn't drop from the shock when he finds out."

"Well, I cannot wait to tell my Sisters!" said Granna as she felt the excitement flood over her. "May I?" she asked. "I cannot tell you how long they have waited for news such as this."

"Tell you what, Granna," said Cherese as new life gleamed in her eyes. "Let's tell everyone together, okay!"

With that, Cherese and Granna turned and walked over to the group of family and friends that had gathered to celebrate the upcoming weddings and gave them the good news! If the screams weren't loud enough when J.D. announced that she was not only betrothed to Sean, but that they were going to wed that night with the others. The screams that followed the announcement that Cherese was going to have a baby, were mind blowing.

Hearing the excited cheers and screams from the women who were in another part of the mountain, the men paused they jovial celebration and listened.

"What…do they have a stripper?" asked Sean as he and the other grooms listened to the women's voices as they reached a crescendo. "No fair!!"

"I do not believe that is so," said Aanon smiling as he joined the grooms. "If you do not already know women by now, you will come to realize that they are ten times more excitable in most situations, than we are. It is, what makes them women."

And as Shiro joined in the conversation, he put one hand onto his friend's shoulder and concurred.

"It is also after all, why they are so endearing to us," said Jules' father. "They bring that joy and unbridled enthusiasm to everything that they do. And I for one would not want to be without it."

"Nor I my friend," said Aanon. "Nor would I."

Then, lifting his glass, Paytric's father offered a prayer.

"To those who are about to go forth and claim the women who have opened their hearts to them. I offer these words to you," he said. "Love today, like there is no tomorrow. For tomorrow is not promised to any of us. And make sure that the love you give to your mate and your family, is above all else, pure of intent, and enduring throughout the years. Do this, and you will find happiness for all time. And may the Creator in all his wisdom, continue to grant us, his children, favor in all that we do in his name. Be blessed!"

The group of men who had gathered around the table, all acknowledged the prayer by lifting their glasses and repeating, "Be blessed!!"

After everyone had raised their glasses and drank to the journey that the grooms were about to embark on, it was time for them to prepare for the ceremony.

The grooms were going to wear the traditional Warrior outfit worn at weddings. Leather chaps with shined and groomed boots, and sleeveless, leather adorned vests. Their wardrobe was practical, yet unpretentious, as Warriors are.

Besides. On such a day as this, it was all about their betroths.

When the women had finished their meal, the betroths went into one of the side rooms to undress. When they returned, they had put on a light material robe, and made their way to an open area within the large cavern that had several raised platforms within it. This was where the betroths were to be dressed for the ceremony. As each of them were directed to step up onto a platform and claimed it, that was when they really started to get nervous.

Because another practice that was also tradition in the Warriors' dimension was that the women did not in any way, choose the dress that they were to wear in their 'joining' ceremony. It was the function of a brilliant crystal known as 'The Rhie-a', to adorn the women in the type of wedding dress that best suited her.

How the crystal did this, was unknown to Amanda and the other betroths. All that they knew was that it was the tradition the Warriors had followed for eons. And far be it for any of them to buck their 'tradition' whether they understood it or not. They hadn't had a problem with any of the other 'traditions' they had encountered so far, so why question them now.

It actually felt good to just go with the flow and let someone else handle all of the details. And that's just what they did.

"I can't believe that I'm going to let a 'crystal' choose my wedding dress!" exclaimed Angi as she stepped up onto the platform that was nearest to her.

"You and me both!" agreed Amanda as she quickly looked over at her mother with a nervous glance.

She had always thought that when the time came for her to be married, it would be her and her mother who would do a whirlwind of shopping and select her dress. But that was not to be. She was just praying this 'crystal', or whatever it was, didn't go 'haywire' and put her into something that was, and she was afraid to think it, but she went there.

"Hideous!!"

"Oh God! Oh God! Oh God!" whispered Amanda under her breath as she closed her eyes and hunched her shoulders. Everyone else stood back, anxious to see what the outcome would be.

For Amanda and the others, as well as their mothers, this was going to be a magical experience they would never forget for as long as they all lived.

As each of the betroths stood in the center of her platform, six women dressed in simple white sheaths, stepped out of one of the side caverns. As each of the women made their way to one of the raised platforms and stood in front of it, she held in front of her what appeared to be a medium sized pouch that was tied at the top.

As each woman knelt down, she set the pouch that she carried down onto the platform in the front of the betroth standing there and untied it. As the sides of the pouch gently felt away, there in its center, was a shimmering, silver crystal all aglow with a life of its own.

"Oh my God!" "Wow!!" exclaimed everyone in the room as they looked on in awe.

And then as they watched, slender threads of silver and gold light gently rose up from each crystal and began to twist and coil themselves around each of the betroths, as if they were gently caressing them. The threads of light continued to wrap themselves around the women until they were completely engulfed from head to toe in a glowing pouch of sparkling luminosity.

"Oh my!" exclaimed Vi as the sensation of the threads began to send subtle vibrations throughout her body. "It feels so…" Vi couldn't even finish her sentence because the sensations were invigorating.

Almost sensual.

"I know what you mean," said Cherese as she too felt what Vi and all of the others were experiencing.

It was phenomenal. Beyond anything she could have ever imagined.

Within minutes, those watching began to see something happen that was so magical, they couldn't find words to express it.

As each of the betroths stood within the swirling, silver and gold threads as they continued to weave themselves around them, the simple robes each of them had donned seemed to fade away into nothingness. And in their place…as if spun out of magic, each of the betroths wedding dresses began to appear as they materialized out of the threads of light.

Then one by one, as the threads of the crystal retracted, each of the betroths dresses were revealed. And the women discovered that despite their concerns, they could not, they would not have wanted it any other way. The crystal, in its wisdom, had given each of them exactly what they had dreamed of.

Angi's strapless dress was made entirely of liquid, glass threads and began to form to her figure as it fell into folds of a white silver material just below her knees and then swept behind her as if the dress itself was in perpetual motion with every movement. She seemed to radiate as the crystal pulled back its threads revealing the first betroth.

Vi's dress also hugged her body, but in a very different fashion. As she looked down, she saw a flowing cascade of a bed of the tiniest, purest white flowers, as they wrapped gently around her and fell to the floor in a cluster. And each flower had a touch of blue, her favorite color, in the middle of it. On each of her wrists, ringlets of the same flowers twisted up her arms and lightly wrapped around her neck, then twisted into beautiful ringlets as they hung softly onto her chest, just above her breast.

Cherese's dress was also strapless and was made of a layered, sheer light gauze material with chocolate crystals embedded in the fabric as it flowed behind her from a gathering of material that began at the top of the bodice above her breasts. Then volumes of the material draped and flowed behind her, moving slightly in an unseen breeze. The dress itself draped down in the front until it almost touched the ground.

The crystal had draped both Amanda and Kenadi in dresses of silver and white. Amanda's dress was off white and fitted on top and then fell to the floor into a wide, full skirt of the lightest material she had ever seen. The skirt was laced with tiny crystals as was Kenadi's dress. But Kenadi's dress was one shouldered and hung delicately from her as it fell to the ground and dipped behind her as it seductively showed just enough of her backside.

And lastly, J.D. was donned in her favorite color of pale pink as she stood looking down at her dress in complete awe. Not only of how she looked, but how she felt.

Her dress seemed to be alive with a life of its own, as it hovered around her body. The flowing, see through threads, some thinner than others, lightly laid themselves across her chest, disappeared over her left shoulder, then reappeared on the other side of her body flowing over her right hip. Then the threads playfully draped in front of her and moved around to her left hip, where they once again disappeared as the they discreetly draped over her backside.

All of the betroths' hair had been gently pulled up and allowed to fall into a cascade of curls except for Kenadi and Vi. Vi's hair was pulled up into a ponytail that bounced playfully behind her, while Kenadi wore a traditional wrap on her head as her hair flowed out over the top and hung down her back.

As Laura stood next to the platform that her sister was standing on, she found herself crying uncontrollably, as just as everyone else in the room was. Never had they witnessed such a sight as their daughters, sisters, friends and loved ones had presented to them at that very moment before their wedding.

All of the betroths were breathtaking and beautiful as they all stood ready for the ceremony.

This was the first part of a night that had proven itself to be a magical surprise for everyone. And it was only the beginning.

~~~~~~~~

As the sun made its way to its final resting place for the evening, it would balance itself on the edge of the horizon, until dawn beckoned for it to once again rise and meet the new day. And just as the ceremony was about to begin, also welcoming in the beginning of a new day, were the women who were about to be joined with their betroths, as they made their way to their appointed spots.

The majestic backdrop of the mountain rose up behind them, and then evened out to various levels of tiered, grassy outcroppings. And looking down from the tiered levels above, as well as from either side of the plateau, were hundreds upon hundreds of guests as they lounged on overstuffed pillows and brightly colored carpets as they sat atop the soft green grass.

Suddenly, a burst of cheers erupted from the guests watching from above, as the betroths made their appearance at the base of the mountain and stepped out onto the plateau. Each of the women were draped behind a delicate veil of twinkling, white and gold lights as they stood in their elegant wedding dresses and gazed out in awe over the plateau.

"Oh God!" exclaimed Vi as she saw how the plateau had been decorated as she looked through the lighted veil that draped in front of her. "It's so…so…!"

"Beautiful!" whispered Amanda softly, as she finished Vi's sentence.

"And then some!" chimed in Angi as she, too, was floored at the sight that she saw before her.

From the base of the mountain where each of the betroths stood, was a wide path that extended out in front of them. And each side of the path was graced with beautifully painted planters, overflowing with flowers of the kind they had never seen before. They were huge, bulb like flowers in the deepest, stunning color of orange they had ever seen before. And accentuating the deep orange color, were a dark green, leafy foliage and what appeared to be pure white, Baby Breaths, as they gently rose up from the groupings of the flowers surrounding them.

Overhead, above each of the paths, was a trellis laden with tons of the same feathery, light Baby Breath flowers, as they allowed the sunset sky above to occasionally peek through. And at the end of each of the trellis that looked out onto the horizon beyond, were masses of cascading Lilacs as they spilled out onto the floor of the plateau, providing a lightly scented, floral carpet for the betroths to walk upon.

And there at the end of each trellis, stood the men.

As the applauding and cheering of the guests began to subside, music gently floated throughout the air. And as the music played, a veil of twinkling lights draped before each of the betroths, slowly began to lift, revealing them for the first time to the grooms.

As each of the betroths took in a deep breath, they felt as if they were taking part in a dream wedding that was surreal. Each of them stepped out underneath the trellis and began to make their way down the flowered path toward the grooms and their loved ones as they stood waiting. Overhead the tiniest bluebirds they had ever seen, fluttered in and around the flower laden trellis' as the betroths took their final walk before being 'joined'. When the women reached the end of the path where the trellis opened up onto the plateau and to the sky above, they each took the hand of their betroth, and turned to face them.

And although everything pertaining to the ceremony was done in the traditional Warrior's way, they wanted to do honor to the 'Humans' participating in the 'joining'. Jerome and Ziggy had made mention of a favorite song from their dimension that all of the girls loved and would swoon whenever they heard it. So as a surprise, in honor of the women before their vows were to be spoken, one of the well-known singers from within the Warriors' dimension, began to sing the song for them.

As the male singer began to voice the lyrics of the song from their dimension, he sang about the melody of a love that had been 'unchained' in the heart of a man for the one that he adored. And in hearing the melody of the song and its words, all of the betroths facing their men, gasped and took a deep breath.

Their faces expressed how they felt about hearing that song at their wedding as the tears began to flow. Even from within the group of family members and friends surrounding the trellis', you could hear the exclamations of astonishment and joy, as the singers' voice caressed the words of the song, and milked the melody for everything it was worth.

One by one each of the men began to softly speak their vows to the one that they were declaring their love to. As the words of the song floated gently through the air, the powerful emotion attached to them caused each of the men to either kneel or fall onto their knees in front of their betroths.

All of the betroths stood looking down at the men as they vowed their undying devotion to them. Amanda tried not to make the 'ugly face' and bawl outright as Jason spoke his vows to her. Angi didn't care as she let the tears flow as she sobbed uncontrollably. Kenadi thought her heart was going to burst right out of her chest as she smiled at Obra through tear filled eyes. Hearing the song that the men had chosen was an unexpected delight as the words being sung expressed everything that she felt.

As Ziggy knelt down in front of Vi and spoke his vows to her, to his surprise Vi fell to her knees with him.

"God, how she loved this Man!" she thought to herself as she threw her arms around his neck when he finished and cried into his shoulder.

Overcome by emotion by what he felt for J.D., Sean fell onto both knees and crossed his hands in front of him onto his chest as he looked up at her. He couldn't help the overflowing of emotion that flooded from his heart as the tears ran down his face. He softly spoke the words he had longed to say to her as they flooded from his heart and joined with the words of the song being sung.

Hearing the song and the soft murmuring of the other men as they cited their vows, Jerome found himself trembling as he also knelt in front of Cherese. As he began to softly speak his vows, he pledged his undying love, until death claimed him. When he had finished, Cherese looked down at him with tears in her eyes and spoke her vows to him as the song continued in the background.

And when she finished, she bent down and whispered something in his ear.

At first, Jerome's father and mother thought that he had had a change of heart when he literally jumped up a took a step backwards, away from Cherese.

And then they heard him exclaim softly, "A baby!! We're gonna have…a baby!!" he said as he grinned from ear to ear. And then he stepped forward and swept Cherese off of her feet as he twirled her around.

Cherese nodded her head in acknowledgement, as the tears began to roll down her face, and she quietly said, "A baby!!"

As Jerome placed her gently back onto the ground, he once again knelt in front of her. Reaching out and drawing her to him, he touched his forehead to her stomach, and wept.

As Paytric and a pregnant Jules looked on while their son Caleb stood in front of them, they understood the joy that Jerome and Cherese were experiencing. That was the way it was when Paytric first found out that Jules was pregnant with their first son. And the joy had not diminished one bit as they looked forward to the birth of their second child.

"Wait a minute!" exclaimed Jerome's mother as she overheard Jerome and Cherese's conversation. She quickly grabbed a hold of her husbands' arm to keep herself from fainting dead away.

"Did..he say, I mean, did she say…Baby. They havin' a Baby!! Oh My Lord!!" exclaimed Carolyn, as Reginald grabbed her to keep her on her feet.

He couldn't believe it himself as he looked proudly over at his son.

"My lord, my lord!" Reginald whispered under his breath. "Will wonders never cease. I'm going to be a Grandfather," he said as he held up his wife. Then looking over at her, he said, "Carolyn, Baby. You're going to be a Grandmother!"

Carolyn partially recovering from the shock of what she had heard, shot a look at her husband. And if looks could kill…

Then she turned to him and said unequivocally, "You call me that one more time, and you won't have to wait for a response when you pray to the Lord. When I'm through with, you can tell him in person. I'm just saying!"

Not caring whether she 'bitched' and moaned about it or not, Reginald grabbed Carolyn and swung her around as he whispered in her ear, "Grandmother! Grandmother! Grandmother! Baby, we're going to be Grandparents!"

Carolyn realized that as Reginald swung her around, she had begun to giggle uncontrollably at the thought. And then she gave in and hugged Reginald tightly.

They were going to be Grandparents!

Even though there were hundreds of guests looking on, what each of the men had to say to their betroths, was for her ears only, and no one else.

As Jesse and Thomas stood between their parents, just to the left of where Amanda and Jason were, they still couldn't hear what was being said.

"I can't hear what he's saying, can you?" asked Jesse as he tried to lean forward.

"That's the idea, Jesse," said Thomas as he looked on. "We don't need to know what their vows to each other are. Only they need to know."

"That's no fun!" exclaimed Jesse, feeling bummed out.

As Jesse's mother wiped her eyes, she leaned her head onto her husband's shoulder.

"Well, I knew this was going to eventually happen," she said as she tried not to bawl outright. "But I didn't think it was going to be so hardddd!" And like any self-respecting Mother of the Bride, Amanda's mother couldn't help it as the tears began to flow.

Jesse knew it was only going to be a matter of time before she broke. He was actually surprised that his mother was able to last this long. For sure he thought she was going to lose it when Amanda first stepped out onto the plateau with the others.

And he had to admit it. His sister looked awesome!

He even found himself holding back a tear or two when Amanda seemed to float past them just before she took Jason's hand. She kind of gave him a quick wink and a smile. And he knew right then and there, that no matter what. She would always be his sister.

Always!

Having finished their vows, everyone felt the joy that this night had brought. And although Granna and her sisters already knew the good news, when they saw Jerome's reaction, it made the blessing of a child even more appreciated.

As the singer finished the song, Aanon stood on the platform and cleared his throat as he faced the betroths. And then he spoke.

"Will the betroths please join hands and step forward," he said.

As the six couples moved forward, they joined hands and faced Paytric's mother and father, Channa and Aanon. The sky behind them became the backdrop for the ceremony. The setting Sun sat on the horizon's edge, giving the striated clouds that stretched across it, a glorious hue of deep yellow and purple.

They could not have picked a more beautiful time of the day to be joined.

And then Channa spoke.

"It is with blessings this day that we bring these couples together tonight to be joined. May the happiness you feel at this moment, increase every day of your lives."

"And may the Creator of all things," added Aanon, "continue to love and keep you safe and focused in all that you and your mate strive to accomplish."

Then looking over at Cherese and Jerome he said, "And may this child that is yet to be born, but whose future will truly be bright, always bring joy to its parents, Cherese and Jerome."

"Wow!" thought Jerome and Cherese.

It was mind blowing to hear for the first time, the two of them being referred to as, parents.

"In the name of the Creator," continued Aanon. "We give our blessings to you and your betroths. Be forever happy, and may you live your lives with respect to your loved ones and your people. Always and forever!" said Aanon as he and Channa smiled at each other and then held hands. "You may kiss you mates."

As each of the couples kissed, the roars of the onlookers was overwhelming. And all of the parents of the couples rushed forward and congratulated each of them with hugs and kisses.

They had been joined. And now they were mates forever!

The crowd cheered as they got to their feet, honoring the newly 'joined' couples.

Aanon and Channa bowed to them, and then directed the couples to decorated carriages that had been drawn up to the edge of the plateau by several of the Warriors' Birds of Prey. Each carriage had colored streamers flowing from the sides as the remainder of the carriage was decorated with Lilac flowers mixed with Baby Breaths as their light scent filled the air.

"As it is in the Warriors tradition," stated Aanon. "And I believe your people also. Your carriage awaits. The Birds of Prey will take you and your mates to a location, that has been selected for each of you. Now is the time for you to begin your lives together, without the outside world looking over your shoulder. Be at peace, children!"

With that, each of the couples headed for a carriage that had been harnessed to a Bird of Prey. And as each carriage slowly rolled forward, and then lifted off of the plateau into the air, the silhouettes of the Birds of Prey could be seen as they were outlined against the setting sun, as they carried the newly wedded couples off to their honeymoon.

Those left behind all waved, as they stood on the plateau, still in awe of the joining ceremony they had just witnessed.

"Things were truly going to change from this point forward," thought Thomas and Jesse as they waved to Amanda and the others as they disappeared into the horizon.

Things weren't going to be the same again! Amanda and the others were off starting their new lives, and it was back to Hampton and school for him and Thomas.

And then Jesse thought for a minute.

"That's right!" he thought to himself as his spirits lifted. "Things weren't going to be the same anymore. Heck! He and Thomas only had the rest of this semester of High School left to finish. And after, that they were planning to train in the Warriors' dimension with Paytric, Remy and Shiro."

"Things 'were' going to change for him and Thomas," thought Jesse excitedly. "But for the better. And that was something they were both had been looking forward to."

As Jesse started to beam uncontrollably, Thomas looked over at him.

"Aw, com'on Jesse! Not again!" exclaimed Thomas. "You're not thinking about you and Shelby 'doing the wedding thing one day, are ya?" he asked. "Because you know I…"

"What?? Noo!!" answered Jesse nonchalantly. "Actually, I kinda forgot all about Shelby."

"Really? Good. 'Cause Amanda was not happy when she heard about the way Shelby was treatin' you."

"Aw, com'on Thomas," exclaimed Jesse as he cast a disappointed look at his best friend. "You didn't tell my Sister about Shelby, did you?"

"You don't know your Sister, Jess!" pleaded Thomas, realizing he had let the cat out of the bag. "She can make the buffalo on a nickel 'poop' if she squeezed it hard enough. And I am not that tough."

Realizing that what Thomas was saying about his sister was true, Jesse shrugged his shoulders.

"It's alright, Thomas," he relented. "I know that when Amanda sets her mind on something, all bets are off."

And then turning back to Thomas, Jesse got excited again.

"Thomas! Do you realize that we only have the rest of this semester to finish, and then it's good-bye Hampton, and hello Warriors' dimension?"

"You're right, Jesse!" exclaimed Thomas as he too beamed with delight. "You are so right, Dude!"

The two teens were beyond excited as they body slammed each other just as a group of girls walked past them.

"Hi Jesse!" "Hi Thomas!" said the girls as they smiled at them.

"We're looking forward to training with you next year when you come back," said the taller of the girls. "It's going to be fun! See you then."

As the girls continued past them, they turned and smiled at them once more, and then disappeared into the crowd. Thomas and Jesse were so flabbergasted that all they could do was to just stand there, staring after them.

After a few seconds had passed, Thomas squealed in a high- pitched voice.

"Ohhh!!!"

He doubled over as he whispered, "Did you hear that, Jesse?" he said. "They're looking forward to training with us! Hot damm!!" he yelled as he did a little skip in place. And then turning to Jesse he exclaimed, "Dude! Let's follow them!"

Jesse couldn't help grinning from ear to ear as he watched his best friend shed his shy self and follow after the girls.

"Heck!" he thought to himself. "Why not! Shelby didn't even know he was alive! It was definitely time to move on."

With that, he and Thomas both rushed into the crowd as they followed behind the group of giggling girls.

As Mrs. and Mr. Carlson stood looking after Jesse, they both gave Thomas' mother and father, 'a look'.

"Ah Boy!" sighed Jesse's mother. "Here we go again!" she said remembering what they had gone through with Amanda when she discovered boys. "And here I thought I was going to be Jesse's favorite girl," she said.

"Well, sweetheart! You'll always be my favorite girl," said Mr. Carlson as he wrapped his arms around his wife. "Will that be enough?" he said as he kissed her lightly on the neck.

"Hmmm! Let me think about it. Okay!" she said quickly as she smiled. "I'm good! But you're going to have give me a lot of attention. Our daughter just got married and I'm missing her already!"

"Done!" said Jesse's father as he kissed his wife once again.

"Well, the two of you are going to have to give me and Jonathan some pointers," said Lillian Gates as she and her husband joined Jesse's parents. "This is new territory for us. I think we're going to need all the help we can get!"

As they all laughed together, they moved themselves out onto the plateau among the other wedding guests, enjoying their evening in the Warriors' dimension.

It had truly been a night to remember for all of them, and one they would never forget.

Chapter X

Return to Hampton

As the yellow bus pulled up in front of the school and opened its doors, the students filed off and flooded out into the cool, brisk Winter air. They mingled with the other students as everyone made their way to their first classes of the day. It was Monday, and while the weekend had passed much too quickly for everyone else, for two of the students, they were just glad it was over.

Well, at least, the first part of the weekend.

Although the last part of the weekend had stretched out to be an additional two months they were able to spend with the Warriors in their dimension, it made all the difference for Thomas and Jesse. With time passing so differently between dimensions, it helped that one hour in their world was the same as seven days in the Warriors' dimension. The eight hours they were gone between four am and Twelve noon on Sunday, allowed them to spend two months' time with their new friends. And of course, taking the time to train with Pauly and the other Birds of Prey, Thomas and Jesse were in 'seventh heaven'.

Taking the additional time also allowed their parents to not only have a well-deserved vacation, but to also be able to see Amanda and the others when they returned from their honeymoon. All in all, it was to date, one of the most spectacular weekends ever.

As Thomas and Jesse walked together, they headed for their first class, going over everything that had happened during their stay in New York City and in the Warriors' dimension.

"Man! Can you believe everything that we went through?" exclaimed Thomas as he tried to shield himself against the cold air.

"You know, when I think about it, it all feels like it was some sort of dream or somethin'. You know?" admitted Jesse.

"Yeah, well, you're not dreaming now!" said Thomas. "We're back at school, ole' buddy." And then as an afterthought, Thomas asked Jesse a question that had been on his mind.

"Hey! Were you trying to contact me last night?"

"Call you last night?" asked Jesse. "Nope!"

"No, I don't mean like calling me on the cell phone," said Thomas trying to clarify what he meant. "I mean, did you try and open a 'mind portal' to me? Cuz' I swear I thought I heard you calling my name last night. It was like you were trying to tell me somethin' I couldn't make out."

"Not me!" exclaimed Jesse. "You sure?" he asked.

"Well, we did have an awesome weekend, and I was kinda knocked out," said Thomas quickly. "I could be wrong."

And then Thomas looking up ahead of them, quickly looked over at Jesse and said, "And what a surprise! There's Shelby Miller!"

And sure enough.

There was Shelby Miller as she stood with some of her girlfriends on the steps leading up to the front door of the school. And for the first time, Jesse realized that it was where they always stood in the morning before classes. It seemed as if it was someplace where they could all stand and be seen by everyone passing by.

"Why didn't he notice that before?" he thought to himself.

"She never did call you like she said, did she?" asked Thomas.

"No, she didn't! Not one message." answered Jesse. "But it doesn't matter. I'm over it, now!"

"For true?" asked Thomas as he looked at his best friend.

"For true," answered Jesse as he beamed at Thomas.

"Alright!" exclaimed Thomas as he kept stride with Jesse as he moved forward.

Just as they approached the group of girls, one of Shelby's friends leaned over and whispered to her.

"How long are you going to keep him dangling, Shelby?" she asked. "He's kinda nice! And he's hecka' cute!" she said as she noticed that he seemed cuter than she had remembered. He looked more…something.

"Could one weekend have made that much of a difference?" she asked herself.

As a matter of fact, even Thomas was looking a little more filled out than any of them had noticed before. And the glasses he wore now seemed to fit his face as they gave him that sexy, studious look.

"Yeah, he is cute, isn't he?" said Shelby as she looked over at her friend. "I don't know," she said as she too found herself looking at Jesse a little differently. "We'll see what I feel like today!"

"Oh, you are so bad!" exclaimed her friend as they all watched Thomas and Jesse come up to them.

"Jesse! I'm so sorry I didn't get to call you this weekend!" exclaimed Shelby as she went into her 'girlie' spin. "I just got so busy and all. You know how it is. Maybe we can talk sometime this week, okay!"

"You know Shelby," said Jesse in a very 'matter of fact' tone as he stopped in front of her. "I didn't even notice."

"What!!" said Shelby in a shocked tone as she got a taste of her own medicine.

"Yeah! Well, you know, after being in New York City for the weekend, Thomas and I got to hang with some pretty awesome girls," admitted Jesse. "Besides, I'm just not that interested in playing games anymore."

"Yeah, right!" shot back Shelby as she tried to regain some of her dignity in front of her friends. "Like New York City girls would be interested in you!"

Jesse just shook his head and smiled as he and Thomas made their way past them. Just as they started to go up the stairs, he heard someone called out his name.

"Jesse! Jesse!!"

Turning toward the voice, everyone stopped as they all stared in disbelief. Especially, Jesse.

Stepping out of a black BMW that had parked at the curb in front of the school, was Kenadi. She was dressed in black leggings, short slouchy boots, and wore a thick, pullover sweater in a soft tangerine color. Her hair had been pulled back into a single ponytail that swung playfully behind her as she slowly walked toward Jesse. On one side of her hair was a royal blue streak of color as it flowed through her ponytail, displaying her family's crest.

"Kenadi!!" exclaimed Jesse out loud as he just stood on the steps staring at her.

"Who the hell is Kenadi?" said Shelby as she looked on with her friends.

"Someone very special to me," said Jesse as he turned around to face Kenadi as she stopped in front of him and the others.

And then before anyone knew it, Kenadi had stepped in close to Jesse and placed her hands on either side of his face as she gave him a long, lingering kiss that would have made most men swoon, including Jesse.

"Oh Man!" "Ahhhh! Why can't that be me!"

Everyone looking on was stunned at how sexy of a kiss it really was.

As she stepped back, Kenadi looked at him intently. She smiled. and said loud enough so that everyone could hear.

"I didn't get to give you that before you left New York City," she said. "See you when you come back! Okay, squirt!"

Totally taken aback by what had just happened, all Jesse could do was to nod his head in astonishment as Kenadi turned and made her way back to the car as she waved at him. And then it hit him.

"She called me, squirt," he thought to himself. "Only Amanda called him that." And then he gave a half of a smile as he whispered under his breath, "Thanks Sis! Thanks for making me look good," said Jesse. "I owe you and Kenadi."

As the BMW pulled away from the curb, Thomas slapped Jesse on the back and yelled out, "Wow!! Now that was some kiss!"

"Yeah, it was.," smiled Jesse as he blushed. "It was."

And then turning to an astonished Shelby Miller and friends, Jesse winked at her and said, "See you around, Shelby," as he and Thomas continued up the stairs together and went into the building.

"And Thomas was right," thought Jesse as he left behind a slightly traumatized Shelby Miller. "Things were never going to be the same again."

They were going to be better because he had so much to look forward to. Graduating High School, and then going off to the Warriors' dimension to train with Pauly. And he couldn't forget about the new friends that he and Thomas had met at the wedding.

It was all good!

And he couldn't wait to experience it all, as he and Thomas started on a new journey together.

As the last bell rang, students began to file into the school on the way to their first class of the day. The muffled sound of a cell phone could be heard ringing in the distance. It was coming from inside of a black SUV with darkened windows, that was parked on the street.

"Hello! We found them," said a female voice. "They live in a small town down on the eastern seaboard. A town called Hampton. Yes. I haven't got a lot on the two kids yet, but we found out an interesting fact about this town. Did you know that three years ago, this town literally disappeared off of the face of the map from six-o-clock pm, on October the twenty ninth, until approximately two-o-clock am October 31? For eight hours there was no contact of any kind with the town or its' residents. There're aren't even satellite records indicating that this town physically existed during that time."

"I know," said the female to an unknown voice on the other end as she listened intently.

After a brief pause, she continued.

"It's an interesting coincidence, Sir. The only images we were able to pull from the satellite feed over Central Park before it changed position, were the faces of these two kids. Two kids from a town that did a weird disappearing act a few years back."

There was another pause as the female listened.

Then she simply said, "Understood. I'll be in touch…" as she ended the call and the SUV silently pulled away from the school.

Epilogue

The young boy was on pins and needles the whole time he was sitting in the museum while he listened to the Professor. When the Professor had stopped speaking, he was abruptly brought back to the present.

"Wait! What happened, Professor?" he exclaimed as he leaned forward yearning for more. "In the SUV! Was that the same detective that Sarge spoke to in Central Park? And who was she talking to? And, and…what happened to Jesse and Thomas? Did they ever find out that someone was following them?"

As the young boy spit out his questions, he looked in earnest at the Professor, hoping that he would continue. His eyes gleamed with excitement.

"So many questions," said the Professor as he smiled at the young boy. "Far too many for me to answer now."

"But why?" pleaded the young boy, not understanding.

"Look up!" said the Professor as he cast his eyes upward. "We've been talking almost all day, and it's already begun to get dark outside. And I'm sure that your parents will be looking for you very soon. And we don't want them to be worried, now do we?"

And sure enough.

When the young boy looked up, dusk had already started to paint the early evening sky, making way for the two moons of their world to rise. And looking around, he saw that they had already started to close the museum up for the day, as people headed for the exits. He had gotten so involved in hearing what other adventures Thomas and Jesse had gotten themselves into, he hadn't realized that time had literally slipped away.

"When can I come back, Professor?" he asked, eager to hear more. "Anytime you want! I can come back!"

Smiling, the Professor slowly stood and looked down at the young student.

"He was so much like the Jesse he had known so long ago," he thought to himself as he saw the energy and passion sparkle in his eyes. "So much like him," he thought.

And he found it very interesting that this young student, also had the same name of his best friend from long ago. Jesse. The same young boy who was straddling the back of Pauly, the Warriors' Bird of Prey that was on display in the museum.

"I can come back, can't I?" asked young Jesse. "I mean if you don't mind talking about the past and all. And your friends. If it doesn't make you sad, does it?"

"Make me sad!" exclaimed the Professor. "No! I wouldn't say that it makes me sad, Jesse," he said slowly. "It actually feels good to remember the good times and the scary times, and the friendships that we shared with each other," he said. "And young man. It's good to share those memories with someone who is so interested."

"Then, I can come back?" he asked.

"Yes. You can come back, Jesse," confirmed the Professor with a smile. "I will not be here for the next couple of days, but when I return, I'll have a surprise for you."

"A surprise!" exclaimed the young student as he popped up off of his seat. "What kind of surprise?"

"Ahh! Now that you will have to wait and see," answered the Professor. "But I promise you, it will be magical."

"Really?? No foolin'!" exclaimed the young student.

The Professor laughed out loud as he looked at the student. It had been a while since he had heard himself laugh so freely.

"No foolin', Jesse!" answered the Professor. "No foolin'!"

"Then I'll be back next week, okay Professor! Next week!" called out Jesse as he ran toward the front door of the museum and headed outside.

Then he stopped at the entrance and turned around.

"Don't forget!" he exclaimed.

"I won't forget, Jesse," called out the Professor as he followed behind the young student. "I won't forget!"

Just as Thomas arrived at the front door of the museum, he looked out as the youngster made his way toward a woman waiting for him in front of a 'portal' that had just opened up on the grassy hillside.

"Hmmm! She looked familiar?" thought Thomas to himself as he watched from the front entrance of the museum.

He had lost track of his friends long ago when he had secluded himself from the outside world to concentrate on his writings to chronicle the history of the Warriors. But for Thomas it was more than just documenting their past. He was looking for something in their ancient history that might give him any kind of information that referred to Jesse and what had really happened to him. It was to that end that he had pretty much kept to himself, secluded inside of the museum with Gharvey by his side.

And as fate would have it, he had come across something most interesting in his search of the Warriors' history that very morning before he had met with young Jesse. Something he was very anxious to explore.

As he brought himself back to the present, he had to stop and think, 'how long it had been' since he had had been in contact with any of his friends?'

He sighed as he thought back to the time right after the battle in Central Park, when he and Jesse had attended the 'joining' ceremony of their friends. The Pre' had been dealt with, and there were new talks with Skalla and his Whre. They had decided that rather than viewing the Gargoyles and the Warriors as their enemy, and the Humans as their prey, trying to find a place among them was to everyone's advantage. And Irina and the Gargoyles had agreed to work with the Whre to that end.

After that, the Warriors had returned to their dimension. Jerome and Cherese, along with the others had remained in New York City. Even Zachery Boyd stayed on to work within the Sanctuary with Granna and her two sisters.

And interestingly enough, both Thomas and Jesse had noticed that Zachery Boyd had taken kind of a shine to J.D.'s sister, Laura. While everyone was recuperating in the Warriors dimension after the fight in Central Park, they had begun to spend a lot of time together. And they had to admit, it looked promising.

Everyone's parents, including his own, had all returned to Hampton to resume their lives, although they knew that nothing would be the same again.

Ever!

And the rest of his friends, after being 'joined', had relocated to the Warriors' dimension to be with their respective mates. After that, everyone had set about to live their lives and raise families of their own, trying not to miss out on a single thing that the Creator had blessed them with.

But even after they had returned to Hampton to finish out their last year of High School, their lives were soon to be disrupted in ways they never thought possible. After graduation, Jesse and Thomas were going to return to the Warriors' dimension for training on their way to becoming full-fledged Warriors.

That was the plan.

"But that was long ago," Thomas thought to himself. "So long ago."

"But, ahh…the times!" he exclaimed to himself, as he closed his eyes and breathed in deeply. "They had such great times together!"

But now, Thomas was reliving his past through this young student, who also had the name of his best friend. And he had to admit that it felt good to his soul, to bring back to life all of the wonderful and fascinating things that he and Jesse and their friends had experienced.

But as he opened his eyes, for some reason the woman young Jesse was talking to, still seemed familiar to him. And although he couldn't see her face, it was just a feeling that swept over him in the flicker of a passing second. He didn't' know why, but he couldn't shake the feeling no matter how hard he tried.

She seemed so familiar to him.

"You old fool!" he whispered to himself. "Now you're seeing things. That can't possibly be who he was thinking it was."

He started to step away from front entrance of the museum and dismiss the errant feeling that had momentarily swept over him.

That was until she looked up.

~~~~~~~~~~

As young Jesse ran to his mother, she knelt down to greet him.

"Did you have a good time?" she asked as she swept the hair from his face.

"Yeah!" exclaimed Jesse. "And guess what?"

"What?"

"The Professor is going away for a few days. But he said when he gets back, he's going to have a surprise for me! A magical surprise!"

"He did?"

"Yeah! I can come back, can't I?" asked the youngster, almost pleading. "Can't I?"

"I'm sure we can work it out, Jesse," said his mother as she looked over at the Professor as he stood in the doorway of the museum.

She wondered if the Professor really knew who the youngster was, that he had been regaling all of his stories of past adventures to. She hadn't really met him before, but she remembered her mother telling her stories about her uncle and his best friend, Thomas. Or Professor, as he was called today. How they had the kind of friendship that bonded them to each other, no matter what the circumstances were, and no matter how much time had passed between them.

She smiled ever so slightly and thought to herself.

"Next time I'm going to have to introduce myself to him," she thought. "Let him know who she and her Son really were? She thought he should know."

Looking down at her son she asked, "Have you told him who your Uncle was?"

Shaking his head, her son answered, "No. Should I have?"

"Well...I'm sure you will do it in your own time, Jesse," she said. "When you're ready. But if you like, maybe I'll come with you next time and we can tell him together. Would that be okay?"

Glancing back over his shoulder to the Professor as he stood in the entrance of the museum, young Jesse waved one more time and smiled.

"I just didn't want to make him sad about what happened to Uncle Jess," he said innocently. "You know?"

"Yes. I know, Jesse," said his mother as she too waved. "I know. But that was a long, long time ago."

"But he still misses him, Mom!" said the youngster as he looked back up at her. "Every time when he talks about him, I see tears come to his eyes. And I know he misses him and feels bad about what happened. Is that why he stays in the museum with Gharvey and hardly ever comes out?" he asked.

"Maybe, Jesse. I don't know," answered his mother as she took his hand and led him to the opening of the 'portal'. "It's hard to say why people do the things they do. But we'd better get home. Dinner's ready and we're late."

As young Jesse walked with his mother to the entrance of the 'portal' that stood waiting for them, he abruptly stopped.

"Jesse, what's wrong?" asked his mother as she turned to face him.

"I...I don't know," he answered as he looked down trying to understand exactly what the feeling was that had swept over him.

Then he looked up with tears in his eyes and exclaimed, "I don't think I'm going to see him again, Mom!" he cried as he tried to turn and go back.

Catching her son before he could break away and run back to the museum, Jesse's mother held him tight and whispered in his ear.

"Jesse! Listen to me!" she said. "You trust the Professor, don't you? Don't you?" she asked intently.

Nodding his head acknowledging that he did, his mother continued.

"Then if he said he was going to be back in a couple of days, he will."

"For true, Mom?" asked young Jesse as he looked at his mother.

Realizing that he was using the secret phrase that her uncle Jesse and his best friend Thomas had used between the two of them, so long ago, she answered.

"For true, Jesse," she said. "For true. Now let's go home, sweetheart."

As the two of them turned and stepped into the entrance of the 'portal', within seconds, the low humming sound slowly faded, as did the 'portal' itself.

~~~~~~~~

Thomas watched as young Jesse and his mother disappeared into the 'portal' opening. He just stood in the entrance of the museum as he looked after them, stunned. He could have sworn that the woman was the spitting image of Amanda, Jesse's sister.

"But was that even possible?" thought Thomas to himself. "And if that was Amanda, she looked the same as she did the day she 'joined' with Jason her betrothed, right after the incident in Central Park."

And Thomas knew that it had to be more than two hundred years ago. More than two hundred years ago, here in the Warriors dimension. Not like it was back in their world where one hour was equal to seven days here.

Amanda would have to be…

As he tried to do the calculations in his head, the thought boggled his mind. He wasn't a mathematician. But he did know that time passed differently when you crossed over into another dimension, and it could distort the calculation of how many years had actually elapsed. It had something to do with the bending of time, and then time itself slowing down after so many years had past. And from what he knew, at least a hundred years had gone by in the Humans' dimension, compared to the two hundred years here in the Warrior's world.

"That can't be!" he thought. "Even though their life expectancy had been extended because of the time that they all had spent in the Warriors' dimension, they were still Human. No way would their life span be anything like the Warriors or the Wielders of

Magic, or for that matter, like any of the other magical creatures."

To say the least, at first Thomas was confused.

Then he had to take a step back when he remembered what Jesse had said to him so long ago. It was almost as if he could hear him speaking to him at that very moment.

"Remember, Thomas! It's Magic! And anything is possible with Magic!" he would say. "You just have to believe. You just have to let yourself believe."

Taking in a deep breath, Thomas once again closed his eyes and nodded his head in silent acknowledgement.

"Thank you, Jesse," he whispered softly to himself. "I had almost forgotten. I had almost forgotten."

It was then that Thomas realized what had happened to him over the years he had secluded himself inside of the museum. While trying to forget what had happened to Jesse and to deal with the guilt that he felt, he had almost forgotten about all of the Magic that had once been a part of his life. And how Magic never followed the rules of the Human world.

And if it hadn't been for young Jesse persuading him to relive those times again, he might have actually lived out the last of his days having forgotten about the amazing and fantastic things that he and Jesse had shared with their friends.

He would have forgotten about the Magic.

And like Jesse had said to him long ago, 'You just have to believe.'

Easing herself up next to Thomas, Gharvey nudged him gently as he stood looking after young Jesse and his mother. After all of this time, she was still able to read what he was thinking.

"Do you think it is her, Master Thomas?" asked Gharvey as she too looked out onto the now empty hillside. "Do you think it was Amanda?"

"She looks very much like her, my friend," answered Thomas as he felt a renewed spirit light up inside of him. "Could it be?" he asked himself. "Perhaps it was it was one of Amanda's children, or her children's children," he thought as he abruptly caught himself.

Now it all made sense to him.

The woman resembling Amanda. And the boy not only having Jesse's name, but some of the same abilities that he had developed.

"Was it possible that some of his other friends were still here in the Warriors' dimension?" he asked himself.

It had been such a long time since he had seen any of them.

"It would be nice to see them again," he thought to himself.

Looking down at Gharvey, he smiled broadly and said, "Well, I guess we'll just have to wait to find out until next time, won't we?" said Thomas.

"You have kept yourself away from everything that you knew for so long, Master Thomas. It has been for far too long," stated Gharvey. "You know they do not blame you for what happened. No one does," said Gharvey as she looked up at Thomas.

"It's not their blame that has kept me secluded here for all of this time, Gharvey," said Thomas sadly. "It is my guilt."

"Guilt, Master Thomas?" said Gharvey. "I do not understand."

"For as long as Jesse and I had known each other, he was always there for me. Always watching my back. Defending me no matter what. There were even times when he would put himself in harms' way to look out for me."

"As you did for him, Master Thomas, when it was needed," said Gharvey, reminding Thomas of his own sacrifice.

"Yes, Gharvey," said Thomas. "But when the time came, it wasn't enough."

"You do not know that, Master Thomas. No one but the Creator knows the impact of the final outcome of things that have transpired. No one," said Gharvey as she felt true sadness for Thomas and the pain that he still felt after all of this time.

Thomas turned and glanced up at the replica of Pauly and Jesse as it hung in the opened aired museum hall. They appeared to be in constant flight, as they seemed to soar effortlessly through the air together.

Forever.

"You told young Jesse you would be away for a few days," said Gharvey quietly. "Is that because you are going to go to the Keep and have the process done?" she asked.

"Yes," said Thomas slowly. "I plan to go to the Keep tomorrow and have the Doctors perform the transfiguration process, one more time. As they used to say back home, 'for old times' sake,'" said Thomas.

Ever since the battle in his hometown of Hampton long ago, he had been making visits to the Keep. That was when he and his friends had first met the Warriors and learned that Magic was in fact, real. After the confrontation with the Dark Dimension in Hampton, his life force had been taken from his body. And the doctors at the Keep in the Warriors' dimension, were able 'renew' him through the transfiguration process. But only temporarily.

He had to return to the Keep every so many years to allow them to 'age' him appropriately so that he could continue his Human life in his dimension, without attracting any undue attention. But so much time had since passed, and he was no longer in his dimension. And because so many things had changed over the years, there was no need for the doctors to 'age' him to keep up appearances.

He was now ready to accept what time, and his creator had intended for him.

"In a couple of days, I will see young Jesse again, as I promised," Thomas said to Gharvey. "I would very much like to spend the day with him like Jesse and I used to do," he said smiling as he thought about the times that he and his best friend had shared with each other.

"After that Gharvey," he said quietly. "I think it will be time to go home. I think I'll be ready then. I have been here for far too long."

"Yes, Master Thomas," said Gharvey as she stood next to him. "It has been a long time."

"Besides," said Thomas as he reached into his pocket and pulled out a chain with a pin attached to the end of it. "I have something I need to return to a good friend," he said.

The pin he held, for sure had seen better days.

It was round shaped and bent on one side. And long ago the writing on the face of the pin had been rubbed off and had faded away. So much so that you could no longer read what had once been written there. But Thomas didn't have to read what had been written on the face of the pin to remember its' significance to him.

This was the same pin he had given to Jesse when they were just kids.

He had won it in a Spelling Bee at school. And when he and Jesse had performed their own 'brotherly bonding' ceremony, they had exchanged items that at the time, each of them cherished more than anything.

The pin was what Thomas had given to Jesse.

"Master Thomas," said Gharvey slowly. "I would be honored to journey home with you, if you would allow me to join you."

Thomas turned to his friend and constant companion as tears filled his eyes.

"Why Gharvey, I wouldn't have it any other way," he said. "It is I who would be honored to have you join me. And if I may say so," said Thomas as he smiled. "Having you by my side all of this time, has been Magical! Thank you!"

In acknowledgement, Gharvey rubbed her head and nose up against Thomas' leg and made a low moaning sound that she made when she was happy.

Before taking his leave, Thomas waved his hand one time activating the door of the museum to seal itself for the evening. And as the fluid door materialized, multicolored patterns flowed and mixed with each other as they cast deliberate shadows into the night.

And as dusk blanketed the Warriors' dimension, their two moons rose gracefully to take their places in the night sky, as a peaceful quiet fell across the land.

And yes. It had been a magical journey.

And Thomas would be more than delighted to share…the end of the story, with his new, young friend before he and Gharvey went home.

After all. He felt he owed it to his best friend, Jesse.

For true! For true!

Made in the USA
Middletown, DE
19 September 2024

61151917R00182